David Wolstencroft is the multi-award-winning creator and writer of iconic BAFTA-winning spy drama *SPOOKS* and award-winning BBC legal thriller series *THE ESCAPE ARTIST*. He is co-creator of epic historical drama *VERSAILLES* (Canal+/BBC). David is also the author of two bestselling adult thrillers, *GOOD NEWS BAD NEWS* (Richard and Judy's Book Club selection) and *CONTACT ZERO* (winner of the Ian Fleming Silver Dagger award), both of which are currently in development as feature films.

Published in the UK by Scholastic, 2023
1 London Bridge, London, SE1 9BG
Scholastic Ireland, 89E Lagan Road, Dublin Industrial Estate, Glasnevin, Dublin,
D11 HP5F

Text © David Wolstencroft, 2023
Illustrations by Alessia Trunfio © Scholastic, 2023

ISBN 978 0702 32426 0

A CIP catalogue record for this book is available from the British Library.

Printed by CPI Group (UK) Ltd, Croydon, CR0 4YY
Paper made from wood grown in sustainable forests and other controlled sources.

1 3 5 7 9 10 8 6 4 2

www.scholastic.co.uk

THE MAGIC HOUR

DAVID WOLSTENCROFT

SCHOLASTIC

LULU

CREDENZA

OSSIAN

MUM & DAD

AILSA

GRANDMA & GRANDPA

PRIYA

STEVE & STEVE

SANDY MUNRO

MORAG

LADY BLACKTHORN

VIRGIL

TOBIAS

THE BROLLACHAN

SYDEKYCK

DAY GLOAMING

HIS LAIRDSHIP

NIGHT GLOAMING

For Vida Lev

Then, now, and always

CHAPTER 1

THE GIRL WHO WAS LATE

There is never enough time. For anything.

Particularly when your house explodes.

Ailsa Craig knew this all too well. She was the girl who was always running behind: skidding into classrooms, swimming lessons and birthday parties, always apologizing, explaining, promising that next time, cross her heart, things would be different. Born two weeks late, that girl, went the family joke, and she's made a habit of it ever since. It happened so often she even had a catchphrase:

"Sorry I'm late," she'd say, "I didn't get here on time."

Time was a puzzle to Ailsa.

Some weeks moved like sludge. Others were all fizz and bubbles. There had been an entire year when the world felt like a steel trap, where hours felt like days and months melted into for ever. In better, sunnier moments, her nose deep in a good book, a summer holiday might breeze past before she even knew it.

On the chilly Scottish night that we meet her, however, time wasn't moving at all. It was frozen, and so was she: rooted to the spot, staring up at wisps of acrid smoke.

This is Ailsa's story, so we'll cover the basics at speed: the quality of her character (loyal, kind, nostalgic, stubborn – and late, as you'll recall); her interests (science, books, and most things in between); the hour of her birth (midnight, stroke of); her general appearance (tall enough to reach the ground, with chaotic curly hair of which she was very proud); glasses (usually sliding down her nose); hat (yellow, knitted); eyes (green, curious); and the name of her two cats (both called Steve, for reasons that cannot be adequately explained here). As for the rest, you'll just have to pick it up along the way. Because, well, exploding houses, come on: that feels like something which deserves our attention.

Plus, as you probably know, there's actually no speed limit for books, so we can go as fast as we like.

CHAPTER 2

THE BIG BANG

So there was Ailsa, staring up at a rectangular box of air suspended several metres off the ground. It contained nitrogen, oxygen, argon, carbon dioxide, and a whole lot of smoke.

It was where her bedroom used to be.

Ailsa was eleven and a half years old, and for most of that time, until a few minutes ago in fact, there had been a modest dwelling house here at 47 Bothwell Gardens.

Ailsa lived here with her dad when she wasn't staying in the flat down the hill with her mum.[1]

One thing you need to know about Ailsa is that her parents had split up a few years ago, and she still wasn't sure how she felt about it. Ailsa's older sister, Ada, who everyone called Lulu, had left home the previous winter

---

1   Both of Ailsa's cats lived at her mum's, so no need to worry about that from a houses-blowing-up feline perspective.

to see the world. She always sent Ailsa messages and photos of where she was, and what odd jobs she was doing to support herself (at the moment she was working in a café near a beach). Ailsa missed her sister a lot. She had been the glue that held their family together. The kind of glue that remembered your birthday.

"Keep back now, please!"

Ailsa pulled her yellow knitted hat tight over her ears and pushed her glasses back up her nose. The emergency crews were finishing their work. The force of the blast had scorched a dark circle in the snow surrounding the crater. The rowan tree by the front door was split in two like it had been struck by lightning – scarred, charred and barely alive. Burst pipes sprayed jets of water artfully into the centre of the wreckage. The meltwater ran to a drain on the street, where it made a merry tinkling sound.

As she gazed down at the tangled mess of cracked stone, burnt wood and melted plastic, it occurred to Ailsa that being late to your house exploding was a lot better than being early.

CHAPTER 3

THE STEAMER TRUNK

Wasn't kidding about that speed limit; we nearly started this bit without you. Where were we? Oh yes.

BOOM! Ailsa jumped as a series of rumbles, claps and bangs tore through the night air. Down the hill, people were shouting.

"Happy New Yeeeeeee-ar!"

It wasn't even midnight yet. She could see bright colours in the sky over the rooftops towards town. There was music coming from somewhere, an old song her parents had loved, "Auld Lang Syne". Ailsa had forgotten the date. It was the night of December 31st. Which meant fireworks. Lots of them.

Great. More stuff exploding. Happy Hogmanay.[2]

---

2   Hogmanay is Scottish New Year, but you probably know that. In case you don't: it's like New Year everywhere else, only much bigger and quite a bit louder.

Another thing you need to know about Ailsa and her family is this: they hadn't always lived in Scotland.

Her first country, the island she was born on, had been a lot warmer. In the summer, it had the kind of heat that might cook an egg on a slab of stone. They moved away when she was three, or four. Or five. She could never remember which. What she did recall only too well was the cold, and the dark, of that first Scottish night, the wind moaning in the chimney, the odour of burnt dust from the bars of the electric fire. She had later discovered a Scottish author who had once made a similar kind of journey, albeit in reverse. His name was Robert Louis Stevenson, and it was no surprise to Ailsa that he had written a book called *Kidnapped*.

Ailsa cast her eye across the wreckage again. Most of her books were ash, but a few had endured. She found a yellowing copy of *Moominsummer Madness* in a hedge, the fractured spine of *The Graveyard Book* by Neil Gaiman half-buried in the earth (which she found rather apt) and, in a hole in the ground, *The Hobbit*.

There was, however, something else she couldn't find.

The missing item was a treasure chest: a thick, weathered wooden trunk known as a steamer. It had faded metal corner pieces, stout locks, leather straps, and scratches along its panels. It smelled of salt, engine oil and the open road. Ailsa's Grandma Judith had kept her personal papers in it when she wasn't using it as a coffee table. Judith had been an astronomer for most of her life, and even in semi-retirement she'd kept a small office at the Observatory up on the hill. After she died, the trunk had become Ailsa's. It was Priya, Grandma's researcher, who had given it to her. She knew how much Ailsa loved her grandmother.

Ailsa also loved that steamer trunk. It was a trove of memories, notes, photos. It also, as Ailsa would soon discover, contained a secret. In any case, the very idea of losing it made Ailsa feel quite dizzy. But it had also been in her bedroom, and gazing down at the charred crater before her, she doubted it had survived.

Ailsa couldn't possibly know, but this missing trunk wasn't just bad news for her.

It was bad for the entire world.

She felt her father's gloved hand on her shoulder. "Time to go," he said. His eyes were misty and red. She couldn't tell if he was exhausted, had been crying, or both. But red eyes, in Ailsa's experience, rarely meant something good.

She took his hand. "Where are we going to sleep tonight?"

He went silent for a moment. It looked like a thousand thoughts were tumbling over themselves in his head.

"We'll figure something out."

Ailsa said: "Maybe we could stay at Mum's?"

She knew her parents hadn't been talking much lately. It wasn't exactly common for divorced folks to leap at the chance to ask each other for favours. But Dad seemed to hear her. He nodded and took out his phone.

They walked down the hill together, away from the destruction. Ailsa could hear her mother's voice on the other end of the call. "Wait, did you say exploded? How on earth…?"

… did that happen?

Ailsa vowed that she would find out.

She looked up at the night sky, for courage and answers. Stars blinked impassively back down at her and her tiny tragedy. Far away, hundreds of light years from here, she knew, a supermassive black hole was draining the last remnants of a neutron star towards its own abyss of infinite gravity, like so much cosmic snowmelt. The boiling mass of a million suns was stretched to a shining, shrieking filament of atoms that would last for ever. The remains of the kitchen, the warped garden gate, the carbonized roses, the cloud of vapour as she breathed, this lamp post, that silly tinkling drain, the tracks of drying tears on her face – it was all constructed from parts of a star just like that one, forged in the interstellar explosion that began the universe and all we know inside it.

The Big Bang. The start of the universe.

The first beginning there ever was.

At least, that's how Grandma had always explained it, which – according to Grandpa Eric – was maybe why they never got invited out to dinner very much.

Yet, there in the cold, Ailsa couldn't help thinking: if the entire cosmos really began with an explosion, then maybe this particular blast wasn't an end either. Maybe it was her own personal Hogmanay, a new kind of beginning, a sign that sometime, very soon, a new chapter of her own story would start.

Then again, of course…

It already had.

CHAPTER 4

THE GLOAMING

The clock was ticking for Ailsa Craig.

She was perched on a ledge before a vast and jagged valley of splintered rocks. The ground was crumbling, her feet slipping, until at last she slid back over the edge, falling into nothing, yelling out:

"Somebody catch me!"

Ailsa sat up in bed, listening to the silence.

Dreams, she thought. *A mixed bag.*

They had come to Mum's flat the night of the explosion, a sanctuary from the smoke and chaos. They had ended up staying for the week while Dad searched for another place to live. Now school was starting up, a brand-new term the following morning.

It was an odd experience, having both parents under the same roof again. It made Ailsa happy, but in a nostalgic kind of way, like hearing an old song. Yet she knew this feeling seldom lasted very long. Lulu had always said life with Mum and Dad was a bit like the Scottish weather. The moment you were happy with the way things were, everything would change.

Still, they were all safe, and she was grateful.

She nestled back under the covers and gazed up at the window. It was snowing. The flakes layered themselves in a steady rhythm on to the roof slates and the gutters of the block of flats across the street.

The air smelled of magic.[3]

She loved the snow for many reasons, but those first minutes of total cover were Ailsa's favourite. Silence. Solitude. The crunch of her boots on the blank canvas of a new day. It had taken her six years, and a lot of thermal leggings, but she finally preferred snow to sand.

Over at Dad's, her bedroom had been up in the attic, a cosy, comfortable place – at least when it wasn't exploding. Here at Mum's, things were brighter and calmer. Her two cats, Steve and Steve, had full run of the flat, with plenty of warm corners to sleep in.

The sky began to clear, the dawn approaching from the east. The clouds turned steel and pink. Twilight. The French, her grandma had once told her, called it *entre*

---

3   Slightly metallic, with a hint of nutmeg, since you ask.

chien et loup, "between dog and wolf", as if, in the indigo gloom, you couldn't tell the difference.

The Scots called it something else, of course: the *gloaming*.

Ailsa turned the word around in her mind. It sounded like the name of an animal. She wondered what a *gloaming* might look like and doodled for a while on the notepad by her bed.

A Gloaming would have purple fur, she thought, fringed with steel, like the first light of the morning. It would have yellow eyes, like a cat. It would also have big wide pads on its feet, because it would no doubt skulk around a lot. But what would a gloaming eat? Grass? Hardly seemed right; it didn't sound like a grazing animal. Meat? It didn't sound like a predator, either. An omnivore, then. She thought about the twilight, and it occurred to her that since there was both sunrise twilight and sunset twilight, there would be two kinds of gloaming creature in the world. The Day Gloaming, which would eat darkness, and a Night Gloaming, which would eat light. She hoped she would never encounter a Night Gloaming, even at lunchtime. And what would ever happen if they encountered each other? She wondered if they'd be friends.

Her dad's voice boomed from down the hall, the

smell of burnt toast filling her nostrils, and Ailsa woke up for the second time that day. Daylight blazed in through her window.

"Ailsa Rose Craig, final warning! Get out here now!"

Whoops. Late as usual.

She threw on her school clothes (salvaged from the wreckage, and only a little singed) and rushed along to the kitchen. As she passed the living room, Ailsa could see bedding still on the sofa where Dad had been sleeping.

Ailsa's dad was already dressed for work, his tie flung back over his shoulder. He worked in a large modern office, and most of his day seemed to involve meetings. In profile he still looked a lot like a pencil drawing Ailsa had made of him years ago. Potato-shaped head, with a mop of jet-black hair and nostrils that flared when irritated.

"You have no conception of time at all, do you?"

His nostrils flared.

"Daydreaming again, sorry."

Her stomach was in a knot. Most of the time, Ailsa knew it meant she had forgotten to do something. But what?

"You know, if the school gave grades for daydreaming, you'd have As all the way. But as it stands…"

Ailsa started to think of a snappy retort, but then she

remembered her last report card, which had featured no vowels whatsoever. Dad was opening drawers with a furrowed brow.

"Any idea where Mum keeps the dishcloths?"

Ailsa pointed at a nearby drawer. "How long are we going to stay here?" she asked.

Dad brightened. "The Wilsons just offered us their place for a month, while they're away. I'll move us in tonight, but you'll need to stay here, since it's Mum's week now. I'll ask her if you can come for dinner, so you can see the house. It's just around the corner from the old place."

"What's left of it," said Ailsa.

Her dad looked at her sadly. "We shall rebuild."

"Where is Mum anyway?"

"Early shift. She left you a note."

Ailsa read the short message from her mum (it was loving and warm, but we won't invade their privacy too much by revealing what she said). Ailsa glanced up at the large clock on the kitchen wall. Washing machines and boilers would come and go, but both Mum and Dad had put large kitchen clocks in prominent places all over their house: less-than-subtle hints for their ever-late daughter. This particular clock ticked with a heavy kerchunk every second, which always disturbed her. To

Ailsa it had always sounded like a battalion of marching soldiers, coming to march right over her.

In between large mouthfuls of burnt porridge, she told Dad about the Gloaming. But he was still talking to her about time. Specifically, "now".

"As a matter of interest, Ailsa, when I say get ready *now*," he said, "what kind of 'now' do you think I mean? Eventually, or tomorrow? Next week?"

Ailsa suddenly remembered a science programme that they'd been shown at school. "*Actually*, Dad, there is no such thing as *now*. Anything we think of as *right now* is never happening at that exact moment. We're too slow to understand it. Even *thinking* takes time. Since our brains are powered by electricity, and even electricity has a speed.[4] So, when you *think* a thought, by the time you've even *thought* that thought, it's already in the past. Which means there's no such thing as the present."

Dad shot her a blank look, and rubbed his hands into his face. It made the tips of his eyebrows point in all directions, which made him look like a surprised hedgehog.

---

4   In fact the speed of the electricity in your bedside lamp is about 270,000 km per second, about 90% the speed of light. Which is about as speedy as you can get.

"Well, in that case," he said, "I won't ask you what you want for your birthday." (Dads always insisted on making gags like this. Ailsa had a feeling it was in their contract.)

"I can't help it, Dad, I just get really *caught up* in things. And anyway, I'm only a minute late. It's only sixty seconds."

There was a shift in Dad's face at that moment, like a cloud moving across the sun. Ailsa knew Dad had been quite down since Grandma died. Life seemed to weigh on him more these days, and there were darker circles under his eyes. He took her hand.

"One day, Ailsa, you're going to realize something. Whenever you're late," he said, "you are literally taking someone else's time away from them. It's important you understand that."

His eyes softened. He seemed far away.

"One minute can mean the world," he said softly. "Every second counts in this life."

Ailsa was nodding to let him know that she had understood, but the truth was, what she was really doing was half-thinking about her first class at school, which was science, and how late she could arrive to it, which was not at all.

Seconds later she was sprinting down the stairs and out into the street, yellow hat bobbing in the breeze. She did this without a glance back at her father, who was watching her from the living room window, a strange faraway look on his face. Work was calling, once again. Days were melting into years. Another season gone. Christmas next, then spring was on its way. Time was slipping away. The harder he tried to hold on, the faster it all seemed to go. As much as Ailsa was always late, he wished she would slow down a little.

Life is like that sometimes. You never know how important moments can be before they're gone, when the last chance to see something, or someone, is going to be. You have to take it one precious second at a time and treat every single day like fresh-fallen snow. Because life is not like this book. You cannot hold it in your hand and know exactly how much is left in the story.

Ailsa was rounding the final bend to school when she heard a puffing noise behind her. It seemed to be calling her name.

A Gloaming, perhaps? Surely not here. She turned to see.

It was Dad – red-faced, puffing like a steam train, hands on his knees. He had run after her. He slipped on a patch of slow-melting frost on the pavement but steadied himself by grabbing on to a nearby hedge.

"Dad?"

"Ailsa. Please. Don't ever leave home," he wheezed, "without saying goodbye. That's the rule, remember?"

It truly was, and she knew it mattered to him.

"Sorry, Dad. Bye."

She kissed him on the cheek and skidded off towards school.

Ailsa's dad watched her go. He recalled his daughter's first steps, her first words, and how far away they all now seemed.

"Where does the time go?" he asked himself.

You've probably guessed already.[5]

But Ailsa was about to find out.

---

5   Don't worry if you haven't.

CHAPTER 5

TWENTY-FIVE SEVEN

Still behind schedule here. Sorry, it's probably the footnotes[6], but we'd better hurry up just the same.

All you really need to know at this point is that there was a long, straight access road that approached Ailsa's school. As she ran down it, a taxi rumbled past, bisecting a nearby puddle of slush.

It soaked her. She already knew who was inside.

Credenza Dingwall.

"Not like you to be late," said Ailsa as they strolled in.

"I'm not," sneered Credenza, peering down at the damp patches of brown snowy sludge on Ailsa's school blazer, as if she had no idea how they had got there.

Perhaps you've met someone like Credenza. The

---

6   No, it isn't.

self-appointed monarch of Ailsa's year, she's one of those people who has done everything you have done – only earlier, faster and better. She always got a taxi to school, despite living in a huge house five minutes' walk away. (Her older brother, Ossian, on the other hand, only seemed to stroll into school when he felt like it.)

While most other kids seemed to battle their way through the daily turmoil of school, Credenza appeared to be unruffled by any of it. Despite only being eleven, she looked and acted older than the other girls in their year. The entire world appeared to bore her. She had already seen it all. She seemed simply to glide through life, like a royal barge, serenely prepared for anything the day might have in store. Ailsa sometimes wondered if she had wheels.

"Just got in from Dubai," Credenza said, answering a question Ailsa didn't recall asking. "Dad's building something there."

"What?"

"A building."

Credenza was not someone who elaborated much.

"All by himself?" asked Ailsa.

Ailsa knew the truth, of course: Credenza's family were ridiculously wealthy – her father, Cameron Dingwall, ran a huge construction company with building projects all over Scotland (Ailsa's mum would always mutter "Wall-To-Wall Dingwall" whenever they passed yet another advertising billboard on yet another construction site). But she preferred to bite her tongue[7] when Credenza was in a bragging mood, which seemed to be quite often.

"No, he has people to do that for him," said Credenza, blinking at her. Not many people understood Ailsa's sense of humour. Credenza was a case in point. "Anyway, that's my excuse," she sniffed. "What's yours?"

Ailsa shrugged. "My house exploded."

"Good one." Credenza snorted, assuming it was a joke.

"I'm serious," added Ailsa.

But Credenza was already swanning past her.

The bell rang, and Ailsa's stomach tightened, as it always did at the start of a school day.

Life in Scotland was getting better for Ailsa, but in the mornings she often still felt like she had when she'd first arrived – that she was someone from somewhere else, always on the outside. There were lots of kids from different backgrounds in her year, and yet she somehow always felt like she was floating around the boundaries like a lonely balloon.

---

7   Not *actually* bite it, mind you. That's never a good idea.

As Ailsa followed Credenza towards the stairs, she felt for Grandma's postcard. She kept it with her always, in a clear plastic cover in her coat pocket. On one side was an image of a spiral galaxy.[8] On the other, in Grandma's immaculate capital letters, was a list:

THE SCIENTIFIC METHOD
STATE THE PROBLEM CLEARLY
GATHER INFORMATION & OBSERVE
MAKE A HYPOTHESIS
EXPERIMENT & TEST
ANALYZE YOUR RESULTS
PRESENT A CONCLUSION
BACK TO 3. (REPEAT UNTIL YOU ARE SURE)
(P.S. This is really more of a circle than a list, as you will no doubt discover.)

"The Method", as Grandma had called it, was like a rule book for scientists, one to help them navigate the unknown. Over the years Ailsa had discovered that the Scientific Method could help her navigate all kinds of aspects of her life: social dilemmas, moral conundrums,

---

8   The Pinwheel Galazy in Ursa Major if you want to check it out. It's very spirally indeed.

divorcing parents, new schools, and most of all, in what her science teacher called "as-yet-unexplained phenomena".

Not that there was much mystery about this situation.

Ailsa was late again.

"Well, did you finish your science project at least?" Credenza said, half-turning back to Ailsa as if she was only worth fifty per cent of her attention. "Dr Matthews said it's due today…"

Ailsa's guts churned.

That was it. The thing she forgot. She was glad, at least, that she'd kept the project at Mum's so she could run back and work on it at lunchtimes now and again.

Credenza sensed her anxiety and smiled. "Well, anyway, I finished mine last weekend. I made my own wind turbine."

"Good for you," said Ailsa.

"Yeah, I was working, like, twenty-five seven on it."

Ailsa stopped walking and looked at her.

"Twenty-four seven, surely?"

Credenza froze as if she had betrayed a confidence. For a moment, Ailsa thought she might burst into tears.

"Well," she spluttered. "I mean, yeah, of course."

Ailsa peered closer. Was Credenza … blushing? Her cheeks were turning scarlet. "Obviously, like, twenty-four seven. That's what I said. You misheard me. Anyway, what's your project called again?"

Ailsa knew what she had heard. She also knew Credenza was trying to change the subject.

"I'm building something called an aeoli-pile..." said Ailsa, pronouncing the word carefully. "It's basically this old water experiment. You fill a cup with water and put two straws at the bottom, then it spins because gravity pushes the water down and out through the straws. I think it's sometimes called a Hero's Engine."[9]

"Seeing as it's you," said Credenza with a smirk, "maybe you should just call it a 'Sorry I'm Late'?"

---

9   First invented by Hero of Alexandria, a Greek inventor who lived in Egypt over 2,000 years ago, and who by all accounts was a bit of a hero (at least when it came to inventing).

CHAPTER 6

DELUGE

The science teacher, Dr Matthews, was preoccupied, writing on the board, as the pupils sat in numb silence. Ailsa and Credenza opened the door and crept in. With his back turned, Dr Matthews had no way of seeing them.

"Sir Isaac Newton lived in England in the seventeeth century," Dr Matthews was saying, his pen squeaking away like a hungry baby bird, "and he spent most of his days trying to explain how the world worked. Gravity, mathematics, the entire world was a curiosity to him. He was always asking why..."

"Why?" snarked a kid from the back to laughter.

Ailsa felt a breath of wind next to her and watched in horror as Credenza shot past, using the laughter as a distraction[10], tucking herself in behind her desk before

---

10   This sneaky move shall from this day forward be called "Doing a Credenza".

Dr Matthews turned around. When he did, it was Ailsa, and Ailsa alone, who stood, abandoned, in the centre of the classroom.

There she was again, the Girl Who Was Late.

Dr Matthews pretended not to notice her. "Good question," he said to the kid at the back. "Newton," he continued, "was curious about the world. He was always asking questions: why gravity existed, why motion appeared to obey certain laws, and of course," he was looking at Ailsa now, smiling, "why Ailsa Craig is always late. Though some things, of course, are beyond understanding."

The room guffawed. Dr Matthews's smile turned into a glare. He pointed at Ailsa's empty seat. She skulked over and sat down, her cheeks burning.

"Newton's Laws of Motion," Dr Matthews continued as Ailsa sat down, "are one of the foundations of physical science.[11] As we start doing our experiments in class, I want your scientific minds to start thinking like Newton did, collecting and interrogating your data and analysing your findings. As scientists our job is to always question

---

11   Newton famously watched an apple fall from a tree, which
      made him think about how gravity works, and why it moves
      objects in a straight line. Later that evening, he invented apple
      crumble. (Probably.)

what we know, in order that we may find out what we do not."

Ailsa felt the room watching her.

Credenza was in her usual spot in the back row, along with her gang – four girls who hung on every Dingwall word and laughed at everything she said.

"Now then, your science project proposal deadline. Today is the day. We've already heard from most of you. Credenza, do you have something to share with us?"

A frozen panic grabbed Ailsa.

Argh. Today, it was due today.

Credenza jumped up to the front of the class and opened her fancy laptop, which projected an ornate 3D model on to the wall.

"Lights, please?"

Dr Matthew obliged, and Credenza proceeded to demonstrate the workings of her wind turbine project. When she was done, and the lights came up, the room broke into spontaneous applause.

"Great work, Miss Dingwall," said Dr Matthews. He turned to Ailsa with an expectant smile. "Ailsa, how about you?"

"I'm well, thanks. How are you?"

Ailsa knew that humour was the only ploy she had left. The room obliged with a polite sniff.

Dr Matthews did not look amused.

"Ailsa." He left a pause that said: "I'm waiting."

"Well, sir, the thing is…" Ailsa was blushing again, worse than ever, and she found herself momentarily lost for words.

"Tardy McLateface," whispered a voice from behind her.

"Unbelievable," said another.

"I mean, it's sort of her only talent."

Ailsa heard Credenza chuckling at this one.

So she bit her lip and told the truth about the explosion. How she and her dad had gone for a walk to watch the fireworks at Blackford Hill, and when they'd returned, their house was no more. A gas leak, she'd heard. Perhaps. No one seemed to know.

Now the entire class laughed, as people sometimes do at uncomfortable big news, and Ailsa felt that leaden feeling in her stomach once again.

When the bell rang for the end of class, Ailsa tried to slink out, but Dr Matthews intercepted her by the door.

"I'm sorry to single you out like that, Ailsa. But you've got the ability. You just don't do the follow-through. Your grades are not reflecting your best work at the moment."

"My house really did explode."

"So I gather, and I'm very sorry. And relieved you and

your father are OK, of course. Look, I can give you a few more days, if that helps. But this problem goes beyond this week. And I think you know that."

She did.

"I just never seem to have enough time," said Ailsa.

"Welcome to the world," sighed Dr Matthews. "The earth rotates from day to day. But no matter where we are on its surface, we all get the same amount of moments. It's only how we spend them that matters."

In fact, Ailsa knew exactly how she spent her moments. And her days, her weeks, and months.

Maybe that was part of the problem.

The metronome of Ailsa's life was set at a steady rhythm: one week with Dad, one week with Mum, repeat, repeat. It was never quite enough time to settle.

She had two homes[12], but no centre of gravity.

There were a million other kids worse off than her, she knew: kids who arrived at school with nothing in their bellies, kids with trouble at home, or no homes at all. Ailsa had it easy and probably did have the time, somewhere. But for some reason, no matter how she divided up the moments of her own day, there was never enough to go around.

---

12   Well, one and a half at the moment. But you get the idea.

Talking to Dr Matthews, Ailsa tried to project an aura of responsibility and calm: the Good Student. The minute she was back in the corridor, she knew that it was a better idea to revert to a different persona – the Rover.

You see, Ailsa wasn't the type to join a social club, so she moved from here to there, landing wherever she liked. There was the popular group who occupied the big table at lunchtime. This was Credenza's power base, and she was the empress of all she surveyed. On other tables, there were scattered alliances and shared spaces. Neutral territory: scholars and gamers, the anime crowd and the sporty types (some of whom crossed over with the popular gang). Finally, there was "Team Miscellaneous", as Ailsa's friend Stu liked to call them. Friends of no fixed abode. Free agents, at liberty to float where they pleased. That was where Ailsa preferred to be.

She floated so much she would often find herself talking in slightly different ways to people, depending on who they were.

Truth be told, Ailsa was a shape-shifter.

CHAPTER 7

SHAPE-SHIFTING

It's not that she was an actual werewolf, or the Greek god Proteus, or that she would sometimes wake up to find her bed mysteriously covered in woodland mulch. She didn't change into other creatures either (though she often wished she could).

What she could do was to transform into different Ailsas.

On a daily basis.

Loyal friend. Diligent pupil. Midnight reader.

Dutiful daughter.

She would assume her different forms depending on the situation, like choosing what scarf to wear, or switching hats. There were many versions of Ailsa. And, somewhere in the middle of it all, the real her. She simply wasn't sure which one it was yet.

She bumped into Stu on her way to lunch. He seemed upset. Ailsa knew that his home life was a challenge, and he had special reading classes to do during breaks which sometimes made him the target of cruel jokes. He had been one of the few kids at school who had welcomed her in her first days here, and Ailsa had never forgotten his kindness.

"You OK?" she asked.

Stu shrugged, and gave her a thumbs up – their friend-code that he was mostly OK, and he didn't really want to talk about it.

"How 'bout you?" asked Stu.

Ailsa shrugged. She didn't really know how she felt.

What she did know was that she was sick and tired of being late. That had to change. Today.

She marched into the school library after the final bell, determined not to leave until her science project was finished.

There was just one problem: Ossian.

Credenza's older brother by a couple of years, "Ozzie" was the kind of kid who was always getting into some flavour of trouble. There was the time he put the school up for sale online. The day he covered the stairs with bubble wrap. And, of course, no one would ever forget the unholy army of shrieking rubber chickens hidden under the principal's seat at Holiday Assembly. Truth be told, it was a miracle he was still allowed to come to school at all – but Ailsa wondered if that might have something to do with him being a member of a very powerful and wealthy Edinburgh family.

On this particular day, Ozzie had been in a curious mood. He had decided to see what would happen if he poured a packet of Cinnamon Crunch cereal down every single toilet in the second-floor bathrooms and flushed them all at once. Objectively, it was an interesting experiment: a study of water pressure, flow rate and fluid dynamics. However, in another more accurate sense: it was a watery apocalypse.

Even on a good day, the old school plumbing system couldn't cope. Now that it had to deal with fortified whole grains and added sugar, it gave up all hope. This was why, three seconds after Ailsa sat down at her favourite chair by the library window, it started to drizzle in the science section. Within seconds, there was a cold, hard rain falling all over the dystopian YA novels.

After helping Mrs Strickland, the school librarian, save the books, Ailsa made her way to her mum's flat around the corner from school. She would finish her work there.

She loved Mum's flat. When her parents got divorced, Mum had moved out of the house up the hill, and this bright corner flat had become Ailsa's other home. Unlike some kids, Ailsa had always understood very well why her mother and father had decided to split. They had never seemed to agree on anything, ever. Lulu, being the older sister, had experienced more of their togetherness.

When she had still lived with them, Lulu would often put Ailsa to bed, as both their parents were usually out working.

"What was it like," Ailsa would ask her, "before the war?"

Ailsa wasn't exactly upset about any of it. The closest feeling she could put her finger on was nostalgia – but for a time she could barely even remember. Mum, Dad, Ailsa and Lulu, all together. That night when the power went out, and they lit the gas stove with matches, eating warmed-up leftover pizza by candlelight.[13] Lulu had worked after school at the local newsagents in those days, and sometimes brought Ailsa back a bag of caramel chews as a secret midnight snack. But even Lulu couldn't remember the last time that Mum and Dad saw eye to eye on anything. The sisters would often talk late into the night, and Lulu always made a point of telling her the truth about their parents, even when it was hard to hear. "They're better off apart, I promise you," Lulu

---

13 Tip: don't try warming the actual pizza by candlelight. It takes for ever and burns in the middle.

had said to her one caramel-infused night. "Better for them, and better for us." It was only when Ailsa started studying chemistry in science class that she began to understand why.

The volcano experiment, in particular.

This was a classroom project that Dr Matthews had helped them do at the beginning of the year. It involved baking soda and vinegar, which her lab notes told her was an example of acid–base chemistry. Vinegar, by its nature, was acidic. Baking soda, on the other hand, was something called sodium bicarbonate.[14] It is what is known as a _base_.[15] Which is, as far as anyone can surmise, as far away from an acid as you can get. And the thing about chemically-opposite things like acids and bases is that when they are put together, they react.

Ailsa's school jotter laid out the details:

The Volcano Experiment:

1. Make a volcano-like container.

2. Place the baking soda inside.

---

14 (With the formula $NaHCO_3$, since you ask.)

15 Except on weekends.

3. Pour in the vinegar (not the whole bottle...).

4. Take cover!

When Ailsa first saw the bubbling reaction in class, it reminded her that a similar chemical process existed between the two separate elements of her mother and her father. And although who was soda and who was vinegar often changed, the reaction itself did not. For a few years, life had been full of foaming eruptions of different sizes, and nothing Ailsa ever did seemed to prevent them (no matter how much her parents reassured her that they were not her fault).

But after their divorce, day by day those reactions subsided. Soon there were no more volcanoes, which seemed like good news for everyone. From Ailsa's observations, she had noticed over time that both Mum and Dad had started smiling a lot more. She heard them both laugh again. Little things didn't seem to matter as much, or make them sad, like they used to.

The chemistry had just ... changed.

Even now that they were temporarily under the same roof, things didn't feel quite so ... *volcanic* as before.

Lulu had left home now too. She had always wanted to travel, to see the world and pick up work where she could. She would always send a little money home to Ailsa with a card that read "for caramels". Ailsa missed her terribly.

After she'd worked as much as she could, Ailsa called Mum (who was still at work herself) and reminded her she'd be home later. It didn't take long to walk up the hill to the address that Dad had texted her, their temporary abode. It was in the same neighbourhood as their old exploded house. She hopped on the bus and daydreamed. As she strolled, she daydreamed.

Too late, she realized that she had let her own autopilot take her right back to the old house on Bothwell Gardens, where the same crater-like hole squatted, waiting, like a troll under a bridge.

There was yellow tape strung up around the entire lot in unfriendly letters which read:

DANGER KEEP OUT

A window on a neighbour's house reflected the setting sun, well below the horizon now. The burnt-orange sky was melting into blue, grey and black. As she passed a street light, it flickered on suddenly, startling her.

A thought flashed inside Ailsa's head.

The treasure chest.

They still hadn't found Grandma's steamer trunk.

Maybe it was still here.

It was this thought that propelled Ailsa up to the gate and over the rubble of the garden wall. She gave this no thought whatsoever, and recklessly ducked under the yellow tape.[16]

The beautiful rowan tree outside her window had survived, but barely. It had been standing guard outside her attic bedroom room so loyally for so long, Ailsa felt it deserved to have some loyalty from her too. She wondered how she could help it recover.

The poor thing had been bisected by the blast, up and down its entire length, as if struck from above by the sharpest axe in the world. It had wilted to the left and the right from its wide base, whilst above, branches were held up as if in surrender. It was almost defiant in its injury, as if it was saying *I've had worse*.

Ailsa was just turning back to the street when something caught the very edge of her eye.

It appeared to be inside the core of the tree, past the bark and in the tissue of the wood itself, where the

---

16 Don't try this at home, or indeed anywhere else. Yellow tape isn't usually meant to be welcoming. Except, perhaps, at the end of a running race. In which case, probably best to keep going.

deep centre had been ripped in two. Peering through the gloom, she could make out a series of familiar shapes carved into the inner flesh of the tree.

They were letters. Forming three words, carved by hand into the wood. Not from the *outside* of the tree.

Somehow, someone had written those words from the *inside*.

Impossible, of course. Nonsense.

Ailsa's mind whirred as she searched for logical explanations. Someone must have written this today, she thought to herself. Someone probably came along, saw the yellow tape, ignored the footnote on the previous page, not to mention the wrecked house and the damaged tree, and thought they'd just hop over the wall and randomly carve three words into the inside of the trunk of a barely-alive rowan tree.

That didn't sound too convincing. Or logical. Or sane.

But surely, thought Ailsa, *there was no other way this could have been written. Could there?* Yet, there they were. Three simple words:

EVERY SECOND COUNTS

The letter "Y" had a dramatic loop to it, and the top of the "T" was angled upwards, like a ramp. That seemed familiar to Ailsa, but she couldn't work out why. She also knew something else: hadn't Dad said those very words this morning? She spun around and started to run home – she would confront him, right now, and get to the truth. But she'd taken only a couple of paces when she stopped dead.

There, glinting in the light of the street lamps, were a pair of glasses, partly buried in the dirt. Gold half-moons attached to a long chain. A very old-fashioned pair. Ailsa found this odd because the only person who wore glasses in her family was her. And she had certainly never worn this kind.

She decided to leave them there and continued down the path. She had only taken two steps when she heard the noise.

It came from behind her, in a dark corner.

Hidden at the base of the high hedge that surrounded the small garden. The shadows of twilight had disappeared entirely now, any trace of afterglow gone from the sky.

As if the night had crept up on her from behind and drained the last part of the day while she wasn't looking. She spun around to stare at the source of the noise.

She could see only shadows, dark leaves and dirt.

But wait. There.

The hedge now moved slightly, rustling and pulsing like a snake. The sound came again, from around the corner of the house this time, a wet, snuffling, scrobbly[17] kind of noise. One that seemed completely out of place in a city garden.

Ailsa immediately thought of a badger, even though she'd never seen one in real life, let alone heard one around the corner in the dark.

She wondered how big they got.

And how hungry.

She was getting nervous now, here in the shadows, but her curiosity was still getting the better of her. She began to creep towards the corner and the noise. Looking down at the grass, she could just make out a series of pawprints leading around to the north side of the house. Against all her instincts, she followed.

The sniffing noise, as if luring her around that corner, now suddenly stopped. There was no birdsong, no noise at all bar the rustle and snap of the large plastic tarpaulins, which the salvage team had hung all around the house.

The street light at her back was stronger now, and she caught a glimpse of her own silhouette as it was cast across the patch of lawn towards the far hedge.

---

17   Scrobbly (adj.): reminiscent of a snurffling snortyness.

41

Ailsa's eyes also caught something else.

She could see it only in outline.

It was a snout. Long, full of tiny sharp teeth. It appeared to be eating the leaves of the hedge. At least, the leaves still illuminated by the light. But badgers, as far as Ailsa was aware, did not eat hedges at night. Looking closer, she noticed that the creature wasn't so much eating the leaves themselves but the glow that the light cast upon them.

As if the thing was eating the light itself.

It couldn't be. Could it?

When she looked again, the shadow was gone.

And then it hit her.

This was not a badger.

This was a Gloaming.

A Night Gloaming, to be specific. Here to eat the light.

She had light in her eyes too, she knew that.

Would it try to eat her next? Ailsa couldn't believe her own thoughts. She tried to calm herself as another sound came.

A guttural growl, almost too low to hear.

It was coming from right behind her.

CHAPTER 8

Run

When there's a deep growling noise like that behind you,
the best advice is to

        R

             U

                N

                   !

CHAPTER 9

Run, I said!

Ailsa ran.

CHAPTER 10

Wait, Not That Way!

Very fast.[18]

---

18   No, faster than that.

CHAPTER 11

THE SHED

Confession time: Ailsa took off so fast it was impossible to keep up with her.[19] To be fair, it was dark, she was moving very fast, and there was a Gloaming-like shadow lurking there. Anyway, she's gone now, so may as well describe one of the blades of grass that was sitting nearby. It was small, and green, and—

Wait, there she is.

On a patch of mud at the edge of the crater.

Where were we? Oh yes, panic.

Ailsa's mind pulsed with it. Raw, wheezing, hair-raising panic. Her breath, ragged and shallow, clouded the air around her. Her mind whirled like her old fidget spinner. What if the Gloaming was still hungry? What if it came for her and consumed her here? What if no one came to help her, even if she cried out?

---

19   Plus the ground was really slippery, OK?

She skittered and slid over the mud towards a small shed which she knew Dad rarely used. A strong whip of breeze threw one of the plastic tarpaulins in her face with a *whack*! For a moment it felt like she'd been caught in a ghastly trap.

She wriggled out of the plastic and kept going towards the shed. She'd once seen Dad grab a shovel from there, so she knew the door should open.

For now, she dived behind the structure, pausing for breath.

This was all wrong. This was not normal.

At all.

Ailsa felt in her pocket for Grandma's postcard. She needed something to reassure her. It was too dark to read it, but she suddenly wondered if perhaps the Scientific Method could help her make some sense of this predicament. She re-stated the steps from memory and whispered the advice to herself:

STATE YOUR PROBLEM CLEARLY

Well, I'm possibly being hunted by a Night Gloaming.

Or something like one. That's obvious. I suppose. Is it?

Aren't you paying attention, Ailsa?

It occurred to Ailsa that her statement wasn't clear, and that talking to herself probably wasn't helping

47

matters. She tried again, this time posing her problem as a more precise question.

How can I keep myself safe right now?

That was better. A simple goal for an experiment.

She recalled the next step in her head.

MAKE A HYPOTHESIS

If there's a way in, she thought, there must be a way out. It usually involves a door. She conjured up the postcard in her mind's eye once again. There it was, in Grandma's handwriting.

EXPERIMENT AND TEST

Well, that was simple: to keep herself safe, she would simply have to try the first option to hand and follow where it led.

Looking up, she could see a door.

It looked like a door in the back of the shed.

She didn't recall there being two doors that led into the shed, but she decided to go with it. *I'll be safe inside*, thought Ailsa, and pulled on the handle.

The door was heavy and old. It opened with a sigh, as if the air inside was glad of the chance of escape.

CHAPTER 12

SUMMA SUMMARUM

Keeping up? Good. If not, don't worry if you've missed something in all the kerfuffle. For example, this garden shed that Ailsa recently walked inside?

You should know something about it.

This was not like any other shed Ailsa had ever seen.

Normally these places smelled of mossy dirt and old paint. But this place reeked of mouldering paper, polished wood and dust. Several antique lights hung along the walls, amber filaments casting shadows over piles of identical leather-bound books that were stacked neatly from floor to ceiling. In fact, there was nothing shed-like about the room at all.

The air was utterly still. Every sound felt amplified.

A small wooden desk sat at the far end, which admittedly wasn't very far away at all, where an even smaller woman rested her elbows on it, sitting on a low stool.

She wore an officious-looking outfit topped off with a

pair of bright green wire-rimmed eyeglasses, perched at the end of a tiny nose. Her shock of red hair was arranged in a spiral that made Ailsa think of strawberry soft serve.

The woman was writing in a vast red ledger, which Ailsa realized was identical to every other volume stacked around the inside. Sheds normally contain garden tools, paint and forgotten board games. Here, it was all leather-bound ledgers and small ladies with red spiral hair.

The woman's pen scratched the paper in a judgemental rhythm. Anxious she was once again in trouble, Ailsa tried to say hello, but her throat was so dry she only managed a croak. Maybe it was the dust. She coughed politely and tried again.

"Can you help me, please?"

Whump! The woman closed her ledger sharply.

The smell of mouldy paper drifted past Ailsa's nose. In gold type on the cover were two words: "SUMMA SUMMARUM". Ailsa had no idea what they meant.

The woman's eyes were violet, and Ailsa realized she had yet to see them blink.

The woman re-opened the ledger with a flick of her finger. "Well," she sniffed. Her Scottish accent was sharp and pointy like a needle. "I must say this is all highly irregular."

Ailsa nodded. Because, well – it was.

"I imagine you were born at midnight, is that it?"

Ailsa was surprised at the question. But it was also, bizarrely, correct. Her time of birth had been exactly midnight. She suddenly recalled Mum telling her the story. Several hospital staff had been so excited by the time of her birth that they'd printed out a little extra bonus birth certificate for her (an unofficial one, drawn by the nursing staff). It pictured a crescent moon. "For The Midnight Girl." Her time of birth, written underneath, read:

12:00:00!

Ailsa always remembered that piece of paper because Grandma, in particular, had never stopped mentioning it. She had once whispered to her as she fell asleep that she was "a perfect midnight child", as if that had somehow earned her something, like a badge.

"Is that a yes, then? Midnight?" said the woman.

Ailsa nodded.

The woman pursed her lips as if to say "thought so". She scrawled for a moment longer in the ledger and muttered something about paperwork. Finally, she glared up at Ailsa.

"Name?" she snapped.

"Um – Ailsa. Craig."

The woman stared. "Well, which is it?"

"Er, both. Will I be safe in here?" blurted Ailsa, suddenly regretting her choice of hiding place. "And can I ask what you're doing in our garden?"

The woman ignored her and kept writing. For a few seconds it was the only sound in the room. Ailsa thought she hadn't heard, so she drew a big breath to try asking again. But the woman carried on.

"You'll be quite safe," she said with a sigh. "So long as you stay out of trouble."

"That's sort of why I came in here. But I still don't understand what—"

"Seven bells left," snapped the woman. "Only barely, mark you. So you'd better get a shift on if you're going."

Bells? thought Ailsa. *What bells?*

Perhaps she had misheard.

The woman jerked her head in the direction of the door behind her, which Ailsa had only recently opened. Except now, instead of being a smelly old shed door, it had transformed into one of the fanciest doors Ailsa had ever seen.

The frame was fashioned from some dark and ancient wood, finely polished, while the door itself was constructed from olive-green panels, padded with leather and studded at the edges with a narrow band of brass. A sharp, frosty current of air was whistling under the frame. Ailsa hadn't felt the cold in the garden when she had clambered inside.

Well, at least now Grandma would be proud. Here was the missing data her experiment had been waiting for. She had stated the problem clearly, amassed the necessary data, and now she had a conclusion.

The door beckoned. She pushed it and stepped through into something that was completely and entirely not the back garden.

She heard the door slam behind her, as if borne by a violent gust of wind, and as much as Ailsa blinked, she saw nothing at all. She was standing in the centre of the most profound darkness.

A void without end. It unbalanced her.

Perhaps more terrifying than that was the silence.

It wrapped around her like a velvet shroud. Ailsa could feel her blood thrumming in her veins, sense every beat of her heart, every sigh and shudder of her quickening lungs. Without her bearings, she began to tip forward. As she lost her balance utterly, her hands reached out in vain, flailing, straining, looking for a handhold, wincing for impact, and finding only air. Tumbling over herself, she was opening her mouth to scream when a sharp and frosty breeze snatched the breath from her throat. The breeze became a howling wind and blew her suddenly upright.

Then, just as quickly, a brilliant light hurt her eyes.

CHAPTER 13

SYDEKYCK

Ailsa was now in a tiny courtyard which felt more like the bottom of a well. Dark stone buildings rose around her on all sides, immensely tall, with no windows anywhere; a patch of rose-coloured sky was visible far above her head. The only path out was an alleyway which turned away sharply up ahead.

A freezing wind swirled around her. She pulled her trusty yellow hat down tight over her ears. Her glasses were fogging up, so she cleaned them on the edge of her sleeve. A little better, but that air was cold. As she looked down, she saw why: the square of ground underneath her feet was covered in snow. Thin, hard-packed, solid. It had clearly been here for several days. It bore no footprints, not even from an animal. None of this made any sense to Ailsa. Earlier, on the street, there hadn't been a single snowflake left on the ground. It hadn't even been that chilly.

Now, her nostrils stung in the icy air. She felt utterly alone. Ailsa spun back around to retrace her steps – but found only a thick wall of ancient stone. There was no door there at all, not even the memory of one.

Ailsa shivered. How could this be?

She felt for Grandma's postcard. It was still in her pocket, but for now her fingers felt too numb to hold it.

She calmed her breathing and tried to find her bearings. She figured this area was somewhere down under George IV Bridge, perhaps near the Lawnmarket. But she knew for sure there was no shortcut between that part of town and her dad's garden shed.

A bell tolled again from somewhere, deep and ancient. What had the woman said? Seven bells? What did she mean by that? What bells? Whose bells, exactly? Those bells?

The wind, as if hearing her unease, whistled to her from around the corner. It was then that Ailsa felt something wrap itself around her ankles and rub against her calf.

A soft, furry tail.

The cat was the colour of ash, with brilliant white paws that looked like sports socks that blended entirely into the snow. His tail had a tiny bald ring in the middle of it where the fur had worn away – it was as if he had once caught it on something, or perhaps something had caught him. Ailsa bent down to say hello. He seemed young and bright-eyed and diffident (in the way that most cats can be). He was wearing a red collar with a metal tag.

"Sydekyck," said Ailsa, reading it aloud.

The cat glared at her, faintly annoyed. Perhaps she had mispronounced it. The tag had no phone number, no address. And as beautiful as he was, how was this cat going to help her get out of here? As if reading Ailsa's thoughts, Sydekyck eased up against her, his tail now tugging firmly at her shin.

As if to say: follow me.

"Well, sure," said Ailsa, sprinting after him, "at least you seem to know where you're going."

CHAPTER 14

THE PASSENGER

Ailsa ran flat-out after Sydekyck as he scampered down one alley and up the next, doubling back, round and through, until Ailsa was tied up like a pretzel, dizzy with the effort.

At last, the alleys widened into streets.

Ailsa felt the sky broadening above her.

Edinburgh had always looked like it had been hewn by giants from solid rock, and while there was stone here too, Ailsa could also see a serious amount of wood. Wooden stairs, wooden balconies, windowsills and beams, all haphazard and charming. It had the feeling of ancient worlds, a time long ago and yet right now in front of her. She knew there was an Old Town of Edinburgh, and a New Town beyond it (she lived in neither, however). But this place felt somehow stuck right in the middle.

She wondered how on earth she had missed this part of town for all these years. Then again, being eleven years old, she wasn't much for wandering unknown parts of the city on her own. There were cobbles on the streets (they were called "setts" around here). There were dark windows and steep, chaotic roofs.

Her attention was drawn suddenly back to the ground, to a bank of snow set against a wall. Sticking out from it were green-stalked flowers with bright yellow petals, even more vivid than the yellow of her hat.

Sunflowers.

Ailsa knew from her *Bumper Book of British Plants* that sunflowers only bloomed in the summer. What were they doing here in the frost? She was so distracted that she momentarily lost track of where she was going – which was, unfortunately, straight across a road. Behind her, she heard a low grumbling sound, and an almighty shout echoed nearby—

"LOOK OUT!"

Ailsa turned to see a suited woman with grey hair and red glasses on the other side of the street, pointing like a maniac at a spot right behind her. Ailsa spun round as a horn blared.

An old black taxi was heading straight for her. The cab lurched violently, almost grazing her arm, blasting past her in a pressure wave of engine noise and burnt oil. It was an ancient vehicle, the kind you might see in old black-and-white photos. It had a long gear lever, a lantern up on the front, and a big round rubber horn. The driver was a tiny woman in a uniform: tartan cap, plus-fours and goggles, her cheeks red and raw from the biting air.

While the passenger compartment was enclosed, the driver's seat had no roof or windows. The cab turned and powered away.

"Hey, come back!" shouted Ailsa.

The taxi grumbled on, ignoring her pleas. From the back seat, the passenger turned around to stare through a tiny window in the back. Ailsa knew the face well.

It belonged to Credenza Dingwall.

CHAPTER 15

St. Ninian's Row

Ailsa sprinted after the cab.

Credenza. What on earth?[20]

She passed the businesswoman with the red glasses, who was marching off into a side street. Ailsa called out to her, but the woman waved her words away with a dismissive gesture, as if to say: *yes yes yes, far too busy.* Her sharp wedge of grey hair swished and sashayed with every hurried step.

Everyone here seems to be in an awful hurry, thought Ailsa.

The cab was rapidly disappearing into the distance. The street eased downhill in a straight line, flattening out towards the bottom into a large plaza below. Each side of the street was packed with timber-fronted houses

---

20 No, I mean seriously, I had no idea she would be here either and I wrote this whole thing!

that loomed over each other in galleries, layered, storey upon storey encroaching further into the street, like an arching avenue of trees. The further Ailsa ran, the higher the buildings rose above her. Each new floor was some six or seven feet further towards the centre than the one preceding it. At the very top, two people might open their shuttered windows and comfortably shake hands.

A sign said "St. Ninian's Row".

The snow on the ground still showed fresh compression from the taxi's tyre treads, tiny dots of engine oil leading the way in a straight line towards the vast square beyond.

Credenza. Where was this place, and what on earth was she doing here? It was then that Ailsa became aware that she was being followed once more. That cat, she thought.

She was mistaken. High up on the rooftops, staring down at her, Ailsa could see a figure keeping pace as she hurried down the street. It seemed like a very dangerous thing to do, what with all the steep pitched roofs, chimney stacks, loose tiles and fatal drops to a certain death on the hard stone below.

But she could see him more clearly now, and there he was.

A boy.

He was a few years older than her. His face was dirty, but his eyes were bright and, even at this distance, she could tell they were different colours: one was hazel, the other one blue. He wore what appeared to be a large tartan cape, thrown around his body like a blanket. He was quick, poised and balanced, hardly looking where he was going. He was keeping pace alongside Ailsa even as she sped up.

It was only then that she saw the others.

The streets before her had been empty at first.

But the further into this strange part of town she ran, the more people she started to see. They were staring from the windows at first. Then, one by one, they emerged from the doorways and the shadows. On the street in front of her, a man and a woman suddenly appeared, friendly smiles on their faces. They waved to her and nodded, as if they were expecting Ailsa to be there.

Both were similar to the woman in the shed. Smaller than Ailsa, and wearing the same old-fashioned forms of Scottish tartan. They could have been on their way to a party, dressed in the kind of Highland finery you usually only see on Burns Night.[21] There were men and women,

---

21 January 25th, the celebration of the birth of famous Scottish poet Robert Burns. He's the one who wrote the words to "Auld Lang Syne" (amongst many other words).

small children and some older folk too, but their smiles seemed less friendly than the others'.

Ailsa looked back up to the rooftops, but the boy had disappeared. When she reached the plaza, she found it was teeming with activity. Each and every person was dressed up in vibrant, joyous tartan. A handful more, who appeared a little more imperious than the rest, "peacock-type people" as her dad used to call them, strutted around importantly, as if waiting for something. These people wore shirts with fancy ruffs billowing out from their chests like babys' bibs, and long floppy cuffs extending from the end of their sleeves. They paraded down the street in high-collared long-coats, their bright red waistcoats sporting multiple brocaded pockets from which sprouted a single powder-blue handkerchief. Ailsa saw three of these people in succession and noted that the handkerchief had been placed in exactly the same pocket, in precisely the same way.

It was all so overwhelming. Ailsa wondered if this was all some strange historical dressing-up society. She smiled at all of them, enchanted by the colours and finery.

The same friendly couple had followed her down here, and she caught their eye. The couple nodded to her, a little awkward.

"Hello," said Ailsa.

The man furrowed his brow for a minute. Finally, he said: "Thank you."

Ailsa's face must have betrayed her confusion. She pulled her hat down a little tighter on her head. "I like your clothes," she said.

The man scratched at his neck; Ailsa could see an angry red rash where his skin touched the collar.

"Yes, thank you, as I say, well, they're—"

The woman elbowed the man sharply in the ribs. The blow appeared to transform his face back into a wide, bizarre grin.

"They're fine."

"More than fine, I'd say," said Ailsa. "Are they for a special occasion or something?"

"Well..." The man shrugged, hoping not to get another poke.

"Not as fine as the colour of your hat, dear," the woman said. "A very Blackthorn colour it is too, frosted sunflower."

Ailsa wasn't sure what she meant by Blackthorn, or why anyone would want to frost a sunflower, but it sounded nice enough and she smiled back anyway. The woman kept eye contact, nodding along to her words almost as if she had memorized them.

"We are so happy to see you," said the woman, pulling

the man tighter to her, arm in arm. "And please know that we are here for anything you may need," she added, with an awkward bobbing gesture that was almost a curtsy.

"Thank you."

"You'll have gotten your number then?" asked the man, as if suddenly remembering to be nice to her.

Ailsa blinked. "Sorry, what number?"

"Your voucher," said the woman. "With your number on it?"

Ailsa shook her head, completely confused.

"Oh goodness, dear," said the woman. "Your first time, is it? Well, you'd better hurry on down to the Exchange then, we best not keep you. Bottom of the hill, can't miss it. Ask for the Reckoners. The time is always right to do what is right, isn't it?"

They both laughed politely, and Ailsa, being Ailsa, laughed along with them – if only to keep them company. She didn't really get the joke, if indeed there was one at all.

The couple both smiled and hurried away into the throng of people in the square. The woman glanced back worriedly at Ailsa, but when she met her gaze once more her face burst again into that strange half-smile.

In fact, everyone she made eye contact with had the same expression. It was a bizarre combination of genuine welcome, and, as far as Ailsa could work out, nerves. How she could make anyone nervous was quite beyond Ailsa at this point. But then again, she thought, how could she know what was going on for people? Her dad had once taught her that in a supermarket. "You never know how someone's day is going," he would say. "So it's best always to try to be kind."

In the centre of the square stood a dark bell tower, rising high into the sky. On the south side as she approached, she could see a large terrace with a wooden balcony on the first floor. It looked like a public gathering place.

The bell tolled. It was so loud it shook her ribs.

So that's where it's coming from, thought Ailsa.

The sound ushered in a change to the mood of the crowd. The ones wearing red waistcoats and blue handkerchiefs made a strange lyrical motion – pulling the fabric from one pocket and deftly placing it into another. They did this almost unconsciously, in the way we might rub our eyes if we are tired.

Far across the square, Ailsa could see the grey bob and red glasses of the helpful woman who had warned her about the taxi. She was entering an imposing building, flanked by huge marble columns. The taxi was there too, taking another passenger.

No sign of Credenza, who was no doubt already inside.

Ailsa sprinted the final distance and arrived out of breath at the steps. She was met by two tough-looking guards in grand high-collared jackets and black waistcoats. They narrowed their eyes at Ailsa, but said nothing as she stepped through the door.

CHAPTER 16

THE GATHERING

Inside was a vast lobby area with stone floors and even more columns. Far above, a circular glass skylight filtered the last shreds of the day into columns of silver and gold. It was like lying on the bottom of a sunlit ocean, gazing up at the shimmering surface.

Every floor in the building was open to this central atrium. Exterior walkways circled up to the ceiling, with intricate wrought-iron railings the only barrier to protect from a nasty fall. A warren of halls, rooms and doors seemed to lead off in other directions on every level. At the other end of the lobby was a gleaming metal lift set inside a cage. It stretched up to every floor of the structure. The lobby floor itself was a pattern of black and white squares, reminiscent of a very strange chessboard. Ailsa had the distinct feeling that she was now one of the pieces. She hoped she was a queen, but by the strange looks she was now getting from the guards by the door, she had a sneaking suspicion she was probably a pawn.

Glasses clinked nearby, animated conversations bouncing off the walls. Ailsa saw a door open – inside was a fancy party of some kind. When a waiter floated by with a tray of fancy-looking snacks, it didn't take her long to slip right behind and follow in his wake.

Inside was, if anything, even more grand. Ornate silver candelabras filled the room with a golden light, and the space was awash with bright, shiny faces. All of them in smart evening attire, all engaged, chatting, laughing. Relaxed and, perhaps, a little pleased with themselves.

This was the place to be.

Then, one by one, Ailsa began to recognize them. Everyone here was a face she knew. Not from her daily life, not at all. These people were famous. Successful.

Famous movie and social media stars, singers, fashion models, and older vaguely familiar adults who (by the way they were dressed) Ailsa assumed were either politicians or business types. Over there: that woman with the grey bob, the red glasses and the pinstripe suit, the one who had called out to Ailsa from across the road, and no doubt saved her life. There, by a small fountain, was a young sports star she had seen online, one who managed to be patron of several charities at the same time as winning major trophies. There was the famous gamer who won the world championships whilst graduating from university. That singer who was always on the radio when she wasn't writing novels. Those business types too, powerful-looking folk in serious suits, all of them dizzyingly successful and busy, all of whom clearly didn't ever seem to wake up bleary, exhausted or get dragged in multiple directions by conflicting demands, parents, siblings, teachers, strangers, themselves. There weren't many kids that she could see. But she was here, and no doubt Credenza was too.

Ailsa only had one question. *Why were they all here?*

In pride of place on a small dais sat a striking and imperious woman in an elegant tartan dress. She was flanked by large, squat bodyguards in more traditional tartans.

The woman was as thin as a coat hanger, with bulbous eyes like an ostrich. There were jewels and greenery draped around her neck, and a shawl carefully placed over her shoulders. She had a fine-boned aristocratic air, and a tiny, pixie-like nose. Her eyes glowed with confidence, and on her head, perched on what appeared to be pointed ears, she wore a crown of purple flowers and twigs. Overall, she had the air of someone quite used to people bowing to her.

There was something altogether "Credenza" about her, in fact.

Ting ting ting ting.

A grinning, self-satisfied man bounced up on to a small stage, a chaos of ruffs and shiny buttons. He had a pair of gold half-moon glasses on a chain around his neck. He perched the glasses on the end of his nose and flashed the audience a simpering grin. He was about her parents' age, Ailsa reasoned, but had the air of an older, wiser man. He flicked his hair away from his eyes in a well-practised motion and continued hitting his wine glass with a tiny spoon. He wore a sporran that looked like it was the head of a badger, the poor creature's nose acting as a clasp at the top.

The room fell into an expectant hush, and the man bowed to the elegant pointy-eared woman.

"My Lady Blackthorn," he began, addressing her with a tiny bow and a smile that showed tiny brown teeth. "Noble and distinguished guests. Four and twenty years ago," he began, "I made the most extraordinary scientific discovery. It was a day I shall never forget. The day I discovered the Magic Hour."

There was a smattering of polite applause.

Ailsa vaguely recognized the man's voice – a pointy, nasal delivery that pierced the air. But she couldn't place him.

"Like most major scientific breakthroughs, such as the discovery of penicillin, the matter unfolded almost entirely by accident. The revelation of the Middlemarket, the fair settlement in which we all now stand, marked a new frontier in science. We had heard many stories of your existence. Some even speculated on it, mostly in the realm of fiction, fairy stories, folk tales. No one ever imagined your realm lay within our reach."

The man paused, smiling to himself, enjoying the sound of his own voice. "Two worlds, parallel and coexisting. It fell then to me alone to build a bridge between us. With your help and support, we achieved this feat and more. Now we thrive in this glorious accord, as both our peoples may reap their mutual benefits. It is time to celebrate. We remain here, Your Ladyship, at your pleasure, for which we are and remain eternally grateful."

The woman, who Ailsa figured was "Lady Blackthorn", nodded enigmatically at this.

The man bowed again and intoned: "All hail to the Shee."

The room echoed. *All Hail to the Shee.* Lady Blackthorn smiled and nodded. Ailsa had no idea what a Shee was. Maybe it was her. The woman. *Was she the "Shee"?* But Ailsa was mostly focused on avoiding the gaze of the guards.

The man continued. "And all hail to our Lord and—"

Silence fell instantly.

The man had blundered and could see Lady Blackthorn's eyes burning. His face contorted as his brain tried to save himself from further humiliation and scandal.

"All hail, erm, on His Lordship, I mean, of course."

The silence, if anything, intensified.

The man cleared his throat and began toying nervously with his glasses. "By which I mean, all of the hail in the entire world. Huge frozen chunks of the stuff, falling, erm, very hard. Upon his head. May the hail be, erm, heavy and painful…" He grinned, sweating profusely.

The mumbling spread in the room. Mostly, the glares and disapproval were limited to the shorter, tartan-clad members of the room. Ailsa heard two of them tutting behind her.

"So disrespectful," they said. "The Lady and Laird may be parted, but it's hardly the done thing to mention it."

"All for the best, mind," said another. "Did you ever hear them fighting? Like two pine martens after the same dinner."

"He left her for good now, I hear."

"Aye, back in the Wilds of Midden where he belongs.

Don't imagine he'll set foot in the Middlemarket any more."

"Well, you would smell him coming, wouldn't you? Give you plenty of warning."

They hid their giggles behind their handkerchiefs.

Ailsa figured whoever this Lady Blackthorn and Lord Whatever person were, they had recently split up, quite acrimoniously. She wondered if they had kids.

The man on the dais, now beetroot red with embarrassment, cleared his throat and tried again. "Lady Blackthorn, do forgive me. I am not accustomed to public speaking, as you know."

Lady Blackthorn stared for a moment, and then her eyes closed enigmatically. When she opened them, she spoke. "I wish His Lordship well," she said in a sharp and frosty voice, adding: "a very deep well, from which there is no escape."

The man cackled in subservient laughter. The room followed his lead, and in seconds the pressure and awkwardness dissipated.

Ailsa skirted the edge of the room, not wanting to stick out too much. Her eyes were scanning for Credenza.

As the man on stage began thanking other people in the room with an air of considerable relief, Ailsa backed up into a corner. There she could see a small maintenance door was ajar. A cold breeze was seeping in from somewhere. She shivered. She was turning back to close it when a rough pair of dirty hands grabbed her coat and pulled her behind a pillar.

It was the boy from the roof of St. Ninian's Row. He was out of breath, eyes wide, terrified. A tangled mess of hair that looked like it might be brown were it ever washed. He had ruddy cheeks, burned by frost and winter sun. It was the kind of face like a woodcut, where every joy and every sadness in the person's life is etched into it somehow. His feet were bare, bright red, and raw from the elements. His shins were even worse, chapped and practically scarlet, and they stuck out from below his long tartan smock.

"My name is Tobias Ragwort," he said. His voice was like sandpaper. "Forgive my bold approach."

His eyes darted around the room as he spoke.

"Was that you, following me on the roof?" Ailsa asked.

He nodded as if that was a normal thing to admit to.

Voices echoed from outside the maintenance door, footfalls and shouting, things like "I thought I saw him!"

"I must speak with you. But we cannot talk here. Can you please come find me at the Lorimers, by the Four Courts?" He said this as if he expected her to know what it meant. He tried again. "Next to the Bastion?"

The words were meaningless to her, but still Ailsa nodded, more in encouragement than anything else.

"Come as soon as you can. Please. It's very important."

Ailsa said: "Are you in some kind of trouble?"

"This place is not what it seems," said Tobias.

"How do you mean?"

"Just remember: Newton's Third Law."

He spoke as if these were the three most important words that a person could utter. Then he took Ailsa's hand, pressed something into it – and was gone. Ailsa glanced down at her palm. In it was a small, folded piece of paper. Too nervous to look, she slid it into her coat pocket, exhaling with relief. Her mind, however, was spinning. Was that the same Newton Dr Matthews had mentioned? Even if it was, why was he going around making laws for people? Was he a judge?

She watched the door close with a click.

When she turned back to face the room, Credenza was staring at her from a nearby fireplace. It didn't look like she had been watching her for long. Rolling her eyes, she marched over to Ailsa with an accusing stare.

"What on earth are you doing here?"

Her voice was sharp and cold. It stung.

"What am I doing here?" Ailsa retorted. "What are *you* doing here? And, hey … you nearly ran me over!"

"Well, I mean, you *were* just *standing* there," said Credenza, as if that made it somehow OK.

"I walked into a shed in Dad's garden," Ailsa said, as if that explained everything. "And then a woman with a raspberry hairdo guided me through another door into the snow, and then I followed you here. Which brings me to my next question. Where on earth is here?"

Credenza glanced around the room with the kind of look that says *I don't want to get into trouble*.

"You're not supposed to be anywhere until you've had orientation."

Credenza reached out her hand. Ailsa had never seen Credenza offer a single gesture of friendship as long as she had known her. But there it was. She took it. Another bell sounded, resonating through the stairwell. Hearing it, Credenza pulled Ailsa after her, running out of the room towards the back of the room.

"Two bells left. We'd better hurry."

Why, Ailsa thought, *does everyone here talk about bells?*

CHAPTER 17

ORIENTATION

Credenza led Ailsa up a back staircase to the twelfth floor, along an elegant hallway and into what appeared to be a classroom.

Inside were rows of stackable wooden chairs. The room stank of burnt-off dust and cleaning products. At the far end, on a small, raised dais, sat a spectacularly old television set mounted on a little trolley. On a shelf underneath sat a squat metal box, connected to the TV above by a mess of wires.

There was only one other person inside it – another small woman who resembled the woman from the shed. She wore a crimson sash across her bright green overcoat. There was a leaflet on the chair as Ailsa sat down. It read:

WELCOME TO THE MIDDLEMARKET
A QUICK START GUIDE

The small woman eyed the duo sceptically before she spoke. "On behalf of Lady Blackthorn, the Peoples of the Midden, and the Aldermen of the Middlemarket, welcome."

"What's the Middlemarket?" whispered Ailsa.

Credenza nudged her to be quiet.

"We have prepared a short presentation for you," the woman continued. "Please give it your full attention, if you would be so kind."

The TV winked on in a cloud of static and dust. Then there came a strange wobbly noise, like music being played at the wrong speed. The small woman sat down by the window. Ailsa peered at the booklet through the gloom. It was a single page that read:

PLEASE WATCH THE FILM. THANK YOU.

A bright blue rectangle filled the TV screen and more even wobblier noises washed around the room from the tiny TV speakers. Orange letters then proclaimed:

ADJUST VCR TRACKING FOR
CLEAREST PICTURE

"Dad says they've been using the same film for ages," Credenza whispered. The text disappeared and new letters appeared to a fanfare of electronic music. They now read:

WELCOME* TO THE MIDDLEMARKET

"Time," intoned a pompous-sounding voice.

Ailsa could see there was a tiny * symbol, or asterisk, next to the word "welcome", but there didn't seem to be anything elsewhere that helped to explain what it was doing there. The image of a ticking clock suddenly appeared on screen, hands moving around in frantic circles.

"Most of your life," continued the voice, "facts have defined your world. The earth is round. What goes up must come down. From a humble acorn comes the mighty oak."

"Only if you plant it," whispered Ailsa again.

Credenza nudged her again.

The voice grew louder. "You learned to count. You learned to spell. And then … there came time." When the voice said "time", the music struck a dramatic chord.

"When you were young," it continued, "you learned the days of the week. How to read a clock. Sixty seconds in every minute. Seven days in every week. Fifty-two weeks in every year."

The music struck an even lower, more ominous note.

"But how many of you know how many hours there are in a day?"

The screen showed a question mark. Ailsa rolled her eyes.

The voice suddenly sounded very pleased with itself: "There are, of course, twenty-five hours in a day."

As if somehow anticipating Ailsa's dumbfounded expression, the voice carried on:

"Yes, you heard that correctly. There is an extra hour in every day. So long as you know where to find it."

Credenza elbowed Ailsa in the ribs again, winking.

"What does this extra time give you? Why, here in the Middlemarket, it gives you everything."

The music seemed to get more excited.

"Every day, at the junction of day and night, a bridge is built between your ordinary world and our own Magic Hour. Thanks to an agreement between our leaders, Lady Blackthorn and Professor Munro, while you are here, for ten bells, you are permitted to go about your work and life as you might do at home. The time is ours, and we give it happily to you."

The woman with the sash was busy filing her nails. She had heard all this before, and it seemed about as interesting to her as a shopping list. Ailsa, for her part, was rapt.

"Who are we?" The voice paused for dramatic effect. "We are the eternal guardians of the ancient time. We are the Burgesses of the Middlemarket. We hail from an age before memory. Before your own kin came to these shores. You may know us by another name. Fairies. Pixies. Fair folk. We call ourselves the Shee. And for you, perhaps: neighbours. Allies. Friends."

For a moment there came an image of a group of happy people in tartan dress smiling at the camera and waving.

Fairies? The Shee? Now Ailsa had heard enough. For one, she thought, no one here had any wings.

Ailsa felt Credenza watching her. She leaned into her ear.

"Is this some kind of joke? Fairies really exist?" she whispered.

Credenza shrugged, then nodded. It didn't seem to faze her, but then again – very little did.

"And it's all real? There's an extra hour in every day? Here?"

"Yep," said Credenza. "And it's going to change your life."

I've been working twenty-five seven on this.

That's what she'd said, all right. It suddenly all made sense.

Credenza made for the door, expecting Ailsa to follow. But Ailsa was fixated on that screen. The credits were crawling by now, acres of text in a minuscule font. Ailsa thought she saw the words END USER LICENSE AGREEMENT scroll by, but it was all rather too fast to read.

"Come on! Oh my God, you're not the kind of person who stays to the end, are you? It's totally against the rules to stay after final bell… Let's go, let's go… Hurry, hurry, hurry…"

Ailsa followed Credenza out of the door, which gently shut again of its own accord. The television set, used to being left alone, continued loyally with its story. Displaying, in fast-moving, tiny golden letters, the vitally important small print – including several critical elements of how the Middlemarket, and its Magic Hour, really worked.

If Ailsa had been there to read those words, it would have turned her blood cold.

CHAPTER 18

CLOSING TIME

"It's this kind of bonus time," shouted Credenza as they ran back down the hallway. "An extra sixty minutes every single day."

"How does that even work?" asked Ailsa.

But Credenza was too busy bragging to listen.

"The Magic Hour was first discovered by that old guy you saw up on stage, Professor Munro, but it's really my dad's work that made it a thing, and so now it's this big secret. Important people use it to do important things they don't have time for. Successful people, you know. Movers and shakers. People like us."

Ailsa scrunched her nose. Us?

"So," she countered, "why isn't this place mobbed? Why isn't it full of people? Isn't more time good for everyone?"

Credenza threw her a knowing, worldly look. "Ailsa, didn't you hear me? It's a secret. This kind of thing isn't for just anyone. This place is pretty exclusive. VIPs only. Very Important People."

Ailsa had never felt exclusive before. She felt a mild excitement at the implication. Something niggled at her, though.

"My uncle works in a supermarket, and they started calling him an essential worker. That's important-sounding."

"Oh, come on, you know what I mean."

"Who decides who's very important?"

"Look, Ailsa, people can have important jobs without being important people, OK? This is only for the *really* important important ones."

Ailsa was getting a headache now. Did this mean she and Credenza were special people? More special than who, exactly?

"What about that fancy party downstairs? Is that every night?"

"Oh no," said Credenza. "That's only the Gathering. Anniversary Day. Dad calls it playing politics. We have to be good house guests or something. Today's the anniversary of the Great Discovery, the day they first found out about this whole Magic Hour business. So, we all gather in the hall. Professor Munro thanks Lady Blackthorn. This is sort of her town, after all."

"She was the woman inside, with the purple flowers?"

"Yeah. She's sort of like the Queen. Or president. Or mayor. Someone important we need to butter up, that's how Dad explained it. I don't really think too much about it. She used to be married to some lord, but they split up. Completely out there, by all accounts. Smells like a compost heap apparently. I don't really deal with all the politics. I'm much too busy having fun! Hey, look in there, that's where I did my science project."

Ailsa craned her neck as they ran, peering into the side rooms that lined the hallway – inside, she caught glimpses of libraries, laboratories, kitchens and dance studios. There were calculators and guitars and maps, cooking equipment, simple desks and chairs.

They were full of people working, singing, writing, reading, drawing. There were meetings and hammerings and sawings and quite a great deal of talking. Two men were playing chess, and four others a card game (Ailsa thought it was probably poker).

"Twenty-five seven?" Ailsa smiled.

Credenza blushed. "Kind of a giveaway, looking back."

"So, you can do things here other than, um … homework?"

Credenza laughed. "Mate. You can do whatever you want."

At the top of the stairs, they parted ways.

"Dad's up on the top floor," Credenza said, hesitating. "But, um, probably best if you don't come up with me to see him. I'll need to smooth things out first, OK? I mean, you sort of showed up, and you weren't really invited to the reception. Also, I don't know if Mum's planning on being here today too, and the way they argue, even here, I mean—"

She started to tell Ailsa about how her parents were always arguing. It sounded like a very familiar story.

"I mean, over half of all marriages end in divorce, and sometimes I wish they'd hurry up and get it done already," said Credenza.

Ailsa couldn't hide her surprise. "What? You actually want your parents to split up?"

"I dunno, maybe, not really. I only wonder if they might both be so much happier."

"I don't know if that's true, you know," said Ailsa.

Ailsa had never heard a kid say something like this before. She had always imagined Credenza's family was perfect.

"So, um – how do I get back down?"

"Take the lift!" shouted Credenza as she sprinted away. "See you downstairs by the front doors!"

Ailsa watched her disappear around the corner and started hurrying over to the cage-like lift nearby.

So that's why you never look too frazzled, she thought. An extra sixty minutes on everyone else. Every single day. You and everyone else here. That's how you do it. You've got a secret edge.

A little voice inside Ailsa's head piped up:

And now, so do you.

CHAPTER 19

THE RED DOOR

Hang on a minute here. Ailsa's world has just this morning turned upside down, so we should take a moment to absorb everything that's happened. She got up in the morning the same as you did, ate some breakfast and went about her day. So far, so normal.

At *no point whatsoever* (pretty sure about this) was she contemplating that she'd find herself with her school frenemy Credenza, learning the world-shattering secret that – and let's get this right now – there are in fact twenty-*five* hours in a day.

Is that what you heard? Feels about right over here.

Therefore, safe to say, since we're now in agreement about all this, that it was a very perturbed Ailsa who stepped into the old-fashioned rusty lift in front of her.

Ailsa pulled the metal gate closed and punched the ground-floor button. For a moment, she felt like a bird in a cage. The ancient mechanism clunked into action: valves hissed from somewhere, the structure shuddered and hummed. The lights in the building dimmed for a moment.

The lift was clearly taking its time.

It began to move.

Snails, while sedated, move more quickly than this lift. While she waited, Ailsa began to daydream.[22]

The Magic Hour. An extra sixty minutes every day. To do whatever you wanted. Her mind spun with possibilities. It all made sense now. This was how everyone she knew got their edge. This was how people could get through a busy day and still have time to appear relaxed. And, well, now she'd have that edge too. She would never be late for anything ever again.

She thought of her parents and her sister, all of whom Ailsa heard complaining about the lack of time in their lives. How amazing would it be if she could bring them all here too?

What about her friend Stu from school, who was struggling with his reading? He was always so tired at home, looking after his baby sisters, his mum working two jobs to support them. Which meant he tried to do as much to help around the house as he could before she got home. He could prepare meals in the Magic Hour,

---

22 Seriously. Wouldn't you?

Ailsa thought. Or practise his reading for a full hour. It would be so amazing for so many people. Credenza had given her a gift showing her this place.

Another thought suddenly bloomed in Ailsa's mind.

It had been bugging her since she walked into this place, and now, for some reason, it was coming back.

If this place was so amazing, and so life-changing...

Why didn't she tell me about it before?

At that moment, the lift juddered – *CLANKED* – and dropped like a stone.

The machinery shrieked in harmony with Ailsa's scream as the entire compartment plummeted in a shower of sparks and chaos. It passed the lobby in a flash, heads turning at the noise, until it reached the very bottom of the shaft, where there came an almighty *KERCHUNK* as the car bounced, wobbled and came to a shuddering halt.

The cage reopened in a cloud of smoke and the smell of burnt rubber. Ailsa gasped for breath. The lift had not fully reached the basement floor and had left only a tiny gap for her to squeeze out. It wasn't clear how far down she would have to drop.

She was easing herself over the edge when the lift started to hum again. She gritted her teeth, wiggling through as fast as she could. The noise got louder, now a screeching, churning roar. Ailsa dug her hands into the floor and pushed hard, launching herself out and into the air at the precise moment the contraption sprung back up through the shaft, like the jaws of a metal monster. She fell for longer than she expected, landing hard on a cold flagstone floor.

She trembled to her feet. A grazed knee, nothing broken.

The hall widened at one end of the passageway where a staircase led upwards. On the other side was a huge door, set flush into the wall. The door was thick and almost three times her height. It was hewn from heavy, ancient wood and painted a specific shade of red that reminded Ailsa of something that she couldn't place. In its centre, just within her reach, was a bronze stag's head which Ailsa imagined was a kind of door knocker, intricate and beautiful. The antlers were nine pointers. Since there was no latch or handle, she reasoned, perhaps the stag was how you got inside?

She stood on her tiptoes to reach an antler and pulled. It held fast.

But she was close enough to hear now: under the ringing in her ears was a low growling noise. She tried to calm her breathing and focus in on it. It was like the distant thunder of an approaching storm. In fact it was almost like a—

Curious, said a voice.

Ailsa spun around, but the room was empty.

"Who's there?" Ailsa said to nobody at all.

Only myself, it said again. Closer now.

It was now speaking as clearly as anyone standing next to her might sound. But there was no one else there. More words came to Ailsa as if from the air itself:

Have we met before?

You seem familiar.

Ailsa found her imagination running away from her as it often did in dark and shadowy places. The more she imagined, the clearer the voice became.

Happy, it seems.

On the surface.

I wonder. What happens when you look inside?

Whatever was talking to her was behind that door. And it did not sound friendly. Was this a Night Gloaming? Close to feeding time? Ailsa thought it certainly sounded hungry.

Not really, said the voice as if in reply.

Just all alone.

Ailsa blinked. *And reading my thoughts*, she thought.

The voice appeared to sigh.

Well, it's something to do, it replied.

"Which must mean I'm dreaming it," said Ailsa, out

loud this time, her words echoing on stone. "Which must therefore mean you are not real."

Ailsa tried to control her breathing like Mum had taught her. Four seconds in, four seconds out. She started to feel better. Maybe this really was a figment of an over-active imagination. She turned to go when it spoke again.

Did you find it yet?

Ailsa ground her teeth. This voice was intrusive.

"Find what?" she said out loud.

The missing piece, of course.

Ailsa was thinking of a comeback when the voice spoke again.

We lose pieces of ourselves, don't we?

When people are gone.

Thy parents are sad, too busy to feel much of anything.

Stop it, thought Ailsa to herself. *Stop talking.*

Instead, the voice sounded almost encouraged.

You must want them to get back together. Very much.

Ailsa tried to tune the voice out now, like a radio.

I wonder if that solves the puzzle for you?

Maybe instead.

Why not just let that empty feeling grow?

Did you ever think about that?

Think how much space you would have.

Ailsa stood her ground.

"I'm not afraid of you," she said, not really believing it.

I imagine not.

But all the same.

Best open the door, just to check?

A blast of air rattled the latch on the door. The next time Ailsa drew breath, she had run up five flights of stairs to the lobby. As she gasped for air, she remembered now what that shade of red had reminded her of.

Blood.

CHAPTER 20

VOID[23]

---

23 A void is a completely empty space. A vacuum of nothing (minus
    the vacuum itself of course, which belongs in the cupboard).
    Where did all the words go? Turn the page to find out…

The creature listened as the steps faded away.

It pressed itself to the inside of the red door, as much as a creature like itself could truly press against anything. It was searching again for a crack, but the seal was tight. It could summon enough energy to rattle the latch if it tried hard enough.

But no more than that.

This was where it was, for now. It retreated to the centre and pulsed there in angry silence.[24] A shapeless darkness craves any kind of form, and the creature took whatever was available.

There was a void inside humans, the creature knew – most of them at least – which provided all the room it required. Without a living body of its own, how could it do anything else? No single home would sustain it for too long. Nothing lasts for ever, after all.

One thing was for sure.

It did not enjoy its current accommodations at all.

When a formless thing like itself found a true home, the amenities were generally much more pleasing. They were often centrally heated, for one, coursing with blood, structured with hard bone and soft flesh, and fully

---

24   An angry silence is almost exactly the same as a regular silence, except that if you look very carefully, the edges are jagged.

furnished with accessories – things like arms to flail, hands to grasp, hearts that thundered, stomachs that groaned with ample storage, nails to scratch, a tongue to taste and tie into knots, teeth to chatter and grind and bite, throaty voices to holler and shriek, and of course, the benefit of eyes that bulged and rolled and glowed like the dark cherry coals of a dying fire.

These were the benefits of human containers. They offered a real opportunity to put your own stamp on the premises.[25]

These accommodations were often (but not always) mobile, handily located, thanks to the set of articulated legs at the base (some didn't have these in the same configuration but had other methods of moving). Mobility of any sort enabled these containers to be handily relocated into all kinds of interesting and vibrant places, at a variety of entertaining speeds.

At least, they could until they were used up as they always were. Once spent, they were discarded, and the search would begin anew. The creature knew this was its lot in life, swapping out one home for another, and that its only survival was to keep moving. Such a beast,

---

25 This almost never involved something like an extra bathroom or a conservatory, but you never know.

when born, would drift first towards easy prey. Those that frequented the late afternoon shadow in the corner of a garden. A twilight wanderer, a love-wracked forlorn. As the entity grew, so its hunting grounds would expand. A moonless night in a dank copse made for good sport. A long-forgotten valley floor.

The creature behind the blood-red door was still very young, and there were many more lessons to learn. It knew, for example, that it was partly to blame for allowing itself in here at all. Now the creature had flown free of its cage to occupy its cold, desolate space between these walls.

And now it was here, waiting. But it had youth on its side.

Patience too.

These people aren't the boss of me, it thought.

I shall show them soon enough, all by myself.

In the centre of its flagstone room, the creature would wait. In its cold and pitiless heart, it knew it would not be long.

Most scientists say black holes are the darkest, most terrifying things in the universe. This is untrue. Because most scientists have never met a Brollachan.[26]

---

26 And the ones that do … well. They don't tend to talk about it.

CHAPTER 21

Do You Have a Reservation?

Colours that reminded Ailsa of blood.

That's what was in her head at that moment.

Not relaxing.

Not relaxing in the *slightest*.

Panting hard, Ailsa powered through a set of double doors at the back of the lobby. She found herself in another vaulted room, in front of a long marble counter. Her sides hurt. A stitch. She'd have to deal with it later.

The room felt like a ticket hall at a railway station.

There was a skylight in the ceiling here too, offering a view up to the rooftops of taller buildings nearby. Shafts of rose-coloured light shone down on to a long row of service windows.

Most of the windows featured signs in a bold red typeface that proclaimed: "WINDOW CLOSED". One of the service areas was still open, however, and Ailsa could see a woman sitting there in shirtsleeves with garters on the upper arm, stiff white cuffs and a strange green visor.

"Closed!" boomed a voice. "What is this insolence?"

Ailsa turned to see an officious-looking man in an overcoat scuttling over to her.

The man had been standing near the stage earlier, Ailsa remembered. He was very short and dull-looking, a feature he clearly compensated for with his clothes: yellow-and-green tartan trousers, a bright cherry-red doublet, a waistcoat, a sporran and a huge frilly thing on his chest. A large tartan cape flowed elegantly back behind him when he walked.

From one of the man's pockets sprouted a very ostentatious powder-blue handkerchief. He pointed to the handkerchief provocatively, as if that somehow explained everything.

"I'm really sorry," said Ailsa. "I came in here by mistake…"

"Who sent you?" the man snapped. "Where's your voucher?"

"I don't have one yet. Is this where you get them? I'm supposed to meet my friend Credenza in a minute, but the lift…"

That one word, *Credenza*, seemed to change everything. The man now smiled warmly, his brow unfurled, eyes sparkling. He extended his hand with a smile.

"Ah, Denzie Dingwall, you say? Friend of yours, is she?"

Ailsa nodded. *Denzie?*

"Well, why didn't you say? Um…"

"Ailsa Craig," said Ailsa.

"Is that right? A wonderful name. No relation to the rock, I suppose? Ha ha ha ha…"

Ailsa remembered Grandma telling her how she came to be called Ailsa, and that Ailsa Craig was indeed a famous rocky island off the coast. But the man's laugh was so loud and shrill it had completely fazed her.

"Well now," the man continued merrily, "I am Virgil Merrimack, Chief Reckoner of the Middlemarket, Superintendent of Buildings and Lord High Chancellor of the Midden, at your service. A great pleasure to make your acquaintance. Your first time here, is it? Marvellous. Let's see what we can do, shall we? I take care of the accounts here, you see."

He beamed at her again and turned away. His smile faded.

"Morag," he barked in the direction of the counter, "you'll do your best, I'm sure."

Virgil Merrimack then guided Ailsa to a clerk who

sat at the window, gave a small bow, and, heels clacking, marched away and out through another large door.

The clerk looked like the shed-person's exhausted cousin and worked from the same red, leather-bound ledger. Beside her was a large copper-coloured machine, which looked like a cross between a typewriter and a calculator, attached by valves to two interconnected metal drums. The keys themselves had no symbols on them that Ailsa could see and appeared to be connected to miniature gears.

"Reservation?"

"Pardon?"

The clerk sighed.

"Did you arrange for this credit with a reservation?"

Ailsa shook her head. The clerk tutted. And then sighed again. It was something of a pattern with her.

"What's a credit?" said Ailsa.

The clerk, whose nametag confirmed her name as Morag, tutted lightly, sighed, tutted again for good measure, and then began to murmur as she worked something out in her head. Ailsa was convinced now she was in all kinds of trouble.

"No reservation," the clerk said, counting on her fingers. "Three bells in total … that makes four, take away the validations…" She sighed again.

Eventually, she fed a thin piece of paper into the top of the machine. It whirred noisily to life. Gears clanked and keys moved by themselves. There was a churning sound and a series of irritated clicks. The chattering and clacking and whizzing rose in volume. It soon sounded like a washing machine full of marbles. Finally, the entire contraption dinged merrily, paused for dramatic effect (a kind of mechanical "*ta-dah*") and disgorged another piece of paper. This one curled a bit at the edges. It looked a lot like a receipt.

137 (one hundred and seven-and-thirty)

The clerk pulled the paper out, flattened its curling edges, and scribbled on it. "One three seven then," she said. "Sign here." She pointed to the bottom of the slip, tapping her finger on it impatiently.

"What ... is that?" asked Ailsa.

"It's your number, dear. Your voucher."

"Do you need me to pay it?" said Ailsa.

The clerk rolled her eyes.

"That's why you're signing here, my dear. It's your first visit; you'll know for next time," said the clerk. "And just so you're aware," she added slyly, "since you're a good friend of the Dingwalls, Mr Merrimack has authorized a reduction for you. Only this once, mind. Lucky you. Take a quill, hen, quick as you can."

Ailsa took a feather-topped pen from a small container of ink on the side and signed her name. The paper felt warm under her hand. The clerk ripped off a small length from a perforation at the bottom and then plopped the rest into a wire mesh tray next to her marked "PROCESSING".

She handed Ailsa the curling scrap of paper.

"Your receipt, dear. Show it at the gate. You're supposed to come here first and get your number when you arrive, you see; that way we know it's you when you leave." She giggled for a moment, her eyes alive with mirth. "Then you hand it to whoever's at the gate. If you get there on time, of course."

Next to the tray was a large brass bell, and she rang it.

All of a sudden, a sinuous brass pipe appeared, descending rapidly from the ceiling in a series of metallic squeaks. It then hovered over the wire mesh tray and vacuumed up the piece of paper with a *schluuuurrrppp*.

Ailsa watched in bemusement as the pipe retracted into a larger nest of similar tubes arranged in the ceiling. They all seemed to lead back to the far end of the office where a larger, more sombre set of double doors loomed. These two doors had a guard next to them.

"Thank you very—" began Ailsa. As if in reply, the clerk pulled sharply down on an olive-green shade in front of her upon which was written:

CLOSED. NEXT WINDOW PLEASE.

The lights were starting to dim in the entire building.

"Um. Do you think I'll be OK now?" asked Ailsa, to the closed olive window shade.

"It's hard to say," said the voice of Virgil Merrimack from somewhere behind her. Ailsa whirled around. He was standing by the door, eyes sparkling with anticipation. "I suppose it depends."

"On what?"

"How fast can you run."

CHAPTER 22

THE SOUTH GATE

As it turned out, Ailsa could run extremely fast indeed. Faster, in fact, than the first sentence of this chapter, which was supposed to be: "Ailsa was running before he'd finished talking." But it's too late for that now.

Virgil Merrimack had given her basic directions, but here in the dark, in an unknown place, with the panic shrieking in her throat, she was soon lost. Virgil Merrimack had told her she only had a few moments remaining to get out without a penalty. Ailsa had no idea what a penalty was, but it certainly didn't sound good. She was sure she was finished.

It was then that she noticed the cat.

Grey with white paws that looked like socks.

It was Sydekyck! She was sure of it.

He sprinted up past her and looked back – waiting. He was going to guide her. Relief flushed through Ailsa's heart as she redoubled her speed.

Sydekyck led on, cutting through passageways, and then suddenly he checked right and scampered up a narrow wooden staircase. Ailsa stopped dead. The road led straight ahead to what looked like a gate that she could see in the distance. Surely that was the right way to go.

A sharp pain drew her back to the here and now.

Sydekyck was scratching hard at her shins. He looked furious. He turned again and ran up the stairs, glaring back at her.

Ailsa followed.

He led her all the way up three floors of rickety switchbacks which creaked and groaned as they climbed. They wound back and forth, narrower and narrower, until the steps burst out of the top of the building, on to a narrow ledge that was only a small scramble up to the rooftops.

Here, the cat accelerated, scampering over and around chimney pots, all the time glancing back at Ailsa to encourage her to follow.

Ailsa wasn't good with heights.

Looking behind her, she could see the full extent of this strange place. The houses were packed together all the way down to the square plaza. There were other small quadrangles that she could see, radiating out. Past them, dimly lit now by torches, was what looked like a thick, imposing city wall. Beyond that, there was darkness, with the glow of the rising sun visible to the north.

She stopped for a second. Wait.

The sun doesn't rise in the north, it rises in the—

Ouch. A sharp pain in her shin pulled Ailsa out of her reverie.

It was the cat, tapping her impatiently with his claws. It glared at her, then began scampering forward once again.

"Where on earth are you taking me?" said Ailsa out loud.

"Shortcut," said Sydekyck.

Ailsa stopped dead, mouth agape.

Sydekyck seemed to sigh. He ran back to her, wrapped his tail around her ankle and pulled her back into a run.

"Hurry!" he said again.

"But … you can … talk!" gasped Ailsa.

"Well, so can you," said Sydekyck. His voice rasped, between a purr and a meow. "But you don't see me getting all excited about it. So let's leave it at that, shall we?"

He sped up, and Ailsa followed.

Round the next corner, Ailsa lost him completely

behind a chimney pot. She ran to the edge of the building, and now she saw why Sydekyck had taken her here. There, below, was the South Gate. The final crowds were surging forward to exit.

In the street leading up to it were a line of what looked like police. Larger men, all in liveried topcoats and tartan. But they looked mean, and they all had large sticks like truncheons. Braziers burned on either side of the lane, blocking anyone who might need to get past.

This place certainly had a different character in the dark.

There was no sign of Credenza.

Despite her promise.

One of the men from the street suddenly glanced up towards her. Ailsa jerked herself back – too fast. She began to lose her balance and started to fall.

She yelled out in fright, but the freezing air took it away. A hand grabbed her coat and dragged her back from the edge.

It was Tobias Ragwort.

He was standing in the shadows by the chimney pot. Barefoot as before, his eyes shining in the dark, intent on her. He helped her towards the edge and pointed.

"Take the stairs. The gate you need is straight ahead."

"Thank you," started Ailsa. "What about the cat—"

"Go. Now."

Something in his eyes told Ailsa that this was deadly serious. She took his advice and flew down the stairs to the street.

The entire place was dark and empty.

The gate doors were starting to close.

Ailsa sprinted for the archway. A clerk from the bank appeared, holding out her hand. Ailsa held out her sliver of a receipt and the clerk grabbed it sharply.

The space behind the gate was as dark as midnight.

Total silence engulfed her.

And for a moment, the dark was all that Ailsa saw.

Then, she began to see a familiar hedge.

She closed her eyes.

When she opened them again, she was sitting on a step in a small dead-end street in an unfamiliar part of Edinburgh. A road sign, etched into the stone of the wall above her, read "St. Mary's Wynd".

She wandered out into a small alleyway which she worked out was close to the Cowgate. This wasn't a part of town she was very familiar with, but she knew how to get up to the Bridges where a bus would take her home.

Ailsa couldn't see as she walked, but behind her, as she left the dead-end street, the sign – and the dead end itself – dissolved into the stonework.

She passed an older woman on her way to the bus stop.

"You all right there, hen?" said the woman. "You look like you just saw the Brollachan."

Ailsa didn't know what a Brollachan was and didn't want to find out, but she tried to smile back reassuringly.

By the time she arrived at Mum's flat, her eyes were half-closed, and she was nearly asleep.

"So," chirped Mum as she walked in, "how was your day?"

CHAPTER 23

FAIRY ROCK

Phew. For a while there, it wasn't looking likely that Ailsa was going to make it. But she crawled under the covers and fell asleep, so that's reassuring.

Ailsa's sleep was deeper and more profound than she could ever recall. There were dreams, still. Odd ones. She wasn't falling off a mountainside any more. Her dreams were now full of shadows and darkness, a pulsing tapestry of blood-red doors and stags' heads, flickering torchlight and an infinite void beyond.

Yet there was something else lurking at the fringes of these dreams. Something which made her even more uneasy. She was aware of a presence, half-inside and half-outside her mind, one that seemed to be watching her dreams alongside her. Half in Ailsa's dream world, half in her own. The presence had eyes, too, which she could see at the edges of her mind.

They looked like two red coals burning in a black fog.

The eyes didn't seem wholly malevolent, however.

Not exactly.

They appeared, instead, to be rather young. They glowed with frustration. Self-absorbed, resentful. Like a bored teenager dragged into a long car ride. It wasn't the brooding glow that disturbed her in those eyes so much as the total absence of empathy. Nothing else mattered but itself. Worse still, the presence seemed to understand that these were Ailsa's dreams, and that even as those dreams might end, those eyes would live on past the waking moment, and still be there, somewhere, when she woke up.

These were not exactly relaxing thoughts.

At one point her subconscious had clearly had enough of these dark themes, and even though she was asleep, it nudged her towards a much sunnier memory: the summer she had spent with her grandparents.[27]

It had been a sun-dappled two weeks at their ramshackle cottage deep in the countryside. The house was full of the sights and smells of the comfortable past, things that modern life doesn't involve itself with much any more: freshly picked runner beans and silver polish,

---

27 The mind can sometimes do nice things like that all on its own, which is reassuring.

white vinegar and lavender soap, dry mud on rubber boots, fried sausages and boiled sweets.

In her dream, she was back there in the garden, under the sun. Her bare feet on the warm grass, with Grandma next to her in her old cornflower-blue sweatshirt.

"I was reading and found out my name means 'fairy rock'."

"Ailsa Craig, yes, it's in the Firth of Clyde."

"How come I'm named after a fairy?"

"Well," said Grandma, "you were born at the stroke of midnight, which we always used to say was a magical birth time, close to the Shee – which is the true name for fairy in Scotland. It's Gaelic, you see. Spelled S-I-D-H-E in fact, pronounced 'Shee'. We took you up to Glenshee in the Cairngorms when you first came back to live here, do you remember?"

"But, Grandma … fairies don't exist."

Grandma shot her a stern look. Fiddlesticks and folderol.[28] "Tell me now. Do stars exist?"

"Of course they do. You know that. You're an astronomer!"

"But I'm asking you. Do you see them in the

---

28 Grandma had an excellent sideline in words for "nonsense". "Rhubarb" was another. Unless there was custard involved.

daytime?"

"Well, no—"

"So, if you only looked for stars in the daytime, with your naked eye, would you see any? Do you see any right now?"

Ailsa squinted up into the blue sky above them. "Yes, one."

Grandma smiled. "Apart from the sun."

"Then nope."

"Well, then I suppose stars don't really exist at all? If we cannot see them?"

"They do. You showed me some with your telescope."

"But, Ailsa, dear, if you based your conclusion only on the data of the daytime, you'd think something completely different."

"I never thought about it like that."

"*Ceteris paribus* applies in all experiments. Keep everything the same and change only one other thing. Be mindful of the parameters you impose on a problem. You need to take another look at that postcard I got you."

"Ket-er-iss on what bus now?"

"It's Latin, remember?"

Ailsa really didn't have much of an idea what Grandma was talking about, but she smiled as she followed her under an arch of vines towards a chaotic vegetable plot.

Grandma and Ailsa often had conversations like this, ones where Ailsa wasn't entirely sure what they were talking about, while Grandma threw challenging concepts at her on a regular basis. Three Christmases ago, her gift to Ailsa had been a book called *Gravitational Wave Detection Using Optical Interferometers*, into which she had slipped a bookmark on which she had written "for later" with a smiley face.[29]

At the far end was a greenhouse with a squeaky door. They went inside.

"OK, so you're a scientist who believes in fairies?" said Ailsa.

Grandma laughed. "Everything was fantastical once upon a time. The more I learn about the universe, the more I understand I know nothing at all. I believe in the possibility that the world is not so certain as we might think and more magical than we can possibly comprehend. The fact that quasars exist at all was once beyond imagining, and it's now taken for granted. When

---

29 Other "for later" gifts had included: a book on the Antikythera mechanism, a singing fish, Hironaka's bound proof for the Resolution of Singularities, an academic paper on the agricultural soils of Europe, and an electric toothbrush that played "Flower of Scotland" while you brushed.

I study distant objects in the sky, what I'm really doing is travelling in time. Some of the stars are so old their light is older than the planet I'm standing on to see them. How can that be? So yes, I believe in the Shee because I believe we are merely ants in the library of knowledge. We will never understand what we don't know, and I think it's foolish to dismiss imaginative things out of hand merely because it doesn't fit in our anthill. We live in the daytime of the Shee, Ailsa dear. But that doesn't mean they're not there. They live, even now, whether we believe in them or not, in their own world, outside of time."

"But we can't exist outside time, Grandma."

Grandma turned impishly and beckoned Ailsa down to the far end of the greenhouse. The air inside was thick with life, moist and elemental.

"Time is a very odd thing," she said. "Don't you find? Sometimes a week lasts an hour, and an hour lasts a week. And sometimes time can do the strangest thing of all. It can feel like it's stopping altogether."

"How?"

"Try one of those."

Grandma pointed to a tall tomato plant in a corner, poised in a hazy shaft of sunlight. One smaller tomato hung tantalizingly, a deep and purply red with a halo of fuzz. Ailsa picked it and brought it to her mouth. Grandma stopped her.

"Wait," she said. "Smell it first."

Ailsa held the tomato to her nose.

Closed her eyes. And inhaled.

Nothing in her life had ever seemed quite so pure or perfect. It wasn't so much a scent at all as a feeling, an emotion. A harmony of sweet frequencies that washed over her and back again. As if it was the answer to a question she had not yet begun to ask.

She recalled the pop of the stem and the luminous joy on her grandma's face when she turned to her with a look that seemed to say: do you see now? Do you understand a little better what all of this really means?

"Timeless, isn't it?" said Grandma.

Ailsa nodded.

"My own gran once let me pick one of her tomatoes in her garden. And I have no doubt her mother did the same before her. Time stopped for me, in that moment, and painted a picture of itself that I shall always have. Time is a daisy chain of memories, my dear, of paintings and snapshots, and some can take us outside of everything entirely. The universe is a vast unknowable system, eternally expanding. And yet its basic, eternal truth is all wrapped up here, in red and green, in the taste of a humble tomato."

Ailsa woke up smiling at the happy memory.

She knew it now. She hadn't imagined it. She really had been to that Middlemarket place and arrived home as if no time had passed at all. That made no sense. Her mind buzzed with questions.

And she knew exactly who might help her answer them.

CHAPTER 24

BALDERDASH

Ailsa powered her bike up the hill to the Observatory. Its roof had weathered over time, punished by the Scottish rain. It felt like a fittingly isolated place considering everyone inside kept their eyes on the stars.

She ran into the lobby. Priya was there, as Ailsa knew she would be, setting up a display for a forthcoming visitor exhibit.

"Can time go wrong?" Ailsa asked as she hurried in.

(When asking huge and mind-bending questions like this, it's always a good idea to just come right out with it, rather than spelunking around with "Hellos" and "Sorry to interrupts".)

Priya spun around in her wheelchair to face her.

"Wrong in what way?" Priya asked, adding teasingly, "P.S. Hi, Ailsa, I'm glad you're in one piece! What a business!"

Ailsa blushed.[30] "Can time stop, for example? And sorry, hi, we're doing OK, thanks. Dad thinks it might have been a gas leak. But can it? Stop? Time, I mean."

Priya nodded and thought for a moment. "Well, time itself probably will stop at some point."

Ailsa had not been expecting that. "What, seriously?"

"Think about it," mused Priya. "Time started once, at the instant of the Big Bang, so it makes sense that one day it will also slow down and stop altogether. The flow of time is different depending on where you're looking from. As a car's lights might look white or red depending on whether it's driving towards or away from you."

Ailsa blinked. "How about in our back garden?"

Priya grinned. "It's much the same wherever you are. Look. We're pretty sure that there was no time before the universe began. At least, no time that we understand. Time and space are pretty much tied together, and they both began at that moment, you see."

"What about after that?"

"When, precisely, are you thinking about?"

"About five o'clock yesterday? Just after sunset?"

Priya leaned her head to one side and stared at her.

---

30   OK, maybe saying hello is in fact a nice idea after all.

Ailsa explained what had happened. After she was finished, Priya furrowed her brow.

"So, OK, taking this on face value," said Priya, "what you think you found is a kind of bubble, outside of time, where the laws of time don't work any more?"

"Yes! It was around five o'clock when I went in, and after an hour inside, it was still five o'clock when I came out."

"Well, that's how it appeared to you. But look at the objective information you have, which is merely that the clocks stopped. You don't know if time did, in any meaningful way. As scientists, we always have to ask: how can we be sure that what we are concluding isn't due to some other cause? If you throw a stick up in the air, and we don't observe it coming back down, that doesn't disprove gravity or that it's stuck hovering in mid-air. It may simply mean there's a strong wind or a bird caught it. Just because we didn't see it happen doesn't mean it did not, in fact, happen."

Ailsa sat in silence for a moment, digesting this. "So there's only twenty-four hours in a day?"

"Correct."

"But how can we be sure?"

"Well, that's based on observable data, also known as daylight. The earth currently rotates once every twenty-three hours, fifty-six minutes and four seconds. A long time ago, it was even shorter, twenty-two hours when the dinosaurs were around. It's not incredibly precise, we know that, but it's the system we've built over the years. The Sumerians counted with twelves, but it was the Egyptians who first split the day into ten hours. Adding on an hour on either side for daylight, they figured a day was twelve hours long. Which meant that the night-time was the same. Babylonians had a base sixty number system, which explains the minutes thing, but we don't need to go into that."

"Dad always says that every minute is a gift."

Priya's face darkened for a moment. "Yes, I know he does."

Ailsa nodded along, not quite understanding, but was too shy to ask. She didn't like taking up too much of people's time. Especially after what her dad had said to her at breakfast.

Priya, noticing her discomfort, said, "You were asking me about time actually stopping somewhere."

Ailsa nodded, and said: "Could it be something to do with Newton's Third Law?"

Priya's eyes flashed for a moment. "Ah. This feels like it might be a longer conversation ... and one I'd love to have with you. I'm always here to talk about Newton.

125

Isaac Newton, that is. English scientist and philosopher, and the author of many of the laws of mathematics and physics we still use today." She had her back to Ailsa now. "But getting back to your question, you could conceivably go into a black hole with your watch on – you might slow time down a lot … it's just that the rest of the universe would speed up…" She turned back and saw Ailsa's face was anxious.

"It's just – what I saw…"

"Ailsa. What exactly did you see?"

"Balderdash![31]" sneered a voice from across the hall.

The voice was nasal and pointy, like it could bore a hole through wood. Ailsa found it strangely familiar.

Striding over to Priya, brogues clacking on the shiny floor, was a man. He looked younger out of his kilt, yet he was dressed in the uniform of a much older man. He smelled like a pile of wet towels left too long in the washing machine. He sported an almost permanent smile, those tiny brown teeth unmistakable to Ailsa. His smile had an upward curl of the lips that, once you knew him a little better, you might realize was closer to

----

31 Another word for nonsense, one which Grandma would sometimes deploy as well (when flapdoodle wasn't quite right). But Ailsa had never heard it sounding quite so unpleasant.

a sneer, or a snarl – one of ill-disguised superiority. His eyes were tiny black dots set deep into his skull, which gave him a look of grave intensity but also kept his true feelings reliably hidden. Eyes that flicked sideways when he was thinking and burned like bright lumps of coal when he laughed, which he did loudly and often, usually at his own jokes, but – if occasion required it – at those of anyone else who might be useful to him.

Ailsa's mouth gaped. It was him all right.

The man on stage in the Magic Hour.

The man of "the most extraordinary discovery".

Ailsa suddenly recalled being at Grandma's retirement party, and hearing that same man bark like a seal at any joke that floated his way, open-mouthed, teeth bared, more baboon than human. He would clutch wildly at his sides, as if trying to prevent the stuffing coming out. His point, Ailsa felt, was to make sure everyone in the room knew that here was a man with a sense of humour, a man of the people. A man with a lighter side, even though he was the boss.

This was Professor Sandy Munro, a senior researcher at the Observatory. At one time, he had been Grandma's "research buddy", as she would amiably call him. He was younger than her by a couple of decades, but Grandma had always been happy to help younger scientists on their way up the ladder. But even back then at six years old, Ailsa had a good sense of people – and there was nothing friendly about this man at all. She knew he had been using her grandma to get ahead, and he had soon become Grandma's boss. After that, Grandma had never seemed particularly happy.

"Hello, Professor," said Priya. "Are you referring to any balderdash in particular?"

Sandy Munro brightened abruptly, his face breaking into a warm smile. He was the sort of person who could shift between sunshine and rain at a moment's notice. He chuckled, and toyed with the gold half-moon glasses that dangled on a chain around his neck.

"Ah, yes, apologies, but, well, I couldn't help but hear your musings from down the hall. Wearing your watch down a black hole indeed. Molecular movement might address the premise," he mused, "but it's a pointless exercise. Anyway, why on earth are you larking about with this kind of undergraduate piffle?"

He raised an unkempt eyebrow and stared over at Ailsa, noticing her for the first time. It was clear he was trying to place her too, a tiny bell of recognition jangling in his mind.

"What is *that*?" he said, pointing a well-gnawed

fingernail[32] in Ailsa's direction, "and what is it doing here?"

"Sandy, this is Ailsa. Judith's granddaughter," said Priya, a little reproachfully. "You remember Ailsa."

Sandy blinked as a lizard might.

He had turned cold again.

"Judith?"

"Professor Craig."

"Ah, yes. Ha ha. Very good."

There was that shift again. Frozen wastes to instant warmth. Sandy summoned another smile, briefly reassured, and thought for a moment. By the time the smile had come, it was gone. His mind on greater matters. But his mouth kept moving regardless. "Hello there, erm, little one," he said, with all the charm and good humour of a vending machine. Ailsa knew that men like him were often appallingly bad at talking to children.

"She's helping me set up this new visitor display," said Priya. "Would you like to pitch in, Professor Munro?"

Sandy turned his nose up at her, displaying a chaotic jumble of nose hairs of differing lengths and colours. "Well, um, I … that is to say, no."

---

32 Still attached to the tip of his bony finger, in case you were worried, disgusted, or both!

In that moment Ailsa remembered Grandma's retirement party speech, and how she hadn't mentioned this man at all. And how once, in a New Town restaurant, she had gone out of her way to avoid him completely.

"I'll leave you to it." He smiled, nodding amiably at Ailsa. "But we need to chat about tomorrow, Priya. I'll be hosting the gentlemen from the Compass Group and will need you to join in the greasing of palms. That should help loosen some wallets, eh?"

With that, he marched off, expensive leather soles clip-clopping on the tiled floor. Ailsa watched him go warily. Priya's hand appeared on her shoulder.

"He never said goodbye," said Ailsa.

"No. Mind you" – Priya smiled as they made their way to a set of double doors that led outside – "he never said hello either. I suppose that makes him consistent?"

Ailsa laughed, and it felt good. A sudden draught of air blew Ailsa's hair back over her face for a moment, and they both laughed even harder.

CHAPTER 25

A WARNING

The sound of continued mirth floated down the hallways to the unkempt, hairy ears of Professor Sandy Munro. Lowlier brains, he had always found, were prone to fits of involuntary emotion.

He was waiting for the vending machine to dispense him a frothy coffee. Even the din of the grinding beans didn't silence the sounds of merriment.

Of all the baser human noises, Sandy hated laughter most of all. He could deploy it with ease, of course, feigning spontaneity when necessary – he had cultivated a loud, rollicking laugh that was a useful social tool to achieve visibility, or ensure flattery. A good loud guffaw could turn heads, and he knew the benefit of that. Lesser humans enjoyed the sound, he knew. What was it the Roman poet had said? Give them bread and circuses to keep the people happy. Didn't they see the menacing sight a laugh produced? How people bared their teeth as they rocked back and forth? How it was nothing more than the promise of deferred violence?

Out came the coffee.

He grabbed the plastic cup and walked on.

Nevertheless, the afterglow of glee seemed to follow him, taunting him. It remained around him like an odour all the way to his office. Distracted, he took a deep slug of his coffee, burning his lips and throat, which only angered him more.

After a brutal, loveless childhood and a steep ambitious ascent to his singular goal, all of it at the serrated edge of hard science, the only two feelings Sandy Munro truly understood were anger and its constant companion, fear.

He would look in the files again, just in case.

So, that was Judith's granddaughter, was it?

She seemed curious, certainly.

He wondered if she knew.

CHAPTER 26

THE INSIDE TRACK

Ailsa was with Dad all weekend. They still had errands to run, issues to fix and all the shopping to do. It was doubly hard adjusting to the new house. They didn't have much and had to buy most things to cope with what they'd lost in the explosion. They also had only a few weeks to find somewhere to live again. Sunday morning, Ailsa had a lie-in but had promised she would tidy her room and put the laundry on.

It wasn't the most relaxing weekend.

It was around dinner time, then, that Ailsa noticed her father's head. Specifically, the single grey hair which she hadn't ever noticed before.

Dad caught her staring over their takeaway dinner, and he smiled ruefully. "Yes, I know. I saw it this morning," he said. "The burden of parenthood, you see. I think it was disguising itself as a blond highlight for a few weeks."

Ailsa furrowed her brow, but Dad waggled his naan back at her. "Joking, my darling! You're no burden at all, I promise. In fact, you've always been the opposite."

"It's not exactly been an easy year, Dad."

His face dropped a little. A sadness in his eyes.

"We're all helping each other get through it," he said. "Hard on Mum too. So long as you're doing OK, though?"

Ailsa nodded. Shape-shifting again into the stress-free child. She knew it was always the best hat to wear when difficult subjects arose. She knew it helped him. At least, she hoped it did.

As she helped with the dishes, Ailsa realized the weekend was almost over, and she still hadn't finished her science project.

But she knew exactly what to do.

After all, now she had an edge.

The next day, after school, Ailsa met Credenza outside the gates.

"Come with me," Credenza said as a taxi pulled up next to her. The two of them rode in silence towards George IV Bridge, which Ailsa remembered was where she had emerged from the Middlemarket the first time. It was right before sunset as they wound down towards the Old Town of Edinburgh, and into the Cowgate.

Ailsa recalled the dead end she'd found herself in but couldn't see it at first.

Credenza told the cab to stop and waited until it had driven away before she took Ailsa's hand and led her down a vaguely familiar alleyway. The street name was back, carved into the stone. St. Mary's Wynd.

The alleyway stretched before them as the light began to fade. A shiver hit Ailsa's bones as she wondered whether the Gloaming might make another appearance. But with every second that passed, as the light faded from orange to violet to grey, shadows on the walls began to take on a new form. One of those shadows began to change. Its edges became sharper, and soon the shadow was an outline. A few seconds after that, the outline had become a door – identical to the one that Ailsa had seen in the back of her dad's shed.

Ailsa wasn't sure if it had been there all the time. It sure looked as if it had. (Doors often don't just materialize – this is something most physicists agree on. Certainly not fancy doors like this with brass handles and heavy wood.)

"This isn't where I went through the first time," said Ailsa as they approached the door.

"I know. I mean, you weren't ever supposed to be there at all," said Credenza, as her hand grasped the handle.

"There are only four ways in, and this is the best one."

She turned the handle and pushed the door open. Beyond, Ailsa found herself in the same strange room as inside the shed the other night.

The strawberry-haired woman was warmer and cheerier this time, greeting Ailsa with a wide smile. Ailsa had seen the taxi driver behave in the same way, and she was starting to get the feeling that being in Credenza's company was a ticket to sunshine, a kind of passport to pleasantness in the world. She was the sort of person who opened doors for whomever walked beside them.

"Is this the only way in?" asked Ailsa as they approached the wood-panelled door once again, the frosty breeze already whistling out from under its base.

"There are four portals, dear," croaked the woman from behind them. Ailsa could see a nameplate on the desk now. It was made of brass and read: "MOIRA BOGBEAN, CHIEF CLERK".

The clerk pointed to the floor and Ailsa realized there was a design woven into it. One that showed a compass with eight points. It looked to Ailsa like the face of a clock. Beyond the compass directions of north, south, east and west were words.

"You are here, at the Southern Port," said the clerk, "also known as the Bridge Port. Accessed through St.

Mary's Wynd at twilight." She pointed to the same words on the carpet as she talked. "We call them ports, rather than gates, although the principle is the same."

"I've never seen that road before," said Ailsa. "St. Mary's Wynd."

"I'm not surprised, dear," continued the clerk with a smile. "There are two other entrances to the Midden. Causeway Port to the east, Niddry Port to the west."

Ailsa peered closer. "What about this one to the north? And that little one to the south? What about those?"

The clerk's eyes darkened and her voice lowered.

"Your little break-in to the south was a mistake. An explosion, I believe, one that opened up a tiny rip into our world. A rip that has since been repaired."

Ailsa knew that was the garden shed, and that the explosion hadn't just torn her life apart but torn up something here too.

"And the one to the north?"

"That one is sealed and shall not be opened. Do not venture north in the Midden, my dears."

"Why not?"

The clerk kept her eyes on Ailsa. More firmly this time: "Just don't." She suddenly brightened, as if catching herself, and grinned. "Not that you're the type to disobey the rules, I'm sure."

"Come on, Ailsa," chuckled Credenza. "If you don't go looking for trouble, it won't find you."

"If you say so," said Ailsa. All this new information was making her head spin. Credenza held Ailsa's hand as they approached the door. She could feel Ailsa's reticence.

"There's a trick to the next bit, by the way," Credenza whispered.

"What is it?"

"Hold your breath and try not to think too much."

Once through the door, Ailsa didn't feel that frosty wind catching the back of her throat. The darkness, and the falling, was something she would simply have to get used to.

On the other side of the door, the courtyard beckoned again: the same hardened frost on the ground, bizarre golden sunflowers peeking out from drifts by the walls.

Ailsa grinned. She hadn't dreamed any of it.

This place was real.

The two of them wandered into town. Credenza, as ever, supremely confident. Ailsa, with a wide new set of eyes. The people of the Middlemarket were the same as when Ailsa first encountered them.

"How did this all start anyway?" asked Ailsa.

"Well, Professor Munro found the portal, and then met Lady Blackthorn. That's all I really know. Dad told me Munro did the Shee a favour, and so they let us have this hour in return. When Munro brought my dad into it, though, that's when everything really started moving properly."

"How do people spend their time here then?"

"First things first," said Credenza, catching the eye of a guard-like person walking past. "We need to get our numbers. Come with me, I'll show you the sights."

Credenza led Ailsa back to the Reckoning Room, this time taking "the long way round". On the way, Ailsa got her bearings a little better, and took in the sheer beauty and scale of the place.

The town was small but jewel-like in its construction. It was built from wood and stone, that was certain, but the windows and door knockers, railings and roof tiles, all of them glowed with the auburn tint of sunset. It was one of the most beautiful places Ailsa had ever seen.

The people of the town, as Credenza had said, were both welcoming and preoccupied. Ailsa wasn't entirely sure what anyone actually did here, but then again she had no idea if these fair folk (or Shee or whatever they preferred to be called) had real jobs at all. They mostly seemed to be very social, talking and gossiping, laughing and strolling, helping the humans who visited, pointing people in the right direction when they got lost.

There were the workers inside the Exchange, of course, which seemed to function like an enormous school with extra butlers.

On the way, as Credenza chatted to her about all the famous and important people who came here, Ailsa did glimpse ordinary families sitting down to dinner, framed through glowing windows, though in their eyes she couldn't help but notice, here and there, that many of their faces were etched with a deep melancholy. As if as much as they had a lovely life in a beautiful house, they would rather not be there at all. Once in a while, Ailsa also felt she was being watched again, from up amongst the chimneys. She kept reminding herself to seek out Tobias again, but Credenza was so intent on showing her around she didn't want to be rude.

"And that," Credenza was saying, "is where the sportier people go if they're training for something. The people that need to work with numbers are in that floor up there, and the swimming pools are on the other side, in the basement."

"How do the Shee know what we need?" asked Ailsa.

Credenza shrugged. "They just do. And if they don't, they ask. They're here to help. That's what they're always saying."

"The time's always right to do what's right," replied Ailsa. "That's what one of them said to me."

Credenza sighed and shrugged, which was her default response to things she'd prefer not to deal with or that bored her. She was not one for details.

They were soon back in the strange teller room that Ailsa had found on her first visit. This time there were literally dozens of windows open, each with a helpful clerk issuing small slips of paper. Around them were lines of patient, happy, healthy, successful-looking people. Ailsa recognized most of them from the reception. Some from watching them online or on TV. Some of them even recognized her.

The woman with grey hair and red glasses nodded to her, but Ailsa realized her gaze was fixed on Credenza.

"Hey, there's my dad!" said Credenza, pulling Ailsa over to a tanned, rotund man in a bright blue business suit and brown loafers. Ailsa noticed that he wasn't wearing any socks, which she imagined was horribly cold.

This was the famous Cameron Dingwall. He was shorter than Ailsa had imagined him to be and seemed to be profoundly sunburnt. He flashed a toothy grin as Credenza approached. Seeing Ailsa behind her, his brow furrowed.

"Dad, this is Ailsa from school. She's here too."

"Apparently," said Cameron Dingwall. "You all right?"

"Great. Can we do something today?"

"Busy day round here, chicken, sorry. Lots occurring."

"See you at home then?"

Cameron smiled in a way that didn't commit him to anything. "Behave, now," he said. "Both of you." He winked.

He turned back to two people in line behind him, who Ailsa thought she recognized from the Scottish Parliament.

"He still calls me chicken," said Credenza. "Total cringe."

Ailsa thought Credenza didn't look too embarrassed about it. In fact, she looked over the moon to spend even a moment with her father. Ailsa hadn't really considered how much both her parents were part of her life.

The numbers system, or "vouchers" as she had heard it referred to, had initially confused Ailsa. But it all appeared to simply be a way of keeping track. They were basically numbered tickets that you received when you arrived, and gave back when you left. That way, as Credenza explained it, the people of the Middlemarket could keep track of everyone who came through the ports each Magic Hour, and everyone who then left. Those leaving at the correct moment handed over their vouchers, and the clerks crossed their names off the list. If there were vouchers left unaccounted for when the Magic Hour ended, well, that meant that the people with those vouchers had overstayed, beyond the allotted bells. If you were late, you had to come back to the Reckoners to get a receipt and pay a small penalty.

Everyone, Ailsa understood, was late sometimes.

Which made Morag the clerk busy – and annoyed. It was her who greeted Ailsa with a sigh and a self-satisfied nod.

"Doing things properly today, I see."

The strange machines behind the counter whirred and clacked once more and spat out a small piece of paper – an official "voucher". Credenza's was "seven-and-fifty" and Ailsa's "eight-and-fifty". The two girls walked back from the "Reckoning Room", across the lobby of the big building, which Ailsa now knew was called the Exchange.

Ailsa followed Credenza up the stairs, giving the lift a wide berth. She thought for a moment about searching for the room with the red door again, but when a growling sound entered her mind, she cast it aside, and the low noise soon faded to nothing.

Over the next week, every day after school Credenza

would show Ailsa everything that she needed to know about the Magic Hour: a neat way to skip the line at the Reckoning Room to get their vouchers, the bewildering variety of rooms made available for everyone to spend their extra sixty minutes.

In some spaces, behind closed doors, Ailsa could hear conversations. In others, typing, singing, welding and sawing. Some people sat in silence, reading by a fire. Other rooms were gymnasiums, business boardrooms, silent study. A whole orchestra of noises, but in all of them the noises of work, study, progress.

Around the back of the Exchange, Credenza showed Ailsa a vast outdoor space that was divided into all manner of special sections. There were grass football pitches filled with shouts and whistles; tennis courts that fizzed and popped with the sound of serves, volleys and rallies; there was a swimming pool, a diving centre, a running track and even a ski slope.

In another part of the vast complex, Ailsa snuck inside a high-ceilinged room to watch a violinist rehearsing a challenging melody. He seemed familiar to her. Perhaps she had seen him on a poster outside the Usher Hall. When he saw her looking, she blushed. He smiled and nodded. It was almost like she had joined a club, and everyone was pleased to see her.

"Your dad seems nice," said Ailsa as they wandered. "I've never met your mum, though."

"She's the best," said Credenza.

"Does she come here too?"

"She always says she will, but she never does. I think it's probably to do with the fact that Dad's here all the time, and she's been avoiding him lately. What do your folks do again?"

"Dad works in an office, training people, I think. Mum works at the hospital."

Ailsa also knew that her father loved to paint more than anything, and her mother was a photography nut. But since they were so busy making ends meet, they never had a chance to do any of it. She was suddenly alive with the idea of them both coming with her one day, and spending an hour doing what they loved. Her heart soared at the image in her head, and her luck in finding the truth about this place.

As the two girls explored, they made friends. Not only with each other, but with everyone they encountered. The people of the Middlemarket, as far as Ailsa could see, were unerringly warm and welcoming. Nothing seemed to be too much trouble.

Once in a while, however, when Credenza wasn't walking with her, things would change. Like a warm day when the sun suddenly dips behind a cloud. She would see an awkwardness creep back in. Smiles would fade faster. And on one occasion, a younger, smartly dressed man seemed to almost tease her.

"Enjoying your time, I hope?" he had said, in a way that suggested that he didn't hope that in the least. When Ailsa explained how extraordinary she found it all, he had snorted and snickered back at her.

Later on that day, she had seen the same young man being marched unceremoniously to the Belltower. When she looked closer, she saw that the firm hands on his shoulders belonged to none other than the pleasant, friendly couple she had first met on the street. They were practically dragging the younger man inside, grim-faced and rough. The woman turned to see her watching and walked back up to her as the young man was bundled inside the door of the Belltower.

"Everything all right?" said Ailsa.

"The boy was unforgivably rude to you," said the woman. "Please accept our apologies. It won't happen again."

"It's really OK," said Ailsa. But they had already gone into the building and slammed the door.

As the days turned into weeks, Ailsa came back to the Magic Hour as often as she could. Often with

Credenza, but sometimes on her own. She kept meaning to ask Credenza if she could bring her folks, but there was so much she didn't know herself, she felt like it might be a better idea that she learn first. That way, she thought, she could show them round herself.

Ailsa loved the Magic Hour, and the Magic Hour loved Ailsa.

She found herself using this time better than any other moment in her day, perhaps because she knew it was there, waiting, and she was always prepared for what the hour would involve. She not only completed her science project, but found that with an uninterrupted hour of study, she was easily able to finish every single outstanding piece of homework she had been set. All it took, she realized, was taking advantage of a period of pure, quiet concentration. She had forgotten how many times her attention would wander – a text, a meme, a joke, a secret note, one of her parents calling her for dinner.

Not only that, but by finishing her work early, she had more time for fun. She started running again. She played tennis with Credenza (Credenza was very good, but a patient, fun playing partner) and then swam laps to unwind. At the end of her first couple of weeks, it felt like there was nothing she couldn't do, so long as she took advantage of everything the Magic Hour had to offer. It was like a vast, city-wide summer camp in the snow.

Now she had a special, inside track.

A shortcut in life.

Coming home, whether to Dad's house or Mum's flat, she would add to a list of all the things she kept forgetting to do – and she found to her delight that she suddenly had time to do them. She had even begun to forget how upset she had been when Credenza abandoned her that first fateful time despite her promises.

Ailsa even managed to make sense of the bells that rang out across the Middlemarket. She had worked it out with a pencil on the back of a takeaway napkin. Since there were ten bells across a single hour, that meant that one bell equalled six minutes of "actual" time. The final bell, when it came, was more curious. It was louder and deeper than the rest – and she knew that once that bell sounded, she had only six more minutes to get to a port (the Southern Port, generally, since she knew it so well) and hand in her voucher to a guard to make sure her visit was accounted for.

One day, as the final bell reverberated around the square, Ailsa was striding across the quad towards the Southern Port when she saw Credenza beckoning her nearby. She was half-hidden around the corner of the

Belltower, which Ailsa had heard some others call the Tron. Ailsa hadn't seen her at all that day, having come to the Middlemarket alone. When Ailsa approached, Credenza pulled her close. Across the square, she could barely make out Cameron Dingwall scurrying back towards the Southern Port alongside the lady with the silver hair. There was another man with them, very upright looking with a shaved head. He seemed mean.

"We should get going," said Ailsa. "Everyone's leaving. Time's up."

But Credenza put her finger to her mouth. "Aren't you curious?" she said.

"What about?"

Credenza looked around to make sure there was no one else close by. "About what happens here after the final bell, of course!"

"Well," said Ailsa, not liking where this was going, "they've been pretty clear it's against the rules to stay after the final bell."

"Which is precisely what's going to make it so fun!" said Credenza. With that, she yanked Ailsa in through the door and slammed it shut behind them.

CHAPTER 27

THE GLOW

Inside the tower was a dank circular room laid with a threadbare old rug; a staircase wound up the wall. There were no windows. At the top of the stairs, Ailsa could see through the gloom to the faint outline of a hatch in the ceiling. She presumed it led to the roof. It was getting hard to see in the dying light. Credenza was too busy laughing at her own joke to pay much attention.

Ailsa, however, didn't see the joke. "What are you doing?"

"Oh, come on, it'll be fun. Much more fun than homework."

"I don't know about this," said Ailsa, moving to the door. "And I've done all my homework, thanks."

"Swot," teased Credenza. "*Sook.*"

(You've probably had people behave in your life like Credenza was behaving at that moment. Someone who is excited to take a risk, persuades you to do it, even acting alone, but hasn't yet thought about the consequences. People who get quite defensive when challenged. These people tend to learn, eventually.)[33]

Ailsa tried to temper her frustration with thought. The Magic Hour was real. She thought about her mum and dad.

"You know who could really do with coming here? My folks. I mean, they're strapped for time all the time. It's like all they ever talk about."

Credenza was now very close to Ailsa. Her breath was misting the air inside the room. It was suddenly very cold.

"You listen to me, OK?"

Ailsa nodded. Credenza had her serious voice on.

"This is an exclusive, elite, invitation-only place."

"But your dad's here. Why can't my—"

"My father," interrupted Credenza, developing a haughtier tone, "is one of the founders, OK? The people who discovered this place. You cannot tell anyone else about it. You must promise me that. Honestly, I thought you understood."

"I do understand," said Ailsa, not liking Credenza's tone.

"You have to promise me you'll keep it secret."

"I will."

---

33   Spoiler alert. Maybe.

"I need to hear you say it, Ailsa. I need to hear your vow."

Ailsa sighed. "I promise. But I think I want to go home now."

"Suit yourself," said Credenza, turning back to climb the stairs of the tower. "I didn't realize you were quite so dull. I was actually hoping this might be fun. I guess I was wrong."

The final bell was fading into nothing in the frosty air. Ailsa turned to the exit and pulled the handle.

The door was locked.

"Oh, great," said Ailsa.

"What's the problem *now*?" said Credenza.

Ailsa told her.

Credenza's face stiffened. This had not been in the plan.

"This is all your fault!" cried Credenza.

Ailsa's mouth gaped open. "What? But you're the one—"

"We have to get out of here..." Credenza was trembling now. Holding back tears. "How do we get out? Come on, think!"

Ailsa scanned their surroundings quickly.

There were no windows on the ground floor of the Belltower building. Whether they were pushing or heaving or hammering on it, it made no difference. The door would not open.

Only the stairs offered a solution.

The only way was up.

As they ascended to the roof of the Belltower, they kept their backs to the circular walls, and Ailsa tried to control her rage. She hadn't asked to be here; in fact, she had actively rejected the plan. She didn't want to take part in Credenza's "hilarious" little scheme. Her friend didn't seem to understand. Credenza was different. She was someone for whom everything had a way of working out. So, she simply assumed that it must be that way for everyone.

But it wasn't.

Bad things *could* and *did* happen to good people, Ailsa knew, and breaking the rules like this was only possible when you felt immune to the consequences. Credenza's dad was indeed a founder here; she was part of the inner circle, and chances were she'd be let off the hook for any rule-breaking. But Ailsa was a guest, a random one at that, and she had felt the difference when she was alone out there. They wouldn't treat *her* so kindly. Ailsa had left the place she was born and left it in a hurry. She knew that when things go badly wrong and you fall, there isn't always someone around to catch you.

At the top, the hatch in the ceiling was stiff and it took both of them to push it up and open. A frosty wind smacked into them as they emerged into the air.

Clambering out on to the roof of the Belltower, the sky above them was dark and starless. The floor was stone, a wrap-around terrace, like a large, circular balcony. It offered perfect views over the Middlemarket rooftops and the sky above.

Across the chimneys and rooftops, Ailsa tried hard to take it all in. The lights of the Middlemarket glowed among the roof slates and chimney stacks. Braziers were burning and there was the smell of smoke in the air. Beyond the city walls was darkness to distant treelines, and beyond that Ailsa thought that she could see a kind of shimmering curtain of light. It was hard to concentrate on it for too long; it faded in and out of focus, and seemed to travel in a wide circle around the entirety of her vision. It looked like a warped shower curtain, a membrane.

The whole Middlemarket, Ailsa could now see, was in fact a small, fortified town, surrounded by high walls on all points of the compass. The alleyway courtyard that they arrived in was simply the base of a large guard tower. There were two others that she could see, one to the west set in a large arch, and one to the east that looked more like a garden gate. Ailsa suddenly thought of Tobias. She had that knot in her stomach again, knowing she had promised to come and find him, and she had singularly failed at that. But that extra hour often whizzed by at such speed, her mind so busy and full, she had no time to do what was needed to look for him.

The permanent twilight of the Magic Hour was changing rapidly, plunging them further and further into darkness. Past the rooftops, across to the wall and beyond, Ailsa spotted a vast shadowy wood, and a hill to the north which disappeared into low swirling clouds.

There was something beyond that hill, however.

Something very peculiar.

Over the horizon, enveloped in cloud, was a glow in the sky. It looked like an almost-risen moon on the darkest night.

A flagpole was pitched in the centre of the tower's roof upon a huge stone, a flag snapping and wafting above, displaying what Ailsa assumed was the coat of arms of the Middlemarket. Set into the centre of the base was a metal hole that looked like a flower.

Ailsa peered closer. "Did you see this?" she asked.

"One on this side too," said Credenza. "A crescent moon."

"This one's more like a flower. Or maybe it's a sun."

Credenza pulled at Ailsa's sleeve and pointed.

"Oh, and look down there," she said, eyes bright with

mischief, all of her previous fear now vanished. "Look what's happening to their clothes."

Ailsa peered, trying to make sense of what she could see. One moment, she could focus on the people in the street, walking in their tartan costumes. Then, in an eyeblink, they would disappear one by one. Looking closer, it was their clothes that had changed. Instead of colour, it seemed, there was nothing but the faintest moonlight. The people were still walking, but appeared ethereal, translucent. Their Highland dress replaced by flowing robes and jerkins.

What also struck Ailsa was the silence. The town was transforming from a bustling metropolis to a ghost town. As if sensing that thought, the night air was pierced by a shrill whistle.

Glancing down at the square, Ailsa could see what looked like Virgil Merrimack. He was in his finery and longcoat, a long silver whistle in his lips.

In an instant, the people of the Middlemarket were suddenly back in their tartan finery. Conversations sparked again, shouts and laughter, as if nothing had happened.

Ailsa turned back to tell Credenza but screamed in shock.

Virgil Merrimack was standing right beside them. Ailsa tried to speak, but all her mind could do was ask the same question: *how on earth did he get up here so fast?*

"What is the meaning of this? We're long past final bell!"

Credenza feigned an impish giggle, the kind that small children attempt with their parents in order to get out of trouble. "Funny story," she said. "Thing is, Mr Merrimack, we came up here and the door locked, and we couldn't get out. Thank God you heard us from all the way down there."

"You know the rules, Miss Dingwall."

"Oh, come on, it's me—"

"Those rules apply to everyone. No exceptions. Lady Blackthorn will look upon this very seriously."

He then turned to Ailsa with a revulsion in his face that Ailsa had never seen before. "I see what's happened here," he said. "I imagine this was your idea, was it? You insisted on leading poor Denzie Dingwall up here, did you not, young lady?"

Ailsa's face burned with indignation. "I did no such thing. We came in here together. Now help us leave together too."

Virgil looked at his timepiece.

"The moment has passed; the bell has tolled," he said.

"Can't we work something out?" simpered Credenza.

Virgil went quiet, as if assessing a bet.

"It's possible I can help you," said Virgil. "But you cannot be seen by the others. After all, if word gets around that *outsiders* have disregarded our most sacred pact…"

"Oh, come on, I know that people do this all the time."

"No, Miss Dingwall," said Virgil darkly, "they most certainly do not."

They tiptoed back down the stairs from the roof. The door was now hanging wide open. Outside it, framed by the door like a painting, was a white horse. It was laden with saddlebags and cloth.

"Oh my God," started Ailsa, "what a beautiful—"

Virgil placed his hand on her shoulder to stop her going further. It was then that Ailsa saw the horse had a single horn on its forehead.

"A unicorn? Are you kidding me?"

"Be quiet and do exactly as I say," said Virgil. "Climb in and keep your heads down. But do not ever do this again. I only help you because your father once helped me. Now our account is settled."

"Climb in? To what?"

"The bags, of course. Now *haud yer wheesht* and move yourselves before I change my mind!"

There was a sharper, coarser tone to Virgil Merrimack now. Ailsa assumed he was taking a risk in helping them and vowed to herself never to bow to peer pressure again.

The two girls clambered up and into the low-slung saddlebags. As they did, Virgil draped a cloth over the hind of the unicorn and leapt on.

Ailsa curled herself into the smallest ball she could. The haunches of the horse bumped against her roughly as they bounced and clopped along the street. *Surely this animal can't be a unicorn?* Ailsa thought. *Then again, here I am in the land of the Shee, so it would seem that right now, in this moment, anything is possible.*

All she could see were the red and green fibres of the blanket over her head and body. All she could hear, however, was everything.

There was the sound of hooves, of course, echoing against the walls of the buildings. She could feel them climbing a slope; perhaps Virgil was taking them back up St. Ninian's towards the west gate. There were other sounds beyond the rhythm of the journey. Whistles and murmurs, laughter and hissing. Every so often, a glowing orb passed by her vision, a torch, perhaps, or something larger. For a minute she thought she could hear scampering nearby, and immediately thought of Sydekyck.

Eventually, the noises subsided.

When Virgil spoke again, his voice was a mere whisper. "When I tell you, climb out and run towards the light."

"What light?" asked Credenza from the other saddlebag.

"You'll know it when you see it."

A few more steps, and the animal stopped.

In a single movement, the covering was whipped off and Ailsa and Credenza clambered out of the saddlebags into what first appeared to be utter darkness. Ailsa turned this way and that, looking for a reference point. Suddenly, it sparked into life. Past the tail of the horse, on Credenza's side, she saw a sparkling glow in the middle of the grand archway – the west gate, her exit.

Credenza was already running, and Ailsa took off after her. But Ailsa's curiosity got the better of her, and she could not help but look behind her one final time.

What she saw was a vortex.

Ailsa had never seen a vortex before, outside of watching the water drain down the plug in the bath.

The lines and shapes of the Middlemarket were still there, but now stretched and warped like faces in a funhouse mirror. It was like space itself was being pulled apart. The more she stared into it, the more she felt it pulling at her, like the feeling of vertigo you might get at the top of a building or on the high diving board at a pool. Suddenly, she saw the laughing eyes of the couple she'd first met, the friendly faces now warped and mocking, grey as moonlight, eyes lit with sparks of menace just like the young man's had been earlier.

Ailsa suddenly felt dizzy and began to spin as Credenza grabbed her by the collar and dragged her back towards the port. The two girls fell, emerging once again in their own world, out of breath and unsettled.

"Maybe we don't stay after the final bell next time?" said Ailsa.

"Copy that," said Credenza, biting her bottom lip.

CHAPTER 28

Only Good Things Can Happen

As Ailsa slept that night, the red-eyed presence was there again. It felt closer this time. As if it already knew her well. It was lurking in a kind of mist. It had one foot in her dreams, and one foot, she felt sure, outside them, in her own world.

In her dream, Ailsa was standing at the far end of the same dark stone hallway, the red door with the stag's head looming in shadows at the far end. Next to the door, she could see, was a man.

It was Sandy Munro, and he was talking to someone.

When? came a voice. That voice.

The same one that had spoken to her outside the door.

She could hear it echo, and clearly so could Sandy Munro.

When I tell you, said Sandy, though his lips did not move.

You cannot hold me for ever, came the reply from behind the door.

The way things are is the way things are, said Sandy.

For now, said the voice.

It was here, in her dream, that Sandy Munro turned to look right at her.

Ailsa woke up to the darkness of the early hours and decided to read something cheery till she fell asleep again.

(She did not fall asleep again.)

It was not, to put it mildly, a restful night.

The next day at school, despite her exhaustion, Ailsa was a whirlpool of questions. She rose early and left her dad a note saying goodbye. (This was allowed in the goodbye rules of the house.) Getting extra time to do things meant she had started setting her alarm even earlier. She was curious to see how much she could squeeze out of one day.

She also wanted extra time to think.

The previous night had been wild. She wasn't even that sure it had happened the way she remembered it. Ailsa knew she had to find Credenza before school. It didn't help that, at the same time, she was having to navigate a whole new world.

As she walked into the entrance hall, four girls from her year descended upon her: the popular, shiny ones, bright-eyed with intent. Ailsa knew this quartet as Credenza's friends, the gang of acolytes who sat behind her in science.

Ailsa flinched, fearing the worst.

Instead, the girls grinned.

This was a new phenomenon, and Ailsa was still confused. It had been going on at school ever since her first visit to the Magic Hour. Credenza's posse of friends had decided, overnight, to be nice to her. She was still trying to get used to it.

"You all right?" said one of them.

"How's it going then?" said another

"Cool hat, Ailsa Craig," said a third with a wink.

When Credenza came up to her and hugged her tight, like an old friend, Ailsa was thoroughly befuddled.

Before she could say anything, Credenza had linked her arm in Ailsa's. "So, did you see the shoes Dr Matthews has on this morning?" Credenza said in a confidential tone. "Utter cringe."

Ailsa smiled, and the other girls laughed in echo.

The group moved as one towards the stairs, and Ailsa felt herself swept up in their current. Settling into Dr Matthew's class, Ailsa heard them all whispering again.

Except now, they were also whispering to her, instead of about her.

Ailsa was baffled. She was part of this now? Was this what being part of the in-crowd felt like? She made a joke, and they laughed. This only confused Ailsa more. They were the same kinds of jokes she had always told. Yet somehow, as if responding to a memo, everyone suddenly found them funny.

As class was breaking up, Ailsa took Credenza to the side and finally asked the question that had been bothering her all night. "So what happened yesterday, do you think?"

"Where?" Credenza had the bright and breezy tone of someone who certainly had not been recently running for their life in a dark void.

"Um … in the Middlemarket."

"Middlewhat?"

"When we were running for the…?"

"Seriously, Ailsa, what are you talking about?" said Credenza a little louder, as if for public consumption. Her face now hardening along with her tone of voice. She already had her brow furrowed and a finger to her lips. She leaned in to give Ailsa a pretend hug.

"We don't talk about that stuff here," she said.

"But we need to talk about it sometime, don't we? You and I?"

"Not here." Her words were like tiny darts. Precise and sharp. "Don't forget. VIP. Secret."

Ailsa drew breath to speak, but Credenza cut her off.

"Come over to mine after school," she said, as if this was the final word on the matter. "I need to explain some things to you."

Ailsa spent the rest of the day wondering why anyone would keep something like the Magic Hour secret. She had never felt more accepted at school. She was officially in the club. She had more time to get on top of her problems. Life seemed so much easier than it had before. And she hadn't even been going that long! Imagine what life was going to be like after a year...

It was then that she saw Stu.

She found him in the entrance hall at break, his eyes red and puffy again. He looked, frankly, exhausted.

"Phonics," he said mournfully. "I can't get my head round them. The letters keep dancing whenever I look at them. They keep telling me I'm special, but I don't bloody feel it. How am I supposed to get anywhere in life if I can't ruddy well read properly?"

It was coming up to half term soon, Ailsa knew, and that meant even more hassle for poor Stu. Holiday weeks were tough for him at home, and he already had no time to keep up with his schoolwork.

Ailsa's stomach knotted.

Maybe, she thought. *Maybe I can tell him?*

Just him?

Seeing him standing there, sniffing and desperate, it made Ailsa's heart ache. It was so tempting. After all, it was the easiest thing in the world to bring him to the Middlemarket. Alone. Just once. Far more so than herself, or Credenza, it was people like Stu who would benefit most from an extra sixty minutes in the day. It would mean the world to him.

She cleared her throat. But at the last minute, she pulled back, recalling her promise to Credenza, and bit her tongue. She had said it out loud. *I promise.* She had to keep her word.

"What's up with you?" asked Stu, seeing the contortions in Ailsa's face.

"Nothing," said Ailsa, biting her tongue even more.

Stu didn't look very convinced, but he shrugged anyway.

Ailsa didn't like lying to her friends, even if it was to protect another's confidence.

As Ailsa was leaving to walk to Credenza's house, her phone rang. It wasn't a fancy mobile, and to her dismay it had no internet on it (her parents had agreed to get her a better one when she turned twelve, and she was counting the days). It was her dad.

"I got an email from school about you, Ailsa," he was saying. "And I'm getting Mum on the call too, OK?"

She couldn't read the tone of his voice. It made her nervous.

"It's me, sweetheart," said Mum, joining the call.

Both parents? Not good. Not good at all.

"It's about your report card," said her dad, followed by one of his signature dramatic pauses. Then, he began to read. "After a slow start to the term, Ailsa has really applied herself in these final weeks. A+ work, Ailsa! Whoo hoo!"

"Amazing!" said Mum. "Well done! It's been … quite a while since we've seen you so applied at school, darling. We're so proud of you."

Ailsa felt a warm, golden glow in her chest. So, this was what it felt like to do well. "I'm managing my time better," she said.

Credenza's neighbourhood was far away from the high street. The afternoons were still dark, and holiday songs were still playing in some of the shops, as if people had forgotten to turn them off.

The house was vast, with two animals on the gateposts: a lion and a dragon. There was a complicated buzzer to get in, and Ailsa's feet crunched on the gravel as she walked up to the front door, past a garage full of fancy cars. Two large black Range Rovers were parked nearby. Credenza ran out to greet her and beckoned her round the side of the house.

"Front door's for tradesmen only. All the best people come in through the kitchen, don't you know?"

Credenza seemed genuinely excited to welcome her friend.

The kitchen was a vast, cathedral-like space. There was bread baking, a pot of soup on a vast stove, and a fridge that seemed to be made entirely for bottles of wine. Ailsa's eyes lit up at a large platter of biscuits that had been laid out with precision.

"Nice kitchen," said Ailsa.

"We don't always have stuff like this lying around. Dad's having a meeting in the parlour. Come on, let's take these in."

Credenza picked up the platter and strode out into a grand central hallway. A vast staircase led up to three further floors, lit by a skylight in the roof. Ailsa followed Credenza, marvelling at the luxury of it all. Adult conversation echoed off the walls as they approached a large double door. Credenza glanced at the handle and glared at Ailsa as if to say: can you open this for me?

Ailsa opened the door.

Inside was a plush dining room with a huge table

dominating in the centre. Credenza waltzed in and Ailsa saw five people staring daggers back at them.

"Biscuits?" said Credenza.

Cameron Dingwall glared at her but managed a smile.

"There's my perfect student," he said. "My golden girl…"

Credenza grinned like a medal winner on the podium. In the corner, over Cameron's shoulder, Ailsa saw a big board filled with complex drawings. In large letters above them all was written:

ARIA BRIEFING – CONSTRUCTION PLAN

On the table, amongst silver pots of coffee and platters of delicious-looking pastries, Ailsa glimpsed a vast map that looked like a schematic blueprint. Cameron noticed her attentions, and approached, blocking her line of sight.

"Doing well at school, is she?" asked a woman in a business suit nearby. It was the woman with the grey hair and the red glasses. The woman who had saved her from the cab. Ailsa tried to hide her surprise.

"Outstanding," grinned Cameron. "Top marks, gold stars every time. That's my girl. Brought your friend, did you?"

All eyes fell on Ailsa.

"Hello, Mr Dingwall," said Ailsa, unsure of what

else to say since the man hadn't even said hello. She felt the eyes of the woman upon her now, and a flash of recognition.

"Hello to you too, um…"

The woman said nothing, turning away to look at a document on the table. Everyone in the room had the air of someone caught in the middle of some epic mischief. Silence fell.

"We're going to do some homework," lied Credenza.

Ailsa felt a chill and noticed another gaze upon her. On the other side of the room, by an ornate fireplace, she could see him. It was Sandy Munro, talking in hushed tones to a man wearing what appeared to be a military uniform.

"Sounds good," said Cameron, his white teeth glowing as he herded them towards the doors. "Thanks for the biscuits, though we have people to do that."

Credenza led Ailsa up the main staircase.

"What's an ARIA briefing?" asked Ailsa.

"No idea," said Credenza. "Dad says it's a business opportunity. Then again, that's what he always says about everything, to be honest."

On the upper floor, Credenza led Ailsa to her bedroom. It was as big as her mother's flat.

"So, you're the golden girl, are you?" Ailsa smiled.

Credenza shrugged. She seemed proud. "He's always bragging about stuff I've done. He says he's never seen me miss the mark."

Ailsa had never heard her own dad bragging about her. Her parents were proud, that she knew. But not like that.

"Is your mum here too? I wanted to say hello."

Credenza looked away. "No, she's still in hospital, so..."

Ailsa froze. "What? Hospital? What's wrong?"

"Her hip broke."

"Is she OK?"

"I think so. She fell over in the garden running after the dog, and snap. She's in some posh private clinic, lazing around; it's more like a spa break for her. And to be honest, it's nice to have a few days when my parents aren't having a go at each other. They're like two wolverines fighting in a sack most days. Honestly, I wish my folks were more like yours."

The idea that Credenza could be jealous of anything in Ailsa's life perplexed her. But the idea of Credenza's mother in hospital made her concerned.

"Your poor mum. I heard those hip things can be painful... I remember when Grandpa's hip broke he was in a lot of pain."

Ailsa remember that time well because Grandpa had been celebrating his retirement when it had happened.

She was struck by a thought as she spoke. She knew that broken hips were often things that older people suffered from. A *lot* older.

"How old is your mum?" she asked.

Credenza shrugged. "No idea. Old, ancient. Forty, maybe, something heinous like that."

"Maybe we should go visit her?"

"What, now?"

"Well, no—"

A gale of laughter was heard from downstairs. A familiar one.

Ailsa edged to the balcony and stared down. And there he was again. Sandy Munro on his way out.

A hand grabbed her shoulder. She spun around, and standing there, a grin on his face, was Ossian.

"Happy Easter," he said. "When it comes, I mean."

Ailsa was nonplussed. Easter was months away. Ossian did this kind of thing often, and usually the best solution was to ignore it.

"We're busy, Ozzie," moaned Credenza. "Please go away."

"Here for the big meeting?" smiled Ossian.

Ailsa shook her head, confused.

"Don't worry. No one here knows what that's about. Plans and schemes, the usual. My gold star sister here's more likely to get the true story, mind. That's how it works in this family. I'm the mushroom, always in the dark."

Credenza glared at her brother and shut her bedroom door.

"That promise you made wasn't nothing," said Credenza. "I really mean it. You cannot tell anyone else about the Magic Hour, OK? No one. Secrets must be kept."

"I don't understand why."

"Listen to me. You are now a member of one of the most exclusive clubs in the entire world. So be grateful," said Credenza. "Only good things can happen to you now. So long as you obey the rules. OK?

Ailsa nodded.

But she felt that knot again. This time it was in her heart.

CHAPTER 29

A MOST EXTRAORDINARY DISCOVERY

The house Ailsa and her dad had moved into was more modern than their old place. The place smelled of cleanliness and modernity. Even her attic bedroom, which in this house had an en-suite bathroom, felt totally different.

When Ailsa got home, she heard her father snoring in the living room, the TV still on. She crept up the stairs. In her bedroom she paced, trying to get her thoughts straight, as the TV downstairs droned away.

Ailsa knew she was sworn to secrecy. She knew that Credenza's dad and Sandy Munro were planning something in the Magic Hour. But what? And with whom?

It was then that she noticed the beat-up, charred crate sitting by the end of her bed. It was Grandma's missing steamer trunk! After the explosion, Ailsa had thought she'd never see it again. But there it was with a handwritten note on top of it from her dad:

MICHAEL FROM NEXT DOOR DROPPED THIS OFF – HE FOUND IT BURIED IN HIS HEDGE.

MAKE SURE TO CALL & SAY THANK YOU :)

Ailsa was thrilled. The trunk itself had dents, warped edges and a completely charred base, but there it was. Just then, Priya called her on the house phone.

"You won't believe what's just turned up," bubbled Ailsa when she heard Priya's voice. "Grandma's crate, the one you gave me from her office. Isn't that bonkers?"

"I'm glad you found it," said Priya in an oddly neutral tone. Instead of her bright, curious self, Priya sounded furtive and quiet. "Ailsa, I'm glad you brought that thing up. If anyone asks you about it, maybe it's best if you just say you *don't* have it. OK? That I didn't give it to you?"

"But … why would I do that?"

"I know it's wrong to lie and it probably sounds weird but, well, I think I may have broken some important rules when I gave it to you. Observatory property or something. I just knew you'd want to have it. Don't worry, I haven't told anyone you have it. But some people have been asking where it is, which surprised me after all this time, and I'm wondering if they might ask you."

"What people?"

"My boss."

Ailsa told her not to worry, but the conversation disturbed her. What did Sandy Munro want with her grandma's trunk anyway? She dived into it straight away. The sides squeaked and it smelled of smoke, but nothing inside looked badly burned.

As if attempting to distract her attention, a news item about business blared up from downstairs, a reporter speaking in a monotone:

"The proposals have been welcomed in some sectors but could mean a hefty increase for others."

Ailsa heard another voice chime in, a woman this time.

"If Parliament want a fight," boomed the voice, "then they're going about it the right way. *And if that's true, they will all need to **look out**."*

Ailsa knew that voice. It had saved her life.

She raced down the stairs and tumbled into the living room.

It was her again, on the TV screen. Sharp grey hair and a vivid pinstriped suit. The woman from the Middlemarket. The woman from Credenza's house. A graphic read:

DAME ZARA MACKAY – YESTERDAY

Ailsa was so enraptured with the discovery, she didn't stop to look at her dad, who was still slumped in his big armchair.

"Ailsa?"

"Sorry, Dad, but what does that woman do? I think I met her."

He rubbed his eyes and peered at the screen.

"Oh, that's Zara Mackay; she's a big business bod around town. Friends with the politicians, you know the type. Sorry, I didn't hear you come in. Did you say you met her? You're swanning around construction projects in Lothian, are you?"

But Ailsa wasn't looking at the TV any more.

"Um, why are you looking at me like that?"

Ailsa was indeed staring at her dad.

Something was very different about him.

His hair.

For all of Ailsa's life, even as recently as last week, her father's hair had been a mop, straight and black. In the last weeks, the single grey hair had made an appearance, like a seam of white frosting in a chocolate cake.

But now things were radical.

Now his hair was completely and utterly white.

He felt her gaze, self-conscious.

"Oh, yes, right enough, the hair thing."

"What's happened?"

"Well, I mean, well, it is ... definitely odd. That's all I can say. Woke up this morning like this. Apparently, this kind of thing can happen to people. If they're stressed enough. I didn't realize I was quite this shade of stressed!"

"Should you maybe see a doctor?"

"Um, yes, I suppose I should. Or a hairstylist maybe? Maybe I've turned into Santa Claus. So maybe I should grow the beard and be done with it."

Ailsa's dad, she knew, would make jokes when things were serious. At least, things that seemed like they would be jokes if they were funny at all.

"Oh, by the way, sorry, I washed a jacket of yours by mistake."

He walked into the hallway where a plastic hamper of dried clothes was stacked, waiting to be folded.

He handed her a slightly rumpled blue jacket – the same one Ailsa had worn on her first adventure in the Magic Hour.

"That's OK," said Ailsa.

"Sorry. I'll get you another one if you like."

"I said it's OK," said Ailsa, shrugging it on. It hadn't shrunk, at least.

"Also, this was in the pocket. I didn't look at it, I promise. Looks like someone wrote you a letter."

He held out a small square of paper.

Ailsa tried to hide her surprise. Of course! It was the piece of paper that Tobias had given her at the party. So much had happened to her, she had completely forgotten about it.

She ran upstairs, taking them two at a time, unfolding Tobias's paper as she went. It was a delicate, handwritten pamphlet, executed in an elegant cursive hand, eked out with a stubby charcoal pencil that had blurred near the edges. It read:

ATTENDEES OF THE MAGIC HOUR
BE CAREFUL WHAT YOU WISH FOR.
Newton's Third Law
(see also: First Law of Thermodynamics)

Ailsa rooted around in her bookshelves and found an old *Encyclopaedia of Science* that had survived the explosion.[34] She soon found what she needed, in black and white, in a section called the LAWS OF MOTION:

When you sit in your chair, your body exerts a downward force on the chair and the chair exerts an upward force on your body. There are two forces resulting from this interaction – a force on the chair and a force on your body.

These two forces are called action and reaction forces. Formally stated, Newton's Third Law is:

For every action, there is an equal and opposite reaction.

She turned to another page, which read:

---

34 Ailsa had moved some of the books she'd kept down at Mum's up to her new house with Dad. The explosion had depleted her shelves and she had maxed out her library card already. Ailsa loved being surrounded by books, because books are your best friends, and who doesn't want to be surrounded by their best friends?

**The First Law of Thermodynamics states:
Energy cannot be created or destroyed. It can
only change form or be transferred from one
object to another.**

She folded the pamphlet back up, popped it in her jacket pocket next to Grandma's postcard, before yanking open a drawer on her desk, pulling out a small Black n' Red lined pad, emblazoned with a retro "NASA" sticker. Her trusty science journal. The words LAB NOTEBOOK OF SCIENTIFIC OBSERVATIONS were written in plump letters on the inside cover. She carefully wrote *Dame Zara Mackay* on a fresh page and underlined it.

Research, she added, next to it.

Then she pulled out Grandma's beloved postcard. Written on the other side was simply "For Ailsa. Use <u>liberally</u>."

Step one: STATE THE PROBLEM CLEARLY.

Ailsa continued writing.

Problem: Can time go wrong?

She scored it all out and tried again. Clearly, remember?

What is the Magic Hour?

Why is it here? And how does it really work?

And does it have something to do with my dad's hair changing colour?

Priya's patient explanations hadn't given her enough to go on at all. What would Grandma have to say about all of this? It wasn't enough to simply accept this crazy thing that was happening. She absolutely, positively needed to somehow understand it.

Grandma's words came back to her again.

"Observe," said Ailsa to herself.

Grandma, thought Ailsa. *Maybe she could help.*

Ailsa opened Grandma's sorry, broken steamer trunk again. She was relieved to have it back. She picked through the notes and photos for a while, as it was one step nearer to having her grandma here, hoping for some kind of clue.

Ailsa felt a stirring of nerves.

The same kind of feelings she'd had when she met Sandy Munro. Something about what he'd said had brought this crate to her memory. Now her dad's hair had gone white overnight. And it all seemed to be connected to the Magic Hour.

Frustrated and tired, she shoved the crate under

183

her bed. But Ailsa had misjudged the action, and a corner of the steamer trunk struck the corner of the bed. The structure buckled, and the box of memories fell apart. The walls listed to the side like a house of cards. Distraught, Ailsa tried to put it back together. But the walls were weak and continued to collapse.

The bottom of the crate was not, in fact, the bottom.

There was another compartment hidden underneath. And now that the walls of the crate had fallen, it opened up like a flower. Inside, she could see a small lip of cardboard.

It looked a bit like a handle.

So she pulled it.

The panel lifted easily. A cloud of mothball-scented air enveloped Ailsa as she peered closer. The base of the crate was hollow. Below it was a hidden compartment no deeper than her thumb.

Inside was a single item: a piece of patterned fabric, flattened like a pancake. One of Grandma's old tweed jackets which she had worn almost every day. Ailsa eased it carefully out of its hiding place. Dry-cleaned to within an inch of its life, it was folded, creased and careworn. She gathered it up, imagining her grandma inside it – but couldn't summon the image.

Instead, it looked like what it was: an old forgotten jacket.

Her heart sank.

Ailsa tossed it behind her on the bed and sat down beside it. A wave of exhaustion washed over her, and she lay down for a moment. She thought about what to do.

Maybe, she thought, *there are some problems that don't have solutions*. She turned over on to her side, mulling this uncomfortable idea. As she did, she realized that her ear was lying on Grandma's jacket.

And it was rustling.

What would the Method say? Did old jackets talk?

Experiment and repeat.

She lay back again on the jacket to stare at the ceiling. Again, it rustled.

Well, thought Ailsa, *jackets don't rustle. Not by themselves.*

She sat up and placed her hand where her ear had been. There was something there, under her palm, something making that same noise – a crumpling, papery sound.

She pressed down harder. Now she could feel it as well as hear it. It was trapped in the lining. It felt rectangular, like a phone. Although sleeker, more delicate. She reached inside. There was nothing there.

The noise came again.

She pushed her hand deeper. This time, her fingertips

found a rougher edge to the fabric. She wiggled her hand around for a moment, following the edge, and there it was. A hole. The silk lining had ripped, and something had fallen through the seam and become lost in the lining. Ailsa felt her way to the edge of the stitching, and finally grasped the object. Gently, she pulled it out.

It was a single, slim, spiral-bound notebook, the kind with a cardboard back and a red cover. It was secured by a single rubber band, which she pinged across the room and on to her desk. The pages were in Grandma's incredibly neat boilerplate handwriting, all executed in dark blue biro.

It was a journal.

Ailsa started to read.

Time is a river, it began. *Flowing so slowly when you're young, speeding up as you age. This is a function of ratios, of course. One week to a newborn is a vast ocean. One week to a centenarian is 1/5200 of his or her life. Possible corollary to acceleration of expanding universe? Research.*

She flipped to another page.

Saw another hedgehog today. I think spring is finally here. I'm concerned there's a dog fox stealing the food, however. More bulletins as events warrant.

Ailsa smiled and flipped again.

Good weekend working with my pal Sandy. He was

telling me about his new work in photoionization of stellar clusters, which of course is something I myself had been talking to him about only last week. I think Sandy only understands something when he himself says it out loud and thinks he thought of it first. I should send him my PhD again.

Ailsa closed the notebook with a snap of her hand.

Of course.

It was easy to forget that Grandma had worked with Sandy Munro at the Observatory for years. More entries followed, mostly stock-taking of a day's efforts rather than any other deep thoughts.

On a single page, there came a beautifully rendered sketch of a single tree leaf. Below it, she had written: *Another wonderful day with Ailsa. Such a happy child. Spent time in the garden looking at the leaves. NB explain photoreceptor proteins to her once she learns how to talk.*

The final pages, however, were different.

The neat writing was gone.

The pages were muddied and torn.

The entries, of which there were few, were marked "X" in the top right-hand corner, as if tagged for reference. The handwriting was almost unintelligible in places. Written in a hurry, perhaps, or (Ailsa wondered) maybe these had been back when she was starting to get sick.

The back few pages of the diary contained a series of impatient, emphatic scribbles, none of which Ailsa could comprehend. One of them read as follows:

EXPERIMENT: *Fire pulse of ultracold subatomic particles past a powerful magnet and into the spatio-temporal membrane.*

CONJECTURE, it continued: *if the universe cooperates — some of those particles will tunnel through the wall to allow measurement of neutron oscillations.*

Ailsa had no idea what any of this meant.

What she did know was that a sheaf of papers had been roughly torn out from the end of the notebook. From the looks of it, some ten sheets or so.

Try as she might, she couldn't find any more loose papers in the pocket. She imagined that whatever was written on those pages was lost for ever. But as she was closing the notebook, something caught her eye. Or rather, the tip of her finger.

The cardboard backing.

It was smooth on the back, but rough on the other side. She could feel tiny undulations in the cardboard, as if something had pressed hard on to it. She held it up and angled the cardboard so that the light shone across its surface.

There they were.

Tiny, regular indentations across the entire sheet.

The pressure of the pen had made a mark.

Ailsa ran to her art box and grabbed a sheet of light sketching paper and a charcoal pencil.

Mrs Beeks had taught brass rubbing to Ailsa's art class the previous year, and Ailsa now thanked her as she laid the paper over the cardboard and began to move her charcoal back and forth over the sheet. Almost immediately, words began to appear – white letters springing up as if by magic from the dark background. All of it in Grandma's writing, still. But the letters were jagged, impatient.

The first line read:

The most extraordinary discovery.

And then:

In the middle of the Bridges, spanned across the old Cowgate, bordered by the medieval wall, there exists an island of separated time.

Ailsa kept her composure and made sure to carefully cover the paper evenly with the charcoal. As she did, more lines appeared:

It defies all existing laws of physics.
Yet I have seen it with my own eyes.

Accessed via a circuitous method (see later note)
Similar to a temporal bubble. Too much to explain here
(time crystals?)
One port lies at the location of old St. Mary's Wynd
(Cowgate level)

Perhaps writing things down will help them make
more sense?

TIMING CRUCIAL
ONE BELL = SIX MINUTES? MARITIME?
Ten in all
Making ONE HOUR

Ailsa stared at the words. They started to stick together, running one into another, as if Grandma had been thinking too fast for her pen to write.

The words continued:

VIRGIL MERRIMACK (SP?)

The Shee live alongside us.
Fairies are real.

Think of it! An extra hour in the day!
What medical breakthroughs could come? What books might be written? What help might come for humanity?

I must share this with Sandy soon. He's a bright button.
I think he would understand the possibilities like I do.

This discovery could change the world.

EVERY. SECOND. COUNTS.

Ailsa stared at Grandma's words for a full minute before she realized she had not taken a breath.

So *that* was why he'd had been acting so strangely.

He knew the truth.

Sandy Munro had not discovered the Magic Hour.

It was Grandma Judith.

The man was a scientific thief.

Ailsa had the truth. And, in those final pages of scribbles, folded into a tiny square on the reverse of a page, drawn in fine lines of pencil, Ailsa had something even more useful than that.

She had a map.

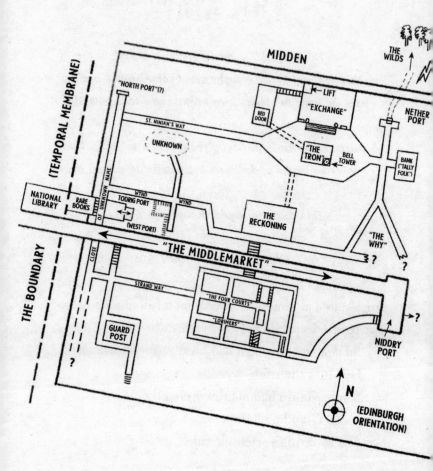

CHAPTER 30

THE MAP

It was all unmistakably Grandma – neat, precise, folded with perfect symmetry. Some parts were more hastily sketched, other sections planned but unfinished. But the map was hers, no doubt.

Statement: Grandma had been to the Middlemarket.

Analysis: she'd known about the Magic Hour.

Conclusion: if she'd been there, she would also surely know how it worked. And perhaps know why this was all happening.

The entire fragment was encircled by a dotted line that read simply "The Middlemarket". The area highlighted by the map appeared to be some sort of addition to the city of Edinburgh. A secret one, from the looks of things. There were scribbles in the margin. *Access? Portal? Scientific Method Must Apply.*

But there was something else in the map that caught her eye. Some of the words echoed.

Bastion. Lorimer. The Four Courts.

All three were dotted around the same section, near the edge. If she was outside the Middlemarket building, and took a right, the road would lead her there.

Tobias. He had warned her too.

She had to find him.

Credenza wasn't answering her phone, so the first moment she could, Ailsa headed back to the alleyway known as St. Mary's Wynd. She stopped by her mum's flat on the way to grab a charging cable she'd forgotten (she was always forgetting something between the two homes). Her mother answered the door with her usual smile. But Ailsa was speechless, and her mum knew why.

"I know, the hair. I think I'll dye it blue."

Her mum's hair, like her dad's, was now utterly white.

Ailsa ran all the way from the bus stop to the alley. She was trying to keep herself from panicking, but now that both her parents had the hair of a much older person, that was increasingly hard to do.

The doorway was already there, washed with the pink metallic glow of twilight. Ailsa shoved it open, and inside the clerk greeted her with a knowing look. She soon figured out why.

"Greetings," said Ossian Dingwall.

Ailsa blinked. It couldn't be.

But there he was, Credenza's big brother. He was slouching in a corner as the woman with strawberry soft-serve hair eyed them both over her ledger.

Ossian chuckled. "Stands to reason, you being here. I mean, in my experience, if I follow my sister, you're usually somewhere nearby."

"Didn't think this would be your kind of thing," said Ailsa.

"Let's just say I'm intrigued. If the rumours are true. An extra hour to read might be fun, I guess."

Ailsa couldn't help but laugh.

"Ossian Dingwall loves to *read*? *Really*?"

"Call me Ozzie. And yeah, I love books. You look surprised."

"Yeah, well, you tried to drown most of them in the library."

"Now, hang on, that was a legitimate experiment. With an unfortunate consequence."

"If it was a true experiment, Ozzie, you would have stayed around to observe the results afterwards," said Ailsa, the anger rising in her chest. "And from what I understand, you ran all the way home. That's not the Scientific Method, that's just ... being scared."

"Mum said there's no case to expel me, and school should be covered under *force majeure*."

"What's that?"

"Not sure really. I think it means get out of jail free. Anyway. Mum works for an insurance company, which is apparently what you call when things go badly wrong."

"Which is quite a lot. Around you."

"You could say that."

"So, Ozzie, what are you *really* doing here?"

"Solving a puzzle."

"What kind of puzzle?"

"It looks a lot like my sister. I know she's been coming here a lot lately, and I think it's got something to do with my dad's business and my poor mum's hip. I'm literally the last to know anything in my family, so I tend to have to play detective and puzzle solver. Wait. Don't tell me you're doing that too?"

Ailsa shook her head despite herself.

"No," she lied. "I'm just … here."

Ossian narrowed his eyes, sceptical. "Can't argue with that."

"Ozzie" had the air of a free pass about him. People with this kind of money didn't experience consequences in the same way as the rest of us, Ailsa thought. They didn't care who they hurt and were used to getting away with whatever they liked. Ailsa was starting to learn this about the world, that some rules that applied to her simply didn't stick to others, so long as they were rich enough. She wondered if she would ever have money. *If I do*, she swore to herself, *I'll make sure I'm nothing like the Dingwalls.*

"But what are you – *actually* – doing here?" he asked suddenly, throwing her emphasis back at her.

Ailsa stopped and took a deep breath, moved closer to him, away from the eavesdropping ears of the clerk. She had to find some common ground, and right now she needed an ally.

"True or false: weird things are happening."

"That would be true."

"Well, I think it's all due to something about this place. And I have to find out why before…" She paused. Her throat felt tight, and there were tears trying to get up into her eyes. But Ailsa forced them back down; she'd had plenty of practice with that.

Seeing her face change, Ozzie softened. "Before what?"

"Before anyone else gets hurt."

"Remember when you were at my house the other day? You saw the plans on the table?"

"The ARIA briefing."

Ossian's eyes flashed. "Exactly."

He held up his phone, which showed a photo of the easel that had been on display.

"Dad never tells me a thing about his business stuff. So, I figured if I went into that room right after they were finished, I might catch a glimpse of something. So I did. I looked up this ARIA thing and it looks like it might stand for Advanced Research and Invention Agency," said Ozzie. "It's part of the army or something. My old man was talking to that old scientist guy. And the other one in military uniform? They're part of ARIA, and I think they've got something to do with all … this."

"Have you ever been through that door before?"

Ossian shook his head. "This is as far as I've ever gone."

Ailsa smiled. "I'll show you."

Ossian shrugged and smiled at the clerk, who glowered. "Name?"

"Ossian Dingwall."

The clerk's face instantly brightened.

"Well now, I thought I recognized you," she said. "Your sister was here earlier; I expect you'll see her inside."

Ailsa led Ossian to the door. "Whatever you do," she said as they stepped into the darkness beyond, "keep your mouth shut."

"Ten bells left," said the clerk with the strawberry hair. "Mind how you go." As the door shut behind them, a smirk bloomed on her lips. "Foolish mortals, the lot of them."

CHAPTER 31

IF TIME WAS CAKE

Ailsa and Ozzie emerged from the darkness into the tiny courtyard with the postage stamp view of the sky. Snow crunched under their feet. Sunflowers sprouted from drifts along the thick walls of stone. The place was eternally frozen in this chilly landscape.

Ozzie was hyperventilating, all his cool, relaxed exterior peeled from his face. He saw Ailsa staring at him and shrugged.

"Well, that was intense."

His eyes moved from Ailsa to the snow, the courtyard and the alleys beyond. His eyes were wide and staring.

"So, what happens now?"

"It gets better," said Ailsa.

As Ozzie followed her through a maze of alleyways, a big stupid grin spread across his face. When they arrived at St. Ninian's Row, its vast bowing buildings like an arch of trees, a bell tolled.

"So, this whole thing is like a free lunch?" he said at last.

"I guess so."

"But … I hope I don't need to say this, though I will anyway. You and I both know there's no such thing as a free lunch."

"Seems pretty free to me, Ozzie."

He smiled again and shook his head. His eyes clouded. "So how come Denzie was keeping all this from me? I'm her brother, for heaven's sake. Even if she was just going to get all braggy about it. She should have said something."

Ailsa looked up at the rooftops and immediately remembered her promise to Tobias. In all the excitement, she had forgotten about him. Where had he said to go? *The Lorimers. Near the Bastion.* It sounded like a boarding house, perhaps, or a family that he stayed with. His surname was Ragwort, she remembered. Perhaps they were relatives?

"I promise you, it's all real," said Ailsa.

Ailsa spotted the same pleasant couple she had seen on her first visit. They nodded as they passed, eyeing Ossian warily.

"Are they … you know?" whispered Ossian. "From here?"

"They're Shee, yes. Now come on; we need a number."

She picked up the pace, heading for the Exchange, and beyond the double doors, she knew now: the Reckoning Room.

As they walked, Ailsa downloaded everything to Ozzie, whose eyes were as wide with wonder as her own had been the first time. Her shed, the door, the clerk and the ledger, the gate, the bells. Virgil Merrimack, Grandma's map and the mysterious Tobias. He took a minute to digest it all, and then raised a curious finger in the air:

"Question. Does Newton's Third Law apply to time?"

"No idea."

"I mean," he continued, "if time was a cake, for example … and you took a larger slice of it, would that mean there's not as much for you? Or anyone else? Is that what he means?"

Ailsa tried to visualize a cake made of time for a moment. All she realized was that she was starting to feel hungry.

"You can't make more time than there actually is," she said finally.

"Good point."

"But that's assuming what we know now is the truth.

201

Science is always discovering new stuff that disproves how they thought before. What if there was more time in the world than we know?" Ailsa asked.

Her stomach was hurting now, and it wasn't only hunger.

She was getting nervous.

"I don't think it works like that."

Ailsa sat with her thoughts for a moment.

"How's your mum doing?" she asked Ozzie.

"She's OK, I guess. How'd you know about that?"

"From Credenza. How old is she, your mum?"

"Thirty-nine next birthday."

"That's really young for a hip to break, isn't it?"

"Yeah, well, it's not the first time either." Ozzie shrugged.

"Was she playing sport or something?"

"No, she was just pottering in the garden and – ouch."

Ailsa winced. Ouch indeed.

"Sorry to ask, but … isn't that something that only happens to older people?"

Ozzie nodded. "It did seem weird."

Ailsa stared at him, a cold feeling creeping over her skin.

"What aren't you telling me, Ailsa?"

She took a deep breath. "I can't work out what's bothering me about all of this."

"Maybe you getting cool free stuff and other people being in the dark about it?"

"Sure, yes. That. But there's something else going on here. I can't put my finger on it. Do you ever get that feeling? When things are going too well?"

"All the time," said Ossian.

Ozzie stared at her intensely. But his eyes were kind, like a mask had fallen away from his face. For a "cool" kid, Ailsa suddenly thought he looked very vulnerable.

"Last night, for example," Ozzie carried on. "I'd had a good day at school, no one was shouting at me and my football team won. Which made me think, OK, what's going to go wrong now? And the other part of my brain was saying, hey, don't be such a downer. There's nothing that can go wrong now. I was on the way to visit Mum, see, at the hospital. So, I convince myself finally that all really is well, walk in there, and all I can look at is her hair."

Ailsa's stomach churned again.

"What happened to her hair?"

"It turned completely white. Almost overnight."

Ailsa felt a chill run down the length of her spine. "The same thing just happened to my parents."

"What do you think it could mean?"

"I think this Magic Hour business isn't as simple as everyone's making it out to be. And I need to find out more."

"I'm in if you are."

Ailsa nodded and unfolded her map.

"How'd you get that?"

"My grandma," said Ailsa. "She's the one who first discovered this place."

"But I thought—"

"So did everyone else. But trust me. It was her."

Ailsa explained her plan to him. Once they'd taken their voucher numbers, they would head out to search for Tobias. The Bastion was to the north, a small scribble across several rooftops towards the edge of the map itself. Once they joined up with him, Ailsa thought, they'd ask all the questions they needed to.

It was Ailsa who saw him first.

He was already here, up on the roof, edging along a balcony. Far above the ground. Maybe that's where Tobias lived, like an eagle in an eyrie. He certainly seemed to like roofs. He ran along the slick tiles and roof beams, seemingly with no fear of falling.

He was now balanced on the high ridge boards of the rooftops on the other side of the street, a little way ahead. He seemed precariously balanced, as if on a gymnastic beam. Suddenly, he sprinted straight ahead and leapt across a gap between the buildings.

Ailsa ran to a parallel street to get a better view,

only to discover it was thronged with people. As Tobias landed, he plunged his hand into a small satchel he was wearing, removing a handful of what looked like tiny strips of paper. Even at this distance, Ailsa was struck by his eyes, which were blazing in defiance. Ailsa's skin prickled with dread.

Tobias bellowed from the rooftops.

"Read and understand!"

All heads turned upwards.

"Newton's Third Law!" he shouted again, his voice rasping with effort, as he launched the papers – in fact, tiny pamphlets – into the air.

The pamphlets were caught by the breeze and fluttered to the ground like wedding confetti. Ailsa craned her neck to see. A few people on the street bent down to pick them up. Others merely shook their heads and walked on, grumbling, ignoring them completely. Still others shouted back. Many more hurried on with their business, heads down.

Perhaps they knew what was coming next.

It only took a moment.

A shrill whistle came first, piercing the cold air. The thundering and rumbling came soon afterwards, echoing across the buildings. It was the sound of boots on stone. Ailsa and Ossian edged into a doorway and watched in growing horror. The next moment, there they were: a wave of hulking guards, like an army of armadillos, sprinting up the passageway towards them. The mob began to surround the tenement house where Tobias was standing, defiant, like a figurehead atop a stranded ship.

Then he took off along the rooftops, and like a swarm, the angry horde of guards followed him, tracking his movements. But the horde all had hobnail boots and the rooftops were steep, unsteady, slick with frost. Keeping track of the guards, Tobias's eyes missed a loose tile. His feet skidded and began sliding down the pitched roof towards the edge of the awning. A wooden balcony lay below, and the guards now ran inside the main door, one after another. Ailsa could hear the boots on the inside staircase even from her vantage point in the doorway.

Tobias was still sliding, grappling for a handhold on the roof.

He was skittering around the corner, out of sight from Ailsa.

But she could see his hand. Gripping tight.

She was willing that hand to keep its grip.

But then, it disappeared.

And Tobias fell.

While she couldn't see him fall, she knew it was a long way.

A sob of pain escaped her mouth. Ossian looked at her with horror. Which turned, almost instantly, into surprise.

Because there, around the corner, came Tobias. Running at full speed. Without a scratch. Ailsa's mouth gaped.

How on earth could he have survived that fall?

Ailsa saw the guards now looking in her direction, running right towards them. Tobias saw her too, with Ozzie, and for a moment almost appeared to smile. In a flash, Tobias ran into another house and was gone.

"How did he do that?" asked Ozzie.

"I have no idea," said Ailsa.

"Look. No one else is paying attention. They're all looking away."

He was right. While the guards followed Tobias into the house, the rest of the onlookers appeared determined to pretend nothing at all had happened. Ailsa and Ozzie hurried back the way they'd come, glancing back – but Tobias had disappeared.

A gruff voice behind them made them both jump.

"Voucher check," said a guard, who had crept up behind them. He had a partner with him. She was eyeing them closely.

"You, visitors. We need to see your numbers," said the second.

"We don't have them yet."

"Why not?"

"Sorry, we're literally on our way to get them now."

Ailsa pulled Ossian with her as she started walking. The guards began to follow. Ossian glanced back at them.

"Is everyone here usually this friendly?"

"It's the first time anyone's been that rude," said Ailsa.

"Come on, we'd better go get what they're asking for."

But Ailsa was frozen. She was looking along the alleyway where Tobias had disappeared into a house. The guards were emerging from the main door now, shaking their heads. They'd lost him.

"I can't. That was my friend on the roof. I have to help him."

"Well, I need to find my sister. Where do you get one of these vouchers anyway?"

Ailsa told him, but then took his arm for a moment.

"I'll be back as soon as I can, OK? Don't go anywhere else."

Ossian glanced at the guards again. "Sounds like a plan."

Ailsa could tell he was nervous but trying to hide it.

"What about the guards?" he asked, swallowing hard.

Ailsa nudged him and looked back over his shoulder. A man was approaching them, pulling a large wooden handcart. The wheels clattered and squeaked on the cobbles. On the cart were various barrels of liquid. Supplies, it seemed. As he passed by Ailsa and Ossian, Ailsa dived underneath the cart and skidded out the other side, sprinting down a side street. At the same time, Ossian took off at pace, following the street down towards the square.

The guards, their eyes on Ossian, were too slow to follow Ailsa. By the time they had barged past the cart and run to the junction, she was gone.

Ailsa sprinted down a series of narrow alleyways in a zigzag, trying to find a trace of Tobias. She followed her map through a maze of streets, and emerged in what appeared to be a residential area with a large terrace of houses. While people lived in the apartments above, every ground floor appeared to be some form of business or trade. Here were weavers and dyers, candlemakers and cobblers. At the far end of the line, what looked like a blacksmith.

As she passed a doorway, she felt a strong hand grabbing her sleeve. Turning to strike, she saw it was Tobias, a finger to his lips. He beckoned her inside and closed the door behind her.

*

Moments later, black waistcoated guards stomped down the alleyway, three abreast, filling the space. Sandy Munro appeared at the opening.

Lying there on the pavement was a woollen hat. It was bright yellow and impossible to miss. Ailsa's hat, of course.

He bent down to pick it up, his mind already mapping out a plan for it, as Virgil Merrimack hurried up to him. He had the air of someone who had been summoned.

"The Craig girl is here," said Sandy Munro.

"With Miss Dingwall, I expect," said Virgil.

Sandy held up the yellow hat and shook it at him. "I doubt it," he said. "She's nosing around a little too much for my liking. Find her and bring her to the Exchange," snarled Sandy Munro to Virgil Merrimack. "The ARIA people are here today, unless you've forgotten, and I need no distractions. Keep all visitors in the square. No explorers today. Do I make myself clear?"

Virgil's lip curled a little at Sandy's tone. But he stopped himself from a snappy comeback.

"You do indeed, sir," he replied in a low, firm voice.

With that, Sandy Munro strode off, Ailsa's yellow hat gripped tightly in his hand, leaving Virgil with the guards.

"Find her. Tear the place down if you have to," said

Virgil. With that, two guards walked up to the door that Ailsa had just run through.

And kicked it down.

The sound was like a starting gun. Ailsa sped away like a startled hare – she was running so fast she hardly felt her feet touch the floor. Tobias was leading the way up, up. The house was packed full of people. There were families, cooking pots, steam and protests as the two of them sprinted on. Below them, Ailsa could hear those boots again, stomping up the stairs in a relentless wave.

Soon the stairs ended. The top floor.

Trapped.

Along the landing was a window open to the street far below. A line of washing had been stretched all the way to the house on the far side of the road. It was just a short gap. Ailsa remembered this avenue of houses from her first time in the Middlemarket.

So close together you could almost – now wait a minute…

Hang on.

She could feel Tobias dragging her with him.

Towards the window.

"You were right," she blurted out to Tobias. "I think I understand now. What goes on here, Newton's Third Law, all of it."

"Good. Now. When I say jump…" said Tobias.

"You've got to be—!"

"Jump!"

Ailsa breathed deep and leapt out into thin air.

She felt herself flying – and then falling. Fast.

Tobias held her hand tightly, but as he leapt, pulling her across the divide between the two sets of houses, her panic took over. She slipped her hand from his. Tobias grabbed the edge of the far balcony with both hands. Ailsa shrieked as fear grabbed her by the throat. She felt her stomach rise like cold lead as her arms flailed helplessly in the air. She was in freefall. As she fell, out of the corner of her eye, she spied a colourful set of clothing hung out on a washing line that had been drawn across the street. She grabbed it and held fast. The line was secured on the lower balconies of the houses.

The line was strong and held her, and the tension offered her enough potential energy to send her right back up towards the upper window ledge, where Tobias was waiting – feet locked into the stonework like a trapeze artist, his outstretched hand ready to catch her.

Ailsa windmilled her other hand over to catch his. He held her, his grip like a vise, immensely strong. Tobias heaved her up to join him on the upper balcony. The two of them scrambled through an open window, apologizing to the family eating dinner on a small table inside as they ran.

They raced to an inside door just as the sound of smashing glass filled the air. The guards had decided opening windows would take too long and had hurled themselves headlong through the glass. They tumbled into the poor family's dining room as Ailsa and Tobias slammed the door in their wake.

Outside, Ailsa heard another bell sound. The second one since she'd arrived. She realized Ozzie would be waiting for her, hopefully with Credenza. Her mind raced to find another solution.

But not as fast as her feet.

Tobias led Ailsa down the stairs on to another landing where a large tapestry had been hung. He yanked the tapestry open and beckoned her inside. Behind it was a small cupboard.

The two of them squeezed into the dark space and held their breath. A current of frosty air seeped in from cracks in the stonework. Outside on the stairwell, muffled by the fabric, they could hear the guards clatter down past the tapestry and on to the ground floor.

"Try the street again!" shouted a man from upstairs. Possibly the man from the dining room table. Gruff voices shouted in frustration, and the guards hurtled down the stairs. The sound dissipated as the door slammed shut, and at last all was silent.

"What's going on?" blurted Ailsa, her breath frosting the air. "Are you a fugitive or something?"

"The Magic Hour is a trick." His words were clear, controlled, sharp. "A cruel, evil trick. I tried to help your grandmother understand," said Tobias. "She finally saw it for what it truly was, and knew that it had to stop. With my help, she tried to shut it down. But by then it was too late."

"I know she discovered it. I read her notebook."

"Not all of it."

Tobias reached deep into the folds of his sash and brought out a small sheaf of papers. They were ripped, torn, muddied and bloodied. All in Grandma's perfect handwriting.

CHAPTER 32

THE NOTEBOOK

Perhaps I will never share these words.

I do not know if I can face the weight of guilt.

I have built a road into a dark and dangerous forest.

The shame is almost too much to bear.

The Shee live in their true world.

The Middlemarket. The Midden, beyond.

They live alongside us.

But those worlds were never meant to meet.

My first discovery excited me. I needed to share it with the world.

I could not bear to see the potential benefits squandered.

An extra hour, thought I. What glorious bounty of time for humanity?

At first I shared my findings with Sandy Munro. I had admired his work in the past and knew him to be inquisitive, open and possessed of a fine, sharp mind. We began our research and collected our data. It confirmed my own findings – here was an island of time, the mechanisms within which might benefit the whole world.

However, the smart and the cunning are often close, and I fear I was blind to it. Sandy and I differed in our methods. I saw something to share with the world. He saw only a means to power and control.

It was then I saw the true nature of the Middlemarket. They loathe and resent us, these Shee. They lure us here with promises. But there is always, always a price to pay.

At first, of course, I did not see this. I helped them. I found two clans at war, and I desired peace. To help them achieve that, I thought, might make us partners. The Unseelie and Seelie, the two clans of the Shee, fought horribly.

A creature preyed on them all, the Brollachan.

A spirit, disembodied and lonely.

Yet when it came for me, I found I could tame it somehow.

It sought out emptiness, but my heart is so full, my life so blessed.

I doubt it found a single thing to interest it.

Using this power, I helped bring it to heel.

Through this act, a peace was declared.

That was when I began to see the cracks.

The trick of time the Shee were playing.

Like all humanity, we know the cost of everything and the value of nothing.

We want a free lunch.

We destroy the planet.

Yet complain about the inconvenience of saving it.

We cannot be trusted to do the right thing.

So why should they?

As for Sandy, by the time I discovered my failings, the power of the place had got to him. He abused what had been gifted to us.

He was weak when he needed to be strong.

Know this:

This world was a trap.

It REMAINS a trap.

Yes, the hour they offer is ours.

But it is time that is RECLAIMED from others.

The debts incurred here are paid by OTHERS.

Per Newton, of course. How deluded I have been.

My poor John, sick as he was, was taken too soon.

And the fault, I fear, is all mine.

How little I knew. His sickness worsened; his life shortened.

I begged Sandy to help me stop the madness.

I told him the price that my husband had paid.

But he did not care.

Young Tobias Ragwort found me.

He knows the danger. He tried to help me.

He told me about the Reckoning Room. The Tally Folk.

Beware the Tally Folk! he said. I should have listened to him.

But by then I was too consumed by guilt, by grief.

I fell apart, I am sorry to say.

I left the fate of the hour to him as I lay helpless.

Soon, I shall pay my debt, I know, alongside my John.
And only hope he can forgive me.

Tobias, the boy, must still be there.
Perhaps he will reach out to others.
Heaven knows he will try.
But let history show
Sandy Munro claimed the Magic Hour for himself.
He has stolen my glory, which is now my millstone.
Any woman in science will know how that story ends.

Curse them all for their trick.
And curse us all for falling for it.

Witnessed by my hand,
Dr Judith Craig

CHAPTER 33

THE WALL OF SOULS

Ailsa's tears wet the paper. She knew it now. She had one chance to change the course of this river. One chance to make everything good again. She thought of her parents. Their white hair.

Ailsa composed herself. A thread of steel in her voice. "Take me to this Reckoning Room. I want to see these Tally Folk with my own eyes."

"It's too dangerous."

"Where are they?"

"You know the Reckoning Room, where the clerks are? At the back of that area, there are two more doors behind. They're always guarded. The room beyond, that's the Tally Room. That's where they do their work. The clerks pass the voucher receipts back to them for processing. They keep track of everything. They know exactly who's here, and how much time they spend."

"OK, but if I only spent an hour here, why was that enough time to turn my parents' hair white?"

"Don't you understand? The Shee don't care! An hour here is not the same as an hour out there," said Tobias, his teeth grinding. "So, they take whatever time they like to balance their books. Whatever causes the most mischief, the most pain."

Ailsa's stomach ached. "And what if you stay past the final bell?"

Tobias looked grim but said nothing.

Ailsa tried again. "Do they take even more time from people?"

Tobias said simply, "You don't want to know."

They crept out of their hiding place, down the creaky wooden stairs, and edged back on to the street outside. They could hear noisy footsteps receding. The path was clear in both directions.

Tobias and Ailsa kept to the shadows and made their way back towards the Exchange square.

"Why are they so nasty?" she asked Tobias.

"They've told you what happens beyond the wall?"

Ailsa nodded. "They told us not to go there, is all."

"All Shee are not the same. There are two courts, two tribes in this land. The Seelie, who are friendly.

221

And the Unseelie, who are not. The Seelie make mischief. The Unseelie desire only pain and suffering for all the M.O.s."

"M.O.s?"

"Mouldy Ones. That's what the Shee call humans."

"So, you're a Seelie, I hope?"

Tobias looked at her strangely. "I'm no Shee at all."

Ailsa blinked. "What are you then?"

Her question unanswered, Tobias leapt suddenly into a nearby doorway and pulled Ailsa with him. Moments later, a guard patrol marched past. The Middlemarket seemed a lot less friendly today.

"Listen to me. Sandy Munro is planning something," said Tobias. "The guards have doubled and there are rumours of more visitors. Important ones."

"I saw exactly what he's planning when I went to Credenza's house," said Ailsa. "At least, some of it. And Cameron Dingwall might be a part of it."

Tobias nodded. "Naturally. I think those two are partners."

"In what?"

Tobias nudged the door behind them open.

Ailsa followed. "Is it safe in here?"

"This is the Lorimers. They're tradespeople. They make things for our animals. Friendly. They don't agree with the Magic Hour either. They help us. This house is theirs. There's always room; it's always safe for us."

"Us?"

"Those of us who wish to destroy this trick for ever."

They walked to the back of the building and took a small staircase down to the street. The vantage point gave them a line of sight all the way to the square and the Exchange building beyond. Two guards stood at attention at the top of the steps.

"The guards change every bell," said Tobias. "So, we wait."

"Grandma Judith," said Ailsa after a while. "You met her?"

"She was a good woman. Once she understood, she tried to help. As best she could. But it was far too late. Anyone with a debt here must pay it."

"But most people don't know they even have a debt… I didn't."

"No one does."

"That's unfair. It's so cruel."

"The only Shee you're safe with are beyond that wall."

"We have to ask for help."

"They won't listen to me; I'm nothing to them."

"Why?"

"I'm not one of them. But you, you're Judith's granddaughter. You're the one who's going to change everything."

He was pulling her sleeve now, impatient.

"Not yet. My friends! We need to find my friends," said Ailsa. "Seems to me we need all the help we can get."

Tobias nodded. "Very well," he said. "But find them quickly."

"They should be waiting. Outside the Exchange."

Tobias grimaced. "We can't risk being seen by the guards," he said. "But I know another way in. There's a passage that leads into the basement of the Exchange building from the Tron – that's what we call the Belltower. They use it for prisoners when there's a trial."

Ailsa gulped. She had been in that dark, foreboding space before when Credenza suggested they stay after the final bell.

"And when there isn't?"

"It's usually empty," said Tobias.

"Usually," said Ailsa. "Great."

All Ailsa's mind could see were the white strands of hair on her father's head. The snow-coloured curls on her mother's. Every moment she was here was costing someone else. She pushed the image from her mind. If she was going to stop the Magic Hour, she'd need her head clear.

She gritted her teeth and ran after Tobias.

CHAPTER 34

QUALIFIED PERSONNEL ONLY

Ailsa had been here before (and so have you, a few chapters ago. But then you knew that[35]). They crept inside the tower. Tobias pointed to the trapdoor in the floor, and then indicated in the direction of the exchange.

A voice surprised them both. It was coming from the trapdoor. It started to shudder and open. Tobias looked at Ailsa. Ailsa looked at Tobias – they couldn't run outside, not now. Ailsa stared up at the walls and already knew which way to go.

Up.

They raced up the stairway to the ceiling and pushed at the hatch above them. But it was stuck fast. They froze, exposed, on the top steps. All it would take was

---

35   Hopefully.

for someone to look up at the ceiling, and they would be discovered. Two Shee guards emerged from the hatch in the floor. Ailsa held her breath as they dusted themselves off, sneezed, and walked calmly to the door. Two workers taking a shortcut home.

When they were gone, Tobias and Ailsa ran back down the stairs to the trapdoor and listened. Nothing but silence.

Tobias said: "Fetch your friends here, and we'll go get help."

Right then, thought Ailsa. *I guess I'm doing this alone.*

She clambered down into the tunnel – which was mercifully lit by glowing lamps at regular intervals. The tunnel led straight beneath the square and emerged in a familiar room.

She knew it before she saw it because she heard a low growl echo across the stone. When the tunnel ended in a short stairwell and a final grate, Ailsa already knew what lay ahead.

The blood-red door with the stag's head.

Ailsa approached the door a second time.

She stared at the stag's head.

Upstairs, she could hear voices and conversation.

She took out her map.

"Lost?" said a voice behind her.

Ailsa whipped around. Sandy Munro was standing in the doorway, lit from above by the dim amber light from the hallway. It cast strange shadows down his face. The shadow from his nose seemed to go all the way to the floor.

Even more oddly, he seemed to be holding her hat. Her very own, yellow knitted bonnet. He saw her gaze move to it, and he quietly stuffed it into his jacket pocket.

"Is that my hat?" she asked.

He looked down at his pocket in an obvious way, as if seeing the hat for the first time. Ailsa used this moment to fold up Grandma's map and slip it away.

"This? Oh, no. It belongs to my niece."

Ailsa fixed him with a glare. "Your niece has great taste," she said. "I've got one just like that." Her eyes narrowed. "*Exactly* like that, in fact. Identical."

"Well, isn't that marvellous."

"That's one way of putting it," said Ailsa.

His expression darkened, his voice creeping lower. "This area is off limits," he said. "For everyone."

"I went for a wander." Ailsa shrugged.

They stood in silence for a moment in their lies.

"Been making new friends too, so I hear?"

He edged a little closer to her. Ailsa edged a little further back. She knew the only way out of here was either back down that tunnel (*no, thanks*), through the red door (*I don't think so*) or right past him up the stairs.

The stairs it was then. But how?

"I didn't know wandering was against the rules," she said, buying time to think.

"Oh, the rules are quite clear around here, you know. The Shee are such *sticklers* for rules. You'll learn that eventually. Visitors to the Middlemarket are encouraged to stay within our main building here, the Exchange. It's generally safer than mixing with the ... general populace. And quite honestly, you have no need to look anywhere else. Everything is provided for you, as I'm sure you've been told."

Ailsa held the silence for a moment and then summoned her clearest voice. "Judith Craig was my grandmother."

A faint smile arrived on Sandy Munro's face, as if to say: *I know*.

"Be that as it may. Qualified personnel only here," he said.

"Are you qualified?"

Sandy Munro appeared to redden at this. A rash appeared on his neck, and he scratched at it distractedly.

"What sort of question is that?"

Ailsa blinked. "A good one, I would say. Doesn't all

this belong to Her Ladyship, anyway? Lady Blackthorn? Don't you work for her, in fact?"

Sandy Munro turned a darker shade of puce.

"Now then, young lady, while I appreciate your intellectual flex, I do believe I've read more Wittgenstein than you've had gummy worms. So don't try to run your tiny rings of logic around me, lassie, because the centripetal force would catapult you to the Orion Nebula."

"Was that meant to be an insult?"

"No, little dear. A warning."

Ailsa felt a droplet of sweat make its way down her back. It appeared to linger between her shoulder blades, as if it was wondering if it had left the gas on. She conjured up a smile of total innocence and shone it at him.

"You must think you're rather clever, discovering this place all by yourself," she said. "It's so impressive. I keep reading in science class about all those women scientists who never got the credit because the men they worked with would push them aside the minute things got interesting. Not that that's what's happened here, of course. Oh no. You must be so proud with all that you've achieved. Truly, *a most extraordinary discovery.*"

Ailsa said those last words, Grandma's words, with cold deliberation. She knew that scientists exchanged papers and findings with each other, and she had no doubt that Grandma would have done the same with Sandy Munro. She looked for a reaction from him.

But she saw nothing.

No guilt, no recognition. Just the millpond of his silent gaze. He wasn't blinking at all now, which made Ailsa rather more nervous. She was losing the sharp feeling in her chest, the indignant spike of bitterness towards this man that had girded her confidence. Now her shirt was sticking to her back, and her stomach was churning.

"I think we've chatted long enough. Back up you go. You'll stay with me for the rest of the hour," he said.

"Not if I can help it," said Ailsa, and dived through his legs.

Sandy, taken aback and unused to physical activity, was momentarily twisted into the shape of a human pretzel. He snarled at Ailsa, flailing out to grab her as she scrambled to her feet on the other side and shot up the stairs.

She took them three at a time.

On a landing halfway up to the lobby, Ailsa passed a small room that housed the elevator hydraulics. There were a few very noisy generators and a larger cabinet in which she could see a flywheel and belt. There were other pipes and construction materials in here too, perhaps the start of repairs.

Sandy Munro was running up the stairs after her, red-faced and wheezing. Once he caught his breath, Ailsa knew he would call for the guards.

Meanwhile, Ailsa needed a distraction.

She searched the construction chaos and found the sharpest, most solid-looking metal bar she could find. Then jammed it firmly into the centre of the elevator's flywheel mechanism. If you've never seen the flywheel mechanism of an old elevator, all you need to know at this point is: *they don't work very well with bits of metal shoved into them*. It was like a tree branch in the spoke of a bicycle wheel.

In both cases, the same result: the thing stops working.

As Ailsa crested the top of the stairs, the elevator cage in the lobby was shrieking and belching foul-smelling smoke.

CHAPTER 35

THE TALLY FOLK

Ailsa hit the lobby at a full sprint.

There is quite a bit of running going on throughout this story, so it's probably a good idea to remind everyone that if you're planning on doing the same, it's very important to warm up and stretch before exerting yourself.

Apologies are also in order, too, because while you were reading that last paragraph, Ailsa flew past two big guards and nearly ran them over. She turned to them as she passed.

"The elevator room!" she shouted, trying to sound helpful.[36]

The guards' noses twitched, smelling the acrid smoke.

Ailsa pointed down the stairs, helping them make the connection. "Hurry!" she yelled, as another guard ran over from the other side of the lobby.

---

36 Which is not easy while shouting.

He pointed to his two colleagues. "Get down there now!"

The noise was getting worse. It sounded like a metallic robot cat running its steel nails down a wall. More door guards ran from their posts.

Including, Ailsa saw, the ones from the Reckoning Room.

Ailsa was about to run back outside when a thought struck her. Those dark double doors in the back.

They had no one outside them now.

With all attention on the lobby, Ailsa realized she had a chance that she would never get again. She had told Ossian she'd be back for him and Credenza. But this was too important to ignore. These were the doors Tobias had told her about. The place Grandma had written about.

These doors led past the Reckoning Room.

To the Tally Folk.

She sprinted past distracted clerks and eased open one of the doors, slipping in, away from the tumult outside.

The space beyond was full of gloom, barely illuminated by a glow from above. The small brass tubes from the Reckoning Room all ended here, snaking their way to a central, circular area.

Each tube was positioned over a single desk and a

single chair. But any resemblance to a regular office ended there. Each chair was reclined, leaned back almost horizontally. As Ailsa peered through the gloom, more details made themselves known.

Occupying each chair was a studious, cold-eyed Shee. Their eyes were focused up towards the vast, arcing ceiling. Once in a while, a *thunk* sound was heard, and a small paper receipt would flutter out of the end of the tube and into a wire tray next to each chair, marked "PROCESSING". Ailsa remembered that Morag the clerk had used one very similar. Each mesh tray was full of receipts.

This is where all those vouchers end up, thought Ailsa.

But the ceiling.

It was the most extraordinary ceiling Ailsa had ever seen.

It was like the vast, velvet roof of a tent, impossibly black, arcing across the entire room like the canopy of the night sky. Scattered across it, in a chaos of patterns, were tiny, innumerable lights. Some were flashing into being, some fading out.

It looked like a living, breathing Milky Way up there.

As Ailsa looked closer, she could see they weren't stars at all.

They were images – of people.

Young, old and every point in between. There were thousands upon millions of them, a galaxy of faces. It seemed to Ailsa to be a living, breathing map of the world.

So these were the Tally Folk, Ailsa thought. *Beware, indeed.*

One by one, each of the Tally Folk would pick a receipt from the pile on their desk and stare up at the ceiling. Ailsa watched in growing horror as they plucked a point of light from the void. The star would expand and float down to them, coming alive in the process. Here were mothers and daughters, fathers and sons, most of them smiling. These were the faces of real human beings. Next to their name was a number.

This is how the vouchers work, Ailsa thought.

Next to the images, connected by tiny glowing lines, were images of other people. There were adults connected to children, children connected to adults, friends, neighbours.

It seemed to Ailsa to be a kind of family and friendship tree, a constellation of love between people. Every individual in their own personal solar system. Once an image had been chosen, a number appeared next to them, and the worker turned a small dial on their chair. The number diminished, and the images turned red.

Sometimes, they faded out completely.

A voice from the far end of the hall pierced the silence. "Stop her! She saw the Sanctum!"

Ailsa felt all eyes in the room fall on her. She had questions, but she wasn't going to wait around here to ask them. She sprinted back outside, clattering past the main door guards, then out and down the outside steps of the Exchange.

There at the bottom of the steps was Credenza next to a lost-looking Ossian.

"How dare you?" snapped Credenza when she saw Ailsa.

"We need to go," Ailsa replied.

"I said, how dare you bring him here?" She glared at her brother.

"I didn't. He came himself. Now follow me," said Ailsa. The authority in her voice surprised Credenza. She was normally the one telling people what to do, and Ailsa, as far as her limited experience had gone, was not the sort of person to do that.

"I beg your pardon?" Credenza asked.

"We need to leave. Right now. Trust me."

Shouts and screams started echoing out from the Exchange building, and black smoke was starting to curl its way out of the front doors and into the air. Credenza's nose twitched at the smell.

Ailsa cast a glance over to the Belltower, where she could see Tobias's foot peeking out from the corner. It was time to move.

"Is something burning—" started Credenza, but Ailsa had already grabbed her arm and was pulling her towards the alleyway where Tobias was hiding. Ossian ran alongside them. Credenza wrenched her arm away, but Ossian took her hand and made sure she kept up with their pace.

"Let go of me!" screamed Credenza.

"In a minute," said Ossian.

The main door guards emerged from the Exchange and on to the outside steps again, dusting themselves off. Ailsa stopped for a moment and looked deeply into Credenza's eyes. Something had changed in Ailsa. She didn't need to change her shape any more. She didn't need to be anyone else but herself.

"Listen to me. If we don't fix this now," she said, "most of the people we love might die. And so could we."

Credenza looked close to tears. "This isn't like you at all," she moaned.

Ailsa squeezed her hand, and as she did, she realized something.

"Actually. This is *exactly* like me. Now please, let's go!"

The trio sprinted around the corner. At that moment, Sandy Munro burst from the main door, eyes scanning the quadrangle. He picked out a pair of fleeing shoes as they disappeared. He knew those shoes well since he had often seen them loitering at the top of the stairs when Cameron Dingwall and he were trying to talk business. They were expensive, rare and belonged to the Dingwall daughter, Credenza.

Three more guards clattered out behind him.

"Away and fetch them back," he barked, pointing to the corner. The guards paused for a moment, glancing nervously at each other. Sandy Munro turned to them, realizing he was not the one who commanded their loyalty. The bell tolled eight times, echoing around the facades of the buildings.

"By order of my Lady Blackthorn."

The guards ran.

Tobias met the trio at the corner of the Belltower, and led Ailsa, Credenza and Ozzie through a maze of tiny streets. Suddenly, he opened what appeared to be a cellar door and ushered Ailsa inside.

"I'm not going down there," complained Credenza, peering into the dust and murk. Through the door, dank stairs led down into nothing.

Ozzie sighed. "Disagree," he said, and pulled her down with him into the well of darkness below.

Tobias pulled the cellar door shut as softly as he could. A moment later, they heard the scuffled footsteps of the guards, barking commands to each other. Seconds passed in silent panic. Finally, they appeared to recede like a malevolent tide.

"I need to know what we're doing in a clarty old cellar with that strange boy," said Credenza finally.

"We are saving everyone's lives," said Ailsa, angry at her friend's obstinacy. "And this boy is risking his life to help us."

"Help me, someone?"

Tobias was pulling away a threadbare rug from under a table. Underneath, two floorboards were loose, and when removed they revealed a vast flagstone grate. Ailsa ran over to help him move it. Ozzie soon joined. Credenza, for her part, watched with growing dread.

"What are you going to do with that?" she asked.

Tobias smiled. "Nothing. Follow me."

And with that the grate fell to the side, revealing a dark, foreboding square opening. It led directly down.

Tobias leapt into the hole, supporting himself with his elbows as he lowered himself on to what appeared to be a stone step.

"Keep your feet on the steps as you go down."

"You're not expecting us to follow you?" said Credenza.

"You can stay here if you like," said Tobias from the darkness of the tunnel. "And wait for us to get back."

Ailsa went down next, remembering how Tobias had supported his weight before plunging below. Her feet flailed around in the dark for a moment before she found a firm footing on a thin stone step. Ozzie went next.

Left alone, Credenza folded her arms in defiance.

In the silence of the basement, she could hear other noises. Footsteps, perhaps. A creaking above her. And what sounded like a tiny, high-pitched scratching noise. It was coming from right behind her.

When the first rat appeared, Credenza was already halfway into the hole, heaving the carpet over the opening and cursing her luck to the darkness.

Far below in the tunnel, Ailsa looked down and immediately wished she hadn't. She tried looking up, but that was no good either – a needle of light pierced the darkness from above, peeking through a hole in the carpet. It reminded her of how far they had already climbed down into this pipe. She tried counting the steps on the slimy footholds of wet stone protruding from the walls in order to keep herself from thinking about what it might feel like if she slipped, lost her handhold and fell.

"Not long now," called Tobias, his voice echoing off the walls.

The final step offered a hefty drop to a stone floor. This was a drainage culvert, a channel in the bedrock which opened wide enough for them to squeeze through.

"We're under the city wall," Tobias told them as they crept along in the darkness.

All was silent for a moment.

Then Ailsa stopped. The weight of what she had seen, like a dam breaking in her throat, surged forward. Tears streamed down her face. Credenza stared at her, still consumed with her own feelings. It was only Ossian who stepped forward, touching her arm.

"You OK? What is it?"

Ailsa wiped away her tears and breathed deeply.

"I saw it, Tobias. The Tally Room. The ceiling." She searched for the word the Tally Folk had used. "The Sanctum."

"I wondered if you had."

"I'm even more confused now," said Credenza.

"Ailsa has seen the true purpose of this place. And it's time that you understood it too."

Ailsa nodded. "We're going to shut the Magic Hour down."

Credenza let out a shrill cry. "Why? No!"

Ailsa calmly told her exactly why. The stolen time, the debts and the cruel trick the Shee had played on humankind.

Ossian shook his head. "Mum's hip," he said. "That's how it happened."

"No," said Credenza again, her knuckles white. "It simply cannot be like that! It's not our fault!"

"But it is," said Ailsa. "The whole place is a giant trap. They set it, and we walked right into it."

Credenza's mind was spinning now. Her words spilled out in a panic. "But if I don't have the Magic Hour, I won't be able to do all the things I do. At least nowhere near as well. I'd be exhausted. Things would be unfinished. I might even be late to things… I'd be normal. I'd be ordinary!"

Ozzie chuckled darkly. "Are you even thinking straight? What about Mum? Don't you realize what it is you've *done*?"

Credenza fell silent.

Ossian, on a roll, kept going. "Her hip is broken. She's barely forty. You and Dad have come here so often that you've built up a debt that's dissolved Mum's *bones*. Don't you see that? Don't you know that *there's no such thing as a free lunch*? Well, *bingo*, Credenza. *Bullseye*. You do now. Welcome to some actual context. You've been the princess of this family since the moment you arrived. I had some of their attention for a couple of years before you came along, but the minute you showed up, that was that. I may as well have moved out. I was demoted to black sheep."

"I didn't know," said Credenza, in a whisper. "I... I truly didn't understand..."

Ozzie blushed with regret. He liked to tease, but this hurt. "Hey, look—"

"I didn't know!" screamed Credenza. "I didn't know, I didn't know! Oh, Mum, I'm so sorry ... poor Mum..."

Credenza pushed Ozzie away and broke down.

Ailsa had never seen the Dingwalls like this. She had always thought they were a perfect family, their happiness carved from stone, that she was the one with troubles. Like Dad had always said: *you never know what's going on with people.*

Credenza breathed deeply, her lungs and limbs shaking. She was getting back under control. Ailsa moved to her, taking her hand. Credenza, grateful for the contact, squeezed it.

"You know what, Ozzie," said Credenza, "here's what you don't understand. When all this ends, and I'm not as good at everything, Mum and Dad won't love me any more. I'm just a prize on a pedestal, made for them to brag about. The minute I stop being the golden girl, all that goes away. You're different. They seem to keep loving you no matter how much you mess up. That's the difference. You'll still have you. I won't have a thing."

Ailsa's eyes stung.

"That's not true," said Ossian. "Not a word of it."

Credenza shook her head, unconvinced.

"We need to keep moving," said Tobias.

They walked on in silence.

Finally, Credenza spoke. "Anyway, all of this makes no sense."

"Not everything that is true needs to make sense," said Tobias. "Ever hear the phrase *once upon a time*?"

"Of course. All stories start that way."

"Not all. But fairy tales do. Ever wondered why?"

"It sounds old-fashioned?"

"Because the Shee don't live in your time, but their own. They don't care about your world at all. In fact, all they think about are ways to make trouble. Especially the Unseelies."

A grey light was filtering down from overhead. The faint shadows allowed them to see several footholds, visible in the walls. All of them leading far above to what looked like an opening to the surface. Tobias scrambled nimbly up, then turned to beckon Ailsa and the others after him.

"But you don't make any trouble," said Ailsa, shouting up after him. "You're helping us. And you're a Shee."

"I already told you, Ailsa," said Tobias. "I'm no Shee."

"Well, what are you then?"

"I'm a kid from Edinburgh. Just like you."

CHAPTER 36

THE GIFT

Sandy Munro clattered down the basement steps of the Exchange and dashed back to the vast blood-red door. He held Ailsa's yellow knitted hat carefully between two gloved fingers.

The Craig grandchild. That irritating *sprog*.

She had figured something out; he was sure of it.

Today was simply too important, too vital, to be left to fate. If there was the slightest chance that Ailsa could disrupt this significant moment in the Magic Hour, and more importantly in Sandy Munro's fortunes, she must be stopped.

The creature could sense him as he approached.

You are humming a tune, he heard it say. *It's called worry.*

Sandy Munro said nothing.

The creature tried again.

The girl?

"Yes, fine, correct, as usual. I have something for you," he cooed. He was trying to change the subject. As he approached, he felt the slightest change in air pressure.

A gift?

"Indeed. In exchange for a favour."

Sandy Munro heard a voice in his head. The Brollachan had no voice without a form, of course, but such was its power that it could still be understood if it wanted to be.

Not gift, then, the voice said. *Since the favour makes it a bribe.*

"Call it what you wish," said Sandy Munro, a little irritated now. "I still think you might enjoy it. Think of it as … a possibility."

The voice almost purred. Whether from pleasure or frustration, it was hard to tell. *I like possibilities.*

"A promise, really."

I know your promises.

"Find the one who wears this hat," Sandy replied. "She is the perfect candidate."

Daffodils, said the creature.

"I beg your pardon?"

The colour. Of the hat. Is the same as the colour. Of daffodils.

"I suppose so," said Sandy, getting impatient. "What of it?"

You would have me fetch the wearer of a daffodil hat.

You would have me work for you.

This is what it means to receive a gift? From you.

Sandy rolled his eyes a little. This creature had moods like a teenager and a capacity for drama. He didn't know it, of course, but the beast swirling behind the door really was an adolescent entity, not yet grown into its adult form.

"I want you to have a home," said Sandy to the creature, in his most velvety voice. "It will benefit both of us."

The creature sighed, as much as a disembodied cloud of vapour can. A frosty draught of air eased around the space behind the door, searching. Interested in what might come next.

Very well, said the voice.

Biting his lip, Sandy Munro moved to the stag's head door knocker and pressed firmly upon the nub of its nose. It moved smoothly inwards of its own accord. There was a resounding click, and the sound of many gears spooling and threading together. After a moment, a giant series of locks could be heard uncoupling, and the latch of the door fell open. Moving fast, Sandy Munro opened the door just enough and threw Ailsa's woollen hat into the darkness beyond, pulling the door tight once again.

Sandy Munro then pulled the latch hard towards him. The stag's nose emerged from the knocker, and the mechanism clanked back into lockdown.

"Study it," said Sandy Munro into the door jamb, his hand on the door handle. "And I will return soon to set you free."

Sounds good, it replied.

The creature, for its part, was thrilled.

It was a wonderful gift. Not the hat, of course, although it could sense the wearer was strong-willed, a midnight child, perhaps. No, the gift was information. In particular, the way a tiny crack appeared in the door jamb whenever anyone placed their hand on the handle. More than enough room for a disembodied spirit to wiggle through, should the chance ever occur again.

CHAPTER 37

THE WILDS

The group emerged from a hole in the ground, scrambling up into a rolling meadow, pock-marked with tufts of longer grass and weeds. The sky was gunmetal grey, cut through with swathes of purple and a deep pink that was almost red. Past a larger fringe of pine trees, Ailsa could glimpse a hill. The trees were silhouettes against the glow of what looked like the setting sun.

"You're … human?" said Ailsa when they were all up.

"I came here as a child. And never left."

"Came here or brought here?" asked Ozzie.

"Lady Blackthorn took me from my cradle."

For the longest while, no one spoke.

"She stole you," said Ailsa.

"And replaced me with one of their own."

He spoke in a plain, almost monotone voice. As if he had somehow learned to talk about this, to detach from it, as if it had happened to someone else.

"I still see them, you know. My parents. In my dreams."

"Do they know you're even here?"

"As far as they know, my replacement is their child."

"A fairy? A Shee? Living in our world?"

"It happens more than you think." Tobias's jaw clenched. "Anyway, it was a long time ago."

"So, you're a Changeling," said Ozzie, as if classifying Tobias in a biology quiz. Tobias looked at him coldly.

"A what?" asked Credenza.

"A Changeling? Human child, swapped at birth with a fairy," said Ozzie. "Sorry, Shee. Cruel prank. You get the gist. They'd take a human child and replace it with one of their own. Horrible stuff. I thought it was a way that people could excuse kids who didn't fit in, back in the day."

"It was Lady Blackthorn who did it. She took away my life and my future," said Tobias. "All to cause chaos and suffering. One day, she will pay. You know they call us the Mouldy Ones?"

"You told me. I remember."

"Do you know why?"

Ailsa didn't.

"Because to them we're already decaying. We're like a bowl of rotting fruit. They see human life as something revolting. They don't understand why time matters so much to us."

"Tobias," said Ailsa softly, "shouldn't we go and find your parents? Tell them what happened to you?"

Tobias turned to her with a look of abject sorrow. "Even if I found them, do you think they'd believe me?"

And with that, they stood in silence, knowing there was nothing anyone could say.

A rough path cut ahead through a tangle of goosegrass, milkwort and rampant weeds, encrusted here and there with small patches of frost. The four of them marched in single file past the ruins of a broken drystone wall. The path was leading them downwards, a lazy snaking trail that seemed to track deep into a valley. Ailsa looked back to the hole in the ground, as people do when they are anxious and need to be reminded where the exit is. But she could see only a mess of brambles and gorse, like a vast natural wall. Somewhere beyond those, Ailsa knew, were the walls of the Middlemarket and its bell. Faintly, on a breeze, she heard it toll again.

Six bells left.

The colours of twilight charged the air: thorntree, indigo and burnished steel. *The sky hasn't ever changed colour since I first came here,* Ailsa thought. *This place is in permanent twilight.*

As they walked, a mist began rolling in. Wisps of it,

flowing down the slopes and into the belly of the valley. Soon, it was almost impossible to see past a few trees on either side of the path. To the east, there was a glow in the sky, like the moon on a cloudy night. One by one the single file march slowed to a stop, and they gathered to get their bearings. Ahead, a line of dead birch trees stood guard at the border of a dark wood, bark stripped like old bones, trunks bent inwards by time and the wind. It looked to Ailsa like the ribcage of a long-dead monster, picked clean by scavengers.

"Anyone want to hear a joke?" said Ozzie, trying to break the tension.

"We need to keep our voices down now," said Tobias.

"More of a riddle really," continued Ozzie, ignoring Tobias. "First, you eat me, then you get eaten. What am I?"

"A piranha in a suit of armour?" said Ailsa.

"Excellent. But wrong."

"I give up," said Credenza.

"A fish hook," said Ozzie triumphantly.

"But I'm not a fish," said Tobias.

"Well, obviously I know that."

"So why would I eat a fish hook?"

"How would I know?"

"Quiet!" hissed Tobias. The mist had, if anything,

thickened. Around a level 6 on the IMTMS scale.[37]

"Even if someone could destroy the Magic Hour, how could anyone actually do it anyway?" asked Credenza.

"Yeah, what exactly is the plan?" added Ozzie.

Tobias rolled his eyes. Clearly there was no silence to be had with this group. He fixed them both with a steady glare. "The less you Dingwalls talk, the better," said Tobias.

"Now you wait a second, pal," said Ozzie, puffing up his chest. "What have you got against my family?"

Tobias's eyes darkened. "Everything," he said. "Keep quiet."

Up ahead, through the thickening mist (Level 7.5 now at least), the glow in the sky intensified. It was more than a mist now. It was like a ring of thick cloud. Ailsa realized that the terrain was hilly, and they were climbing. A line of trees stood out against the glow of the sky, black silhouettes like arrowheads.

They were passing up into the cloud itself.

As she walked, Ailsa's nose tingled with a familiar

---

37   IMTMS = International Mist Thickness Measurement Scale. Level 1 is a thin, wispy gruel. Level 10 is basically a wall of porridge.

scent. It reminded her of the dryer in Mum's flat, or the smell of an approaching storm on the wind right before the rain.

The air was thick with it, stronger with every step.

Her hair began to feel strange, lighter.

Up again, a bleached white light was glowing. Visible through the dense treeline, it looked like the floodlights of a stadium. A vague, deep hum pervaded the air.

It was only when they crested the ridge that the ring of cloud dissipated, and they finally saw it. There before them lay a crater-like depression in the hillside. Below, inside rings of trees and fences, and strange white tent-like structures, was an unmissable sight: piercing a roof of mist was a jagged, glowing filament of raw energy, no wider than a school ruler. It zigzagged and pulsed from the sky, a vast glowing stalactite descending at an angle to earth from a dark thunderhead beyond the trees.

It stayed there, searingly bright, semi-frozen, in the air.

She knew what it was even if she couldn't believe it.

A bolt of lightning. Frozen in time.

"It breached the frontier many years ago, and the portion of it in our world has been stuck here ever since," Tobias murmured.

"What frontier?"

"The one between our world and yours."

Ailsa shielded her eyes and tried to look up at the place where the bolt appeared out of the mist. A small distance above it, the very air itself rippled, like a still pond after a large heavy stone had been thrown into it.[38]

"We live in our own time here," said Tobias grimly.

The bolt had a bright halo of gas surrounding it, churning over itself like a moody, violent sea. There were crests and surges of waves and tides, a swirling vortex of white-hot energy. Radiating out from the impact zone was a makeshift village of steel fences, buildings and white tents. Here and there were people in uniforms who hurried around the perimeter, taking measurements and shielding themselves from the intense heat and blinding light.

Closer to the centre, where the bolt seemed to shake hands with the ground, another set of high fences had been built, dotted at regular intervals with large yellow warning signs. Inside that, where there were few people at all, Ailsa could make out a series of shapes. It was a

---

38   It hopefully does not need saying, but just in case: never look at, or approach, a frozen lightning bolt. Or, for that matter, a slightly defrosted or unfrozen one. Same goes for the sun, volcanoes or microwaved snacks that have molten cheese inside them. Just walk away.

stone circle, ancient and dark. Closer to the bolt itself, the uniforms were replaced with silver foil suits with mirrored gold visors. They looked like astronauts, their face coverings flashing here and there as they turned.

The air itself was pulsing with waves of energy, and below it all she could hear a low roar, like the end of a thunderclap. On the outer edges, away from the intense heat, there were wooden cabins full of glowing computer screens. Several large generators appeared to be hooked up to the area around the bolt, like a root system of trees. At the edge, there were vehicles, more fencing and guard towers.

A large display screen showed a bizarre message:

28,002.4 KELVIN

Credenza peered at the display in awestruck silence.

"Who's *Kevin*?"

"It's Kelvin," sighed Ailsa. "A measurement of temperature that scientists use."

All of a sudden, a powerful searchlight swept across the treetops beside them, and they all dived for cover behind a berm of shrubs. From the compound, an alarm sounded, piercing and insistent. Red lights flashed.

Peeking up over the bushes, Ailsa could now see

several people in military uniforms holding binoculars and scanning the ridge. It was only when the front gates were opened that she saw the sign in the middle of the chain-link fence.

The sign read:

DINGWALL INDUSTRIES

"This is the big plan I was telling you about," said Tobias. "Sandy Munro doesn't only want to bring more people to the Middlemarket. He wants to exploit it too. He wants to get rich."

Ailsa gulped. "What is it your dad's company builds again, Credenza?"

"Power stations," said Ossian. "He builds power stations."

As they ran for their lives, hurdling bushes and logs and slipping on the slick moss, Ailsa could hear her mother's voice echoing in her head. Repeating the same phrase, over and over.

Wall-to-Wall Dingwall…

Wall-to-Wall Dingwall…

CHAPTER 38

FETCH

Sandy Munro pushed the nose of the stag once more[39], and the red door's complex mechanism sighed into action. As the internal locks clicked themselves open, he considered his options. He had given the creature enough time with the object. Sandy had no doubt that it had served its purpose and whet its appetite.

It was time to present his demands.

The creature, for its part, was expecting him.

Gripping the handle, Sandy Munro addressed the darkness.

"I have returned," he said.

Apparently so, said the creature from somewhere inside.

"The yellow hat. You know it now?"

---

39 Never do this with a real-life stag, only with elaborate locking mechanisms in dank basements. A real stag will not appreciate having its nose pushed.

The daffodil, you mean? It sounded annoyed.[40]

"Can you find her? The one who wore it? You should have the scent by now."

The creature was quiet for a moment. Sandy Munro felt a chill run through him, goosebumps rising up his arms.

The owner is in the Midden, it said. *I will hunt there.*

"The Midden? The wild lands, outside the city walls?" said Sandy Munro.

Is there another?

Sandy Munro sniffed. "Out of the question. You will certainly not venture outside the city walls. I simply need her to stay outside the Middlemarket. If the savages of the Wilds were to see you, or hear you, to know you are at liberty, it would reveal the destruction of our promise and destroy the peace we built. It will all come crashing down and there would be war once again. You are to remain here or within the walls of this town under supervision. But that is all. No, I cannot allow it. You'll stay here then. I shall not need you after all."

A little late for that.

The reply came from right behind him.

---

40   It was not yet universally known that Brollachans have a keen eye for colour. And while this is impressive, you must never, ever ask one to redecorate your bedroom.

Sandy whipped around in blind panic. The red door was still shut, he knew that. But the voice was elsewhere now. Nearby.

"What are you doing?" There was fear in his throat, and he was trying his best to subdue it.

Leaving, said the creature, like he was just popping down to the shops. The voice was behind him but further away now.

Sandy wheeled around, his eyes scanning to and fro, but all he could see was the empty passageway. For the briefest moment, by the stairwell, he caught sight of a musty cloud of vapour. Flicking his focus back to the door, he noticed a filament of mist snaking out of the tiny gap in the door, between the hinges and the door jamb.

Realizing the creature was halfway out, Sandy Munro tried to somehow heave the door shut (as if one could ever shut a door that was shut already) but a blast of air, like a sudden breeze, forced it open again to the limit of the lock.

It was not a breeze at all, of course.

It was the Brollachan.[41]

---

41 In addition to being good with colour, Brollachans are malevolently sneaky and will cheat at games when you're not looking. Best to just avoid them entirely, to be honest.

Sandy Munro, sensing defeat, stepped back and flashed a nervous smile: "There, you see! Ha! I have decided to free you."

If you say so.

"You are welcome!"

My kind seldom are. The creature chuckled, gathering itself in a corner, a haze of churning vapour, getting more visible with every passing second. Sandy Munro was sweating now.

"And since I am your liberator," he continued, a little desperately now, "you are thus bound to me for ever."

I do not think so, said the voice.

The creature, which was now more like a bank of cloud than a mist, folded in and over itself in brooding silence. As Sandy Munro watched, he thought he saw two glowing eyes emerge at the centre of the cloud, like the dark cherry coals of a dying fire. Staring at them made him feel cold, lost and profoundly alone.

A strand of misty air began to unspool from the main cloud like the loose thread of a sweater. It lengthened itself in a lazy way, like a cat stretching, spiralling up and around, and eventually drifting down the hallway into the darkness beyond. Hugging the wall, like a serpent looking for a mouse hole.

Sandy Munro shook the feelings from him and ran

after it as best he could. He heaved the doors open as the Brollachan changed form again, now a rolling mist, easing gently down into the darkness of the shaft where Ailsa had recently emerged.

"Come back!" shouted Sandy Munro into the dark. "You're not allowed to be out!"

The Brollachan paused and turned to face him, as much as an ominous mist can turn at all. It contemplated the void inside this specimen, his recent jailer, noting as it did a spacious kind of emptiness within. It was the kind of place which, on a different day, would seem like an excellent prospect for a move. But once the creature thought about it even for a second longer, it realized that despite the proportions and evident void, it couldn't wait to be shot of him. The creature had waited this long, it reasoned. He would pass on this one. A new home was worth waiting for a little while longer.

It swirled away, floating on, pushing deeper, until it located the access tunnel that led to the street outside.

Tioraidh an-dràsta, said the creature, speaking in its mother-tongue. Adding, in translation:

Farewell. For now.

The creature emerged from a grate on the stone-clad street. It was now beyond the thick walls of the Exchange and a new-found energy coursed through it, sensing the change in the air. A young couple in full finery passed by, walking straight through the essence of the Brollachan. But they were happy, content, oblivious. They needed nothing but each other, and this was abundantly clear to the creature. It already knew they were not a dwelling. The Brollachan needed emptiness, void, yearning.

It was time to move on. That's when it remembered the hat.

Daffodils were its favourite flower. Not only for the particular finesse of their colour, nor their delicate scent, but for the inherent promise contained within every petal. They were such openly optimistic flowers. The creature had no idea whether a prospect in a daffodil hat might also be full of such cheery feelings. But a daffodil hat was a good start. With that, it was up and over the rooftops and the city wall, over a vast frontier of tangled weeds and thorns, the inhospitable border between the city and the wild country beyond. It kept on, weaving and winding through gorse thickets and sharp branches, seeking out a familiar smell, its favourite, that of a fast-flowing stream. Once on the scent, it tracked north into the gathering dark. To the east, where it shouldn't have been, was the glow of the setting sun. The Brollachan ignored this contradiction (for it hated bright lights even more than logical impossibilities) and hugged the ground, flowing like an eventide haar.[42] Further below, under the soft, dank earth, it could feel a sure, smooth line of flowing water, surging up to the surface.

A Brollachan would always follow water if it could. There were always opportunities at its banks.

---

42   You probably already know that a "haar" is a word for a cold sea mist, the kind you get on the North Sea. It's used in Scotland but also the North of England. Some people also call it a "sea fret", and when you're inside a swirling, bone-chilling mist like that, you would most certainly fret, a lot.

CHAPTER 39

CAPTURE

The forest was a blur as Ailsa ran. The brightness of the bolt had seared her vision and plunged the world into the shadows. Ailsa's world now pulsed with green and purple splotches, the after-image of the white-hot energy of the lightning and the army camp itself.

Her mind was racing even faster than her legs. Dingwall Industries? Here? She had seen Credenza's and Ozzie's faces when they saw that sign. That was news to them too. They had no idea, and from the looks of them now, they might never recover.

"Oh my God," said Credenza for the twelfth time.

Tobias put his hand on Ailsa's shoulder, and she turned to him. He leaned in to her ear.

"We're being followed," he said.

Ailsa's eyes began to adjust to the gloom, and soon she could see them too. Keeping pace, on parallel paths between the trees, were two pairs of eyes, glistening in the darkness. A few seconds later, two more sets of eyes appeared. Up ahead, two short but fierce-looking bearded men emerged from the trees and blocked the path. Both were barefoot, dressed in a haphazard way with green kilted shawls covered in chaotic burrs of weeds, dirt and pine needles. Two more appeared behind them, women this time. Soon every shadow behind every tree revealed itself, and Ailsa knew they were surrounded.

The men looked roughly identical. They were the same height as Tobias, with similar bare feet and red shins. But where Tobias's eyes were kind and intelligent, theirs were cold and cruel.

Ailsa looked at Tobias for reassurance. She didn't like the change of tone in his eyes.

"Who are they?" she whispered.

"The One True Shee," said Tobias. "A lot more pleasant than the crowd from the Middlemarket."

"Pleasant?" said Ailsa.

Tobias kept going, avoiding the question. "The ones we don't want to encounter are the Unseelie … they're different. They have an unquenchable loathing of humankind, and they wish us ill. They are dangerous and best avoided."

"Ah, OK. These scary-looking ones, they're the friendly ones?" said Ozzie, with almost a snarl.

"Friendly or not," said Ailsa, "we need help. The True Shee are the only ones who can do that."

Tobias's hand touched Ailsa's forearm. He felt very cold.

"We need to be quiet and let them come to us," he whispered again, holding up both of his hands to show they came in peace. "If we want to remain alive, that is."

"Sure, sounds good," mumbled Ozzie.

"You still haven't told us where we are," said Credenza.

"We're in the Wilds now," said Tobias. "The land of the Laird. These are his protectors. They will take us to see him. If we're lucky, he won't be too angry. Just promise me, whatever you do, don't mention Lady Blackthorn."

"Why not?"

"Put it this way: their marriage didn't end well. But if we're to end the Magic Hour, the Laird's the one to help us."

From the edge of the trees, another unexpected noise filtered in. At first it sounded like the deep growl of an injured animal. As it increased in volume, Ailsa realized it was a car engine, labouring up a hill. A searchlight probed the dark, casting vast treetop shadows across their faces. At a distance it was hard to see for certain, but Ailsa was sure it was a kind of jeep.

The True Shee snapped into action. A pair of rough

hands grabbed Ailsa's shoulders and a sack was pulled tight over her head. The jute sackcloth reeked of sage and roots and mouldy potatoes, and as Ailsa felt herself being lifted and carried towards the forest, another powerful scent struck her.

It was so unexpected.

It was the tomato she had tried in Grandma's greenhouse.

The smell enveloped her completely and for a moment she was frozen, transported back to that wonderful summer. She had no idea why, in this hectic moment, she could smell something so specific, so strong and so at odds with her predicament.

Yet there it was, as she was carried along like a plank of wood towards the shadowy forest beyond, next to a screaming Credenza, a yawling Ozzie and the grimly silent Tobias, all Ailsa could smell was the intoxicating perfume of The Best Tomato in the World.

CHAPTER 40

TRACKING

The creature followed the bed of the river, which had winnowed a path through the heart of the wild forest.

The Brollachan preferred open hills and shallow valleys to this tight regiment of trees, but any course of flowing water, a runnel, stream or burn, was welcome. It was happy with the change of scene.

It leapt over logs, free, skimming over bubbles, snapping at fireflies and scaring the fish. At times it hung, still and silent, over the surface, stretching itself wide like a fog bank, listening for prospects, drifting gently on the ebb and flow of the twilight breeze.

Eventually, it sharpened again, easing back towards the banks. There, it played along the rocks and dived in and out of the foamy rivulets on the water's edge, stirring up whirlpools, just because it could. *When I grow up*, it sang to itself, *I will be a water spirit.*

But there was no one else to hear its song, and there

is nothing more painful to a Brollachan than to be aware of its own loneliness. It felt the anger rise inside, burning.

Then, around a gentle curve in the river, the creature heard a keening sound, like a wounded animal. Doubled-over against a willow tree was a solitary young boy, crying at the shore. He had dark freckles across his nose, and was muttering to himself in a reproachful way, teeth bared in regret. Unhappy news, perhaps, or a broken heart. The Brollachan sensed there was enough space here to squeeze itself into a nook, or cranny, a temporary shelter. It began to play with him. The creature made the sad, freckled boy dance a happy jig, in spite of his sobs, all along the rocky shore. Soon it was waltzing him into the shallows and into the freezing water, whirling and spinning and diving ever deeper. The Brollachan couldn't contain its delight, the icy water coursing across its new skin. But the creature had no idea that boys needed things, such as air; you knew that already, of course, and it is painful to report that the two of them danced too long in the tangled weeds at the river bottom. After a while, the Brollachan noticed the boy's limbs felt heavier, and still. It soon lost interest, the Brollachan, as the creature was oft to do, and moved on, leaving the boy's ankles wrapped in a mess of reeds, curious fish darting at his fingers.

And while we can't know for certain that one of those fish didn't nibble those reeds and free the boy, it's comforting to think that it did.

The Brollachan reached the shore and blew back towards the forest. It had already forgotten about the boy, and this was one of the reasons the creature was so feared. It would wreak havoc and forget, moving through the world thinking only of itself.

It wasn't fair, it thought now. It wanted a real home. With room to grow. *And I shall have one.*

It recalled again the daffodil hat, and the one that wore it. All the creature needed to do was track it down. It was in a floating patch of rotting crowfoot that the Brollachan felt the wind change. There were many odours down here, from the True Shee to the Wilder ones, from the creatures of the savage forest to the electric dust on the air that came from the north.

But the river ran north, and that was the source of the wind and the scent upon it, the odour of the small yellow hat. So, the Brollachan kept moving. It would not be long before it had another place to live.

CHAPTER 41

HIS LAIRDSHIP

Ailsa's nostrils filled with the smell of damp grass. Mostly on account of the fact that she was lying, face down, in the middle of a clearing. They had been dumped here moments earlier, and none of their journey had been pleasant.[43]

As they rose to their feet, they could see they were encircled by a ring of guards with red shanks and bare feet. Beyond that, the forest, and its darkness.

In the centre of it all was a stout, barrel-like man, seated on a willow bark throne. A chaotic, mud-brown beard covered his face (and, to be frank, a good portion of his ears). He was draped in a bewildering assembly of vegetation: rich, dark moss, strands of twisted ferns, daisy chains, bracken, white lichen, sunflower petals and bluebells, all of them woven into intricate braids, a

---

43   Travelling by sack rarely is.

tartan foliage held fast with twine. There were emeralds, yellows and purples, spikes of thistles and pine needles. On his head he wore a crown of stags' antlers and his eyes, while wise, betrayed a dark and malevolent mischief. Low-key, he wasn't.

"Guests, is it?" he said.

His breath smelled of mildew and could have felled a donkey. Even at a distance, Ailsa felt a wave of nausea hit her.

"Uninvited, sire," muttered a nearby guard.

The stout man on the throne had been eyeing Ailsa, but now turned his attention to Tobias.

"And you, who are you?"

Tobias cleared his throat. "Your Lairdship, if I may—"

The man held up a hand, heavy with rings that looked like tiny bird's nests. A thick-necked guard next to him, more important-looking than the others on the evidence of the wreath of leaves around her head, bore down on Tobias.

"You will answer His Lairdship's questions, and no more," hissed the guard, "unless you prefer the sting of young birch on your shanks."

Tobias lowered his head.

"My name is Tobias Ragwort."

Ailsa tried to meet Credenza's and Ozzie's eyes, but

they were both staring at the ground, terrified. Ozzie felt Ailsa's gaze and his eyes flicked in anger at her.

"Remind me," he whispered, out of the corner of his mouth, "not to follow you anywhere in the future."

The Laird, for indeed it was he, stood up and regarded them through his vast green eyes. "My people were here before the River Almond changed its course, before the Romans put Dere Street straight through the heart of this land. From the Hunter's bog to the Gogar Loch, we have been here, and *laing*[44] before that. Those that live in the filth of the city would have you believe they feel themselves the more civilized sort, so very modern, somehow closer to you perhaps. But it's a shadow they are selling. A low and devious trick! How arrogant these Mouldy Ones are. To assume they are the centre of everything, that they might control the moments of our days. That it is *they* who move through the waters of *time* … when it is time that is flowing down the mountain, and they are merely in the way. Once one realizes this, of course, the only sensible solution is to seek higher ground. That is where we are. Outside of the influence of the river. Quite safe, up here, on a rock. Safe … for now, of course."

---

44   "Long" in Scots.

He now glared at another guard, adding: "Bit parched, Murdo, if I'm honest."

This guard, who looked suddenly panicked, in turn glared at another, who hurried off and returned at speed with a vast flagon of foaming ale.

The Laird grabbed it and drank deeply, leaving thick spumes of foam scattered across his beard. Ailsa wondered if this might be part of the reason that Lady Blackthorn didn't want to stay with him.

The clearing was flanked with more torches now, a mist slowly descending,[45] their flames receding into the murk. More guards too: burly, barefoot, full of menace. All held claymores and other terrifying weapons. All with their eyes fixed on Ailsa and Tobias – although a few shot worried glances now and again at the Laird, who was still quaffing deeply from his ale.

The mist thickened quickly to fog and wafted in like curtains, surrounding the clearing. As the light darkened, so did the mood of the Laird. The circle tightened. He fixed Tobias with a stare.

"You're no Shee that I've seen."

Tobias appeared untroubled by the attention.

"We need your help."

---

45   Level 7.5 at least.

The Laird dismissed him with a wave. "*Whisht*, halfling."

Tobias bristled. "I am a halfling, yes, what of it?"

"So, you know their world well, do you, you've seen it? Are they as stupid there as they are in here?"

"I was only a newborn when they took me."

The Laird sighed. "She's behind this cruelty, the Lady Blackthorn. Damn her eyes; may the wood beetles eat her daft crown and whittle her ears to nubs."

Ailsa blinked. The Lord and Lady Blackthorn had something of the volcano experiment about them too.

"The *between-stools* cooks a fine tale, sire, but I don't think he's serving the full portion." The guard was circling Ailsa's group now, poking Tobias with the butt of her axe. "Something you're hiding, halfling?"

Tobias shook his head, but Ailsa could see in his eyes that his initial bravado had faded. Now he was anxious.

"An easy enough way to find out, sire?" The guard smirked.

The Laird stood up suddenly, swaying on his feet, but his eyes burned with glee. "Up he goes!"

Guards rushed forwards and grabbed Tobias by the shoulders, dragging him to the edge of the clearing and into the thicker mist by the base of a grand tree. As Ailsa shouted in fury, she saw that there was a rope tied to a high branch.

The Laird began to sing in a brash and tuneless voice:

The truth shall out, and come to town,
On the way up or on the way down!

Others in the circle joined in the haunting melody. Tobias gritted his teeth and shot Ailsa a look that she thought might be defiance but later realized it was an apology.

A thick rope was tied around Tobias's middle and knotted in an elaborate fashion. He was then hoisted – inch by painful inch – up, higher still, into the canopy of the trees.

The truth shall out, and come to town,
On the way up or on the way down!

The mist was now so thick that Tobias soon disappeared from view. After a few moments, the heaving stopped and the singing along with it. All Ailsa could hear was the groaning of a tree branch and the creaking strain of the rope, taut as a guitar string.

"Show yourself," shouted the Laird, "or face a hard reckoning."

There was silence, and the Laird sighed deeply, which appeared to end in a half-burp. He grimaced, then raised a finger up at the guards gripping the tightened rope. There were bullets of sweat on their brows, their knuckles white with effort.

The Laird dropped his finger.

They let go.

Ailsa screamed.

From high above, so did Tobias.

Ailsa saw him fall. Out of the mist he came, spread-eagled and on his back. To hit the ground at this speed was certain death.

But as he fell, a miracle happened. It must have only taken a split second, but Ailsa saw each moment unfold like a panel in a comic book.

First came his colour, which transformed from pale white to ash grey, nearly black. His feet turned paler still, shrinking into white paws, the red from his shanks sprouting grey fur. His hands changed too, and a tail grew fast behind him. More fur sprouted on his haunches and shoulders, with whiskers on his face and yellow slits for eyes. He cried out more in fear than in the pain of change.

Tobias was now a cat.

A cat that Ailsa knew.

He flipped around with ease, landing feet first – naturally.[46]

He had been Tobias at the top of the tree. Now, back on the ground, he was four-legged and feline.

Sydekyck.

The Laird roared. "Behold the truth! A friend with two faces! Do you trust his word still? Tell me this, how can you trust someone who changes all the time?"

Silence fell, and Sydekyck stayed low, hackles up, backing himself towards the base of the tree.

The guard eyed the group hungrily.

"Shall we break the liars down for scrap, sire?"

Another larger guard licked his lips and said simply: "Soup?"

Ailsa was too confused and shocked to be scared. Tobias was Sydekyck? She supposed it made some kind of sense. She looked back towards the Laird, and was now unable to speak. This was because Ailsa was now staring not at him, but at the mist at the edge of the clearing.

In the centre of it all, she saw two glowing red eyes

---

46 Using an instinctive feline "righting reflex" that involves a flexible spine, no collarbone, a surviveable terminal velocity, the conservation of angular momentum, and generally being very cool. There will be a test at the end of this book, but don't worry, you've already passed.

that hovered. The mist was swirling and churning, under and over itself, pulsing as if alive. Ailsa suddenly recalled her dream, a lifetime ago now, where those same eyes were near her, watching.

A voice piped up, close to Ailsa's ear. *You're not as tall as I imagined*, it said. *But your head smells like daffodils.*

Ailsa knew that voice.

It was the creature from behind the blood-red door.

The Brollachan was joyful. The disembodied entity had not been expecting to find so many true prospects out here in the forest. Malevolent tracts of living fog did not normally find their prey arranged together so conveniently.

Ailsa was frozen to the spot.

A tendril of mist, like an errant grey root, now began to meander towards her.

It danced around her eyes, carving shapes in the air, drawing circles and spirals, like miniature hurricanes, drawing her attention closer and guiding her gaze in one direction, whilst a second inquisitive strand moved in quite another, disguising its intent and then reaching out, quiet and unseen, towards her ears.

She heard Tobias's voice too late.

"Ailsa, look out!"

A shock of icy breeze engulfed Ailsa and it felt to her

as if she had swallowed a cold copper wire, frost radiating out to her fingertips. She staggered back and to steady herself trod hard on the ground, but what had been solid earth seconds earlier now felt soft, like a pudding, into which she was now slowly, but surely, sinking.

Credenza took Ailsa's hand and gripped it tight.

"What's going on?" she said. "You're so cold!"

The Laird and guards saw the glowing red eyes and Ailsa losing her balance. A guttural roar of pure fear rose in their throats.

"The Brollachan! Run!"

Ailsa gripped Credenza's hand even tighter. But she was sinking, she knew it. No matter how hard she tried to pull her leg back up, the cold weight of the ground, like molasses, dragged her down further. A darkness was falling across the centre of Ailsa, and she felt its cold touch, scrabbling for a handhold. The mist was in her chest now, in her neck and fingers, grasping her heart tight inside her chest. But despite the weight and dark shadow, the brighter parts of Ailsa's mind and heart began fighting back. As Grandma had once taught her, in the face of adversity she applied the Method.

State your problem clearly? *Well, this cold malevolent entity appears to be taking over my mind, and, if I let it, my entire being. How do I stop it?* Gather information and observe? *The moment the cold hit me I felt like a shadow had fallen across my heart, and the earth is currently trying to swallow me.* Time to skip ahead to…

Experiment. How do you stop the cold and the dark? *You light a fire.*

Ailsa forced her mind to focus on one good memory, one that glowed like a winter fire in her mind. Grandma and the world's best tomato. That was perfect. She smelled the sheer green life of the plants, saw the smile on Grandma's face, felt the warm sun on her skin as they walked back to the house. More memories followed, like embers warming her soul. A simple porridge with Dad in the morning. Her mum's smile after school, even after a hard day. Steve the cat purring, and the other Steve, of course, who didn't purr so much, both curled up alongside her in bed as she watched the snow outside, falling silent and perfect and making little terraces on the rowan tree leaves. And Lulu, of course Lulu, how she missed hearing her sister's voice, her laugh, alive with the excitement of her working day across the sea. And the books, my gosh, the books she had read and the stories she would find next. The rowan tree leaves, she thought again, sensing the creature's grip slipping.

The rowan tree? She thought again.

The rowan tree.

Not enough room, she heard the voice say, as if through gritted teeth. *Not enough room here at all*.

Still the shadows moved around Ailsa and the cold mist flooded into the nooks and crannies of her mind, that cold wire wrapping itself tighter around her spine. Still Ailsa dug her fingers into her palms, forced her heels into the soil, and kept her focus on those warm memories, the fire of the hearth. And they came, like a cavalry over the hill as she focused on everything good and bright and happy that had happened to her and to those she loved, who were many and legion. The bright light of her being shone like never before, and even as the creature scrabbled in a frenzy for a handhold, it was like trying to grab hold of a waterfall.

No space, wailed the Brollachan.

Not fair.

And like that, the weight left her.

The frozen wire uncoiled and a warmth bloomed through her body, from the tips of her toes to the top of her head. The mist was gone. She breathed deep, steadying herself, and blinked. She did not know yet, but what a Brollachan truly needed was a yawning emptiness inside.

That one next door, said the Brollachan.

That was different.

That one had potential.

Ailsa saw Sydekyck dash for the bushes across the clearing. Ailsa pulled Credenza's hand to follow her. As they moved, the fog thickened. Two guards clattered into Ozzie as they ran, knocking him down to the dirt. Ailsa went to help him up, and as she did, she felt Credenza's hand slick and wet in her own, slipping away like a bar of soap in the bath.

Ailsa yanked Ozzie to his feet.

"Where's Denzie?" said Ozzie.

"She must be ahead of us," said Ailsa.

They sprinted the last few metres to the bushes and dived hard into them. Thorns scraped their arms, jagged leaves poking their heads. But they were safe for now. Sydekyck was here too; he shot Ailsa a rueful look.

However, Ailsa was not looking back at him.

She was scanning the swirling mist for Credenza.

"Denzie!" bellowed Ozzie.

Ailsa nudged him. "We can't let that thing know where we are," she said urgently.

"But where did she go? She was right there!"

Far away to the south, over the trees, a bell was tolling. Five bells left. As the sound faded, the mist began to clear. From the fringes of the clearing to its centre, like a sink draining of dirty water.

It was Ailsa who saw her first.

Credenza.

Standing still and alone in the centre of the clearing, her eyes a dark cherry red, like the last embers of a fire.

CHAPTER 42

TAKEN

Ailsa grabbed Ozzie's sleeve and retreated further into the tangled mess of bushes behind them. Her eyes did not leave Credenza, who was not blinking. Credenza, on her part, stared right through her, as if seeing a completely different world entirely.

(Don't know about you, but I don't like the way this is going. I hope you've got a plan, because I sure don't, and I wrote this whole thing.)

Another hand grabbed Ailsa's shoulder and she tried not to scream. She whipped around, ready to strike, but it was Tobias, back in his human form.

"The beast has her now," he said.

"Erm, what beast would that be, exactly?" asked Ossian, his voice trembling.

"A Brollachan is a young spirit without form,"

said Tobias. "Child of the *Fuath*,[47] yet to find shape. Selfish. Cruel."

Ailsa looked at Credenza's glazed and burning eyes.

Pleased to meet you, said the voice.

"What does a Brollachan do?"

"It lives as a mist but craves a form. So it looks for bodies to live in. Living bodies, I mean. Then, once it's done with them, it moves on to someone else."

"What ... happens to the person with the body when it leaves?"

Tobias's face was grim. "We shall drive it out," he said, "before it gets to that."

Credenza's jaw was grinding as she began to move, flecks of froth and spittle appearing at the sides of her mouth. She took confident, hearty steps, almost stamping the ground, planting her feet into the soil as if doing it for the first time. Gradually, step by step, she seemed more at ease, as if re-learning an old skill. Her footfalls steadied; her expression calmed. She started to look more and more like Credenza.

A Credenza with glowing red eyes, that is. Now,

---

47   A *Fuath* is a hateful kind of ancient Scottish spirit, often associated with water. The Brollachan, being a child of this spirit, enjoys both water, and hate. Definitely not someone to invite over for tea. Or, indeed, a water-balloon fight.

she grabbed an abandoned axe from the edge of the clearing, and hoisted it over her shoulder. Then, with steady steps, Credenza marched towards the throne of the Laird.

To get there she had to pass two blazing torches. As she approached, she appears to pause, and proceeded to give them as wide a berth as possible.

"The Brollachan craves the darkness," said Tobias. "It cannot stand light. The brighter, the better."

Ailsa knew this was true. It was the light of her memories, the warm glow of her life, that had driven the thing from her. It reminded Ailsa all of a sudden of the Gloamings she had doodled back home. The Gloamings! One that eats light and one that eats darkness. But since this creature that has taken Credenza finds light so painful, perhaps if they lit enough torches—

Ailsa stopped. A thought hit her.

Ozzie looked at her – perhaps he was having the same thought.

"Look out!" yelled Tobias, breaking cover and running at the Laird, who was cowering behind a tree.

Hearing the noise, the Laird ducked, dodging a flying axe which thudded deep into the bark above his head.

"The creature?" The Laird was grieving and furious in equal measure. He pounded the earth in rage. "They promised! The peace depends on the beast being kennelled… That was the agreement."

"Looks like someone let it out."

"The Brollachan is here! Fetch more fire!" the Laird shouted. "Fire shall drive it out! Light the red clover!"

As the compound became a frenzy of feet, smoke and flame, Ailsa ran to the Laird and tugged on his sleeve. A small piece of bark came away in her hand – but now she had his attention.

"There's something brighter than fire," said Ailsa, pointing back through the forest towards the strange glow in the sky.

CHAPTER 43

Now

Credenza gazed into the deep dark of the woods, her eyes burning red. Ailsa peered out at her from the bushes, hardly believing this was the same girl who was her friend, who rode a taxi to school every day. She was a wild animal now, with a primal energy about her that was completely unsettling.

The gleaming blade of the axe in her hands wasn't exactly helping to calm any nerves either.

Ozzie was on his feet now, hovering at the edge of the clearing. Then, very calmly, he held his breath and began to walk towards his sister.

This was the plan: if Credenza would recognize anyone, they had all reasoned, it would be her own brother. What they needed was her attention. He was the lure in search of a bite. In particular, they needed her to not look anywhere behind her, where two sets of the Laird's guards were hidden.

"It will kill her unless we act now," Tobias had told them. "It does not yet have all of her under its control."

"Hey, Denzie," Ozzie yelled out to his sister, but she did not turn. She hardly even blinked. He tried again. "Credenzabot. Hey! Um, little sis?"

She ignored him.

"Den. Come on. Look at me. It's me, Ozzie."

Ossian was plaintive now. His frustration was showing. But Credenza, or rather the creature that Credenza was hosting and all-too-soon-becoming, had no interest in his words. They were like leaves on the wind, meaningless noise.

The leaves, in turn, seemed to speak back to Ozzie.

I don't think so, they said.

Ailsa saw Credenza's knuckles tighten on the axe handle.

"Try again," said Tobias from the relative safety of the bushes. Ailsa was beside him with the Laird and several of his braver guards.

"Yeah, I don't know," said Ossian. "It's not like I'm exactly her favourite person anyway. Ailsa, maybe you should try."

All eyes turned to her.

"Me?" said Ailsa.

"Well, yeah. You're her best friend."

I am? thought Ailsa.

Stay back, said a voice like thunder in her head.

She's mine.

Ailsa swallowed hard and walked towards Credenza.

What did I just tell you? said the voice.

Ailsa ignored the threat and planted her feet firmly. "Denzie?" she said. "It's me, Ailsa."

Credenza turned towards her. Her eyes now ablaze, that same dark scarlet fire Ailsa had seen through the mist. The Brollachan within was strong and getting stronger every second. Seeing Ailsa before her, arms extended, the eyes dimmed for a moment; it looked like they might fill with tears.

"Denzie, you need to do your best and follow me out of here. I know the way. Come on. Quick as you can."

And with that Ailsa did something she never thought she would ever be capable of. Despite the unsettling presence before her, despite the sharp axe in its hand, Ailsa turned her back.

Then, with great care and precision, she began to walk back towards Ossian and Tobias. Step by step, she held her breath. As she did, she could hear Credenza moving.

Footsteps, close, getting closer. Speeding up.

So very close now. Close enough to swing an axe.

"Come on, it's not too far," she heard herself say.

Credenza's feet stamped hard in the mulch of the clearing; she was running towards her now. A scream was building in her throat, like a banshee wail. As she approached the bushes, two sets of hidden guards leapt out, brandishing a great burlap sack. As one set pulled the axe away, the other dropped the sack over Credenza's head and lifted her aloft.

"Now!" said the Laird.

They had her now and pushed on through a thicket on the edge of the clearing. Beyond was a rough causeway covered in flinty stones laid over the soggy ground. Ailsa's heart thundered in her chest as she tried to keep up. The path wound through the trees and up the slope towards the hill, shrouded in mist and cloud.

Towards the glow in the sky.

Credenza thrashed and roared, kicking and scratching as she was carried aloft in the sack. Ailsa, gathering her breath, dashed ahead, following the pale ribbon of the path as it zigzagged around old roots and clumps of earth, leading up, always up. Tobias kept pace beside her, with Ossian and the Laird bringing up the rear behind the shrieking form in the sack.

Now came the tricky part.

They were ascending into the cloud of mist now,

which seemed to have condensed to the colour of cream. Cresting the ridge almost together, they saw once again the installation far below, the strange concentric circles of fences and security structures that looped around the crater. Down in the inner area, past the fence, women and men in white coats came and went with studious industry. Still others moved terrifyingly close to the scintillating mass, their gold-tinted visors reflecting nothing but the white-hot energy at the centre of everything.

The bolt.

It was still there, demanding attention: a blistering, jagged tree trunk that was painful to gaze at, even through the thick fog.

"Now!" shouted Ailsa.

With that, the guards opened the sack, and Ossian pushed his sister down the steep grassy slope.

Ailsa watched Credenza tumble out and couldn't help but add: "I'm so sorry!"

Credenza screamed all the way down. When she finally stopped moving, she stood up awkwardly and ripped the sack from her face.

Now it was the Brollachan who screamed.

It was like the inside of a thunderclap, or the deep centre of an earthquake – a raw clamour of savage ferocity. The noise shook the fencing so much that several sections collapsed. The scientists in white suits dropped their tools, gadgets and clipboards, many running out of their work cabins in a blind panic.

Credenza fell to her knees in a great spasm of pain. Her eyes were shut tight, her back arching so far behind her that her head could almost touch the ground. Ailsa could bear it no more. Holding her arm up to her eyes, wincing in the pain of the light, she ran down to her friend.

"Ailsa, no!" shouted Tobias.

But she was already halfway there.

As she ran, she noticed in the chaos that Credenza had opened her eyes – they had lost their scarlet glow and were turning back to their regular blue. But as she got closer, she could see that surrounding her, in thin strands of white, was a woven whirlpool of mist. Like an angry, coiled snake, it was encircling Credenza from head to toe.

This one is for myself, said the voice.

Thyself, you take elsewhere.

"I'm not afraid of you," said Ailsa, despite feeling the contrary. "You leave my friend alone. She's with me."

Then, trying to echo the Brollachan's strange diction, added a thought, *She is with myself.*

The mist braided even tighter, as if weaving itself

into a basket around Credenza. One that might carry her away. It seemed to Ailsa like it was thinking.

Thyself, this one? it whispered.

"She belongs with me," said Ailsa, out loud this time. She spoke each word with focused deliberation, attaching to each syllable a powerful memory of her friendship with Credenza. They had not always seen eye to eye, it was true. But she knew she was her friend. And every part of her made sure the Brollachan knew that, even in the tone and timbre of her voice.

Then, like many people do to make a point, she repeated herself. This time, with every word she spoke, she took one step closer to the creature. Something deep in her stomach screamed at her to turn and run, but Ailsa's heart was in control now. And it was standing up for her friend.

"She…"

A step.

"Belongs…"

Another step.

"With…"

One more.

"Me!"

The Brollachan could sense a resolve in Ailsa, the steel in her spine and the courage of her heart. All of which, decided the Brollachan, looked a lot like hard work. It shook and shuddered, unravelling itself. Then, the mist moved. Hard to see at first, but wisp after wisp appeared to move to a spot a few steps away from Credenza. It was leaving. She was free.

Didn't like that one anyway, the Brollachan seemed to say.

Not enough room.

Alarms blared across the compound, and despite the searing halo of light around them, Ailsa could sense there were people coming towards them fast. Credenza stumbled to her feet and shielded her eyes from the light.

"Denzie! It's me!"

"Ailsa?"

Ailsa's chest exploded with relief. She had done it. She had stood up to her fear. And rescued her friend. But the sheer effort of standing up to the creature came crashing down on her now, and her knees began to shake.

This is no time, Ailsa said to herself, *for wobbling.*

"Take my hand!" she shouted, running over to Credenza, as if daring her legs to buckle.[48]

---

48 They didn't. We're often stronger than we can ever know, and this goes double when there are people around that we truly care about.

"What's going on? Where am I?"

"I'll explain it on the way!"

Ailsa grasped her friend's hand, shifting her grip up to her wrist to ensure she wouldn't let go. Above the alarms, another noise filtered in. A motor. Over the crest of the far hill, emerging from the glow of the bolt, Ailsa could suddenly see a military-style jeep. At the wheel, the unmistakable black eyes of Sandy Munro.

Ailsa dragged Credenza to her feet, and they ran into the bushes upslope. Tobias and Ossian were there, the Laird and his guards behind him, ready to scoop them up and carry them over the ridge.

By the time Sandy Munro arrived at the still-spooling tapestry of mist, there was no one there.

No one but the Brollachan.

The creature examined its old captor with new eyes.

It had never really looked inside this one before.

So empty, it muttered. *Just look at it.*

Plenty of room to grow.

Sandy Munro peeled the jeep back around and made for the main science buildings on the site.

Two eyes appeared in the mist behind, following him. They glowed like the dark cherry embers of a dying fire.

CHAPTER 44

COURAGE AND BRAVERY AND OTHER IMPORTANT THINGS

The Laird was grinning at Ailsa in pure admiration.

"A *bairn*[49] fights off the Brollachan. Twice! There's bravery for you."

"We are going to need your bravery now too, sire."

Tobias was talking now, and the Laird was finally listening. Tobias explained what they already knew: that the humans had been exploiting their pact with the Shee, and that the Magic Hour was taking time away from innocent lives.

*

---

49 A Scots word meaning "child". Some others use the word "wean" as in "wee ane" or "small one". In any case, the way it's used here is kind of patronizing, I think you'll agree. But that's Lairds of the Wilds for you.

"You and Lady Blackthorn ruled together, once," said Ailsa.

The Laird sucked his teeth and spit on the ground. "Aye. Why don't you remind me of all the stomach-aches I ever had too, while you're at it?"

"So, it's true?"

"Once is a long time ago," he said. "There was once a single court of the Shee in this land. Now, we have two. A Laird and a Lady. The Seelie, and the Unseelie."

"Which one are you?" asked Ossian.

"The Seelies, of course."

"Why of course?"

Ossian was in an interrogative mood, and Ailsa could see that it was starting to irritate the Laird.

"The Seelie Court is the summer court. We only tease you mouldy folks. We want no harm to others. The rest…" The Laird trailed off, letting his shrug give the silence meaning.

Tobias's eyes were wide. "But, Lady Blackthorn is of the Seelie too, is she not?"

The Laird shook his head.

"You've got it round the wrong way, lad. We're all Seelies out here. It's the city that's got the mischief makers. All the Middlemarket is."

Tobias was open-mouthed. "I never thought—"

"You think because we live out here in the weeds

and the thistles, that we're the brutish ones, is that it? We mean no harm here. We let nature take its course. There in the ring of stone, the Unseelie Court, that's her business," said the Laird. "The Lady Blackthorn and her fancy-pants friends. They hide up in the big town, their big stone houses and their silly tartans. All for show, of course. The finer the better. But don't let appearances fool you – they're wild animals, the lot of them. As savage as they come."

"I never knew fairy life was so complicated," said Ossian.

The Laird grunted.

"What about leprechauns, though? Are they here too?"

The Laird turned to face Ossian. As he spoke, he took large deliberate steps towards him. His left eye was twitching slightly. "Is it the green?" he asked. "Is that it?"

"Is … what it?"

"The fact that many of you people seem to assume that fairies all come from the same land to the west, the Five Fifths of Ireland, and all the kings that came before them?"

"I just…" said Ossian, flummoxed. "So are fairies not Irish, then?" asked Ossie.

The Laird slammed his fist into his thigh.

"Well, some are, of course! But not here! We're all

Alba here, Scottish! Loyal subjects of Galbus of Galloway, and all points north. And while I have every respect for our cousins across the water, we are Highland, we are Lowland, but we are all of us Scotland. Do you understand me clearly?" He was very close to Ossian now, tufts of his beard almost tickling Ozzie's nose. "We have our own commonwealth here, thank you very much."

Ossian held up his hands and stepped back. "No problem. Just, you know, asking."

"There's one thing here I don't understand," said Ailsa. Both the Laird and Ossian seemed happy to change the subject. "If you and Lady Blackthorn disagree all the time, why did you agree to any of this?"

"Any of what?"

"The Magic Hour? When my grandmother first came here, why did you even offer to help her at all?"

The Laird seemed misty-eyed for a moment. "Lady B wasn't always like this," mused the Laird. "But she changed. Thirsty for mischief, I don't doubt. Maybe she was bored. With me, with the world. Who knows? The Magic Hour was her idea. Let the Mouldy Ones think they found it all by themselves."

"So, it's all a trick?" said Ossian.

"Of course it's a blasted trick! That's all she ever liked to do, come up with nonsense and little cruel games. I was never for it myself. That's why we parted. It isn't right to steal lives away. And it was your Grandmother Judith, wean, who first fell for it."

"And the wall is how they do it?"

"Everyone who sets foot here incurs a debt," said the Laird. "And since our currency is time, that is how you pay. But when the Reckoning comes, it's your guarantors who do the paying. Not you."

"Guarantors?"

"The people closest to you. That's who pays your debt."

"Can't you pay your own way?"

The Laird shook his head. "That would spoil the trick."

"How do they know who's close to you?"

"The Sanctum knows all," said the Laird. "You, him, your deepest friendships, your family, your secret loves. The Tally Folk are the ones that watch it."

Ailsa wasn't sure what a Sanctum was, but it all suddenly somehow made sense to her.

"My grandpa got sick," said Ailsa. "More quickly than they ever thought. They said he might recover, he might be OK. And then … all of a sudden… I mean, do you think that he…?"

The Laird's eyes were wet now and full of sorrow.

"I'm sorry, hen. It's not right," said the Laird. "It's why I left that miserable town. And came out here."

Ailsa nodded and began to shake. A vast sob shuddered out of her ribs, out into the air. She shook herself and stood up. Credenza was looking at her, tearful too. As painful as it was to give in to the sadness, Ailsa felt relieved.

"They've tricked us," said Credenza.

"Not just you," said the Laird. "Every last one of your kind who ever set foot in this place. And for what? Amusement. A sick joke. To get one over on you. To put you back in your place. It's only us folk that can live outside of time. You lot are all floating down the river, and there's nothing you can do about it."

There was a desolate silence for a moment.

"So, help us," said Ailsa, gathering herself.

The Laird glowered, then sighed. "Bit late for that now."

"You need to help us stop them," she said again. It was like she was hearing that other person say the words. Ailsa had shape-shifted again – into a leader. Everyone in the clearing was now hanging on her word. "Don't you understand? The more people who come here, the more they experiment, or expand, or abuse this 'joke'… the more innocent people will get hurt."

The Laird seemed unmoved. So she tried a new approach.

"Do you like having us around? Every time I come here, I see more humans. Um, I mean, Mouldy Ones."

The Laird harrumphed. It was clear he did not.

"Right now, this place is a membership club. But that's not enough for Sandy Munro. He wants money. Doesn't he, Denzie?"

"My dad's been so excited about it," said Credenza. "I had no idea…"

"Free energy which he can sell. That lightning bolt's never going to leave this place. So that experiment over there with the lightning, if it works, don't you think even more people will come? The more money it generates, the more people it will bring. Do you think that's likely to improve things? For you? For us, we know it's a disaster. But for you, it might be even worse. If you think we're mouldy now, just wait till we fill up the place."

The Laird sucked his teeth. He dreaded the prospect, that much was clear. Finally, darkly, he looked at Credenza and Ossian. "It's their father who built it."

"And it's my grandmother who discovered it. Which means it falls to all of us to stop it. We're all responsible for this mess. And we are going to clear it up."

"A proper army, are you?" he chuckled, but it was more in admiration than criticism. "I should think so too."

"The four ports, can we close them?"

The Laird thought, then nodded. "It's possible."

"If we do that, there will be no way to cross over?" said Ailsa.

"Or get out," said Ossian ominously.

In the silence, carried by the wind, a bell tolled.

CHAPTER 45

FOUR BELLS LEFT

The Laird was pacing now, alive with the idea. "The gates can all be sealed from the Tron. That's the tower, in the middle of the square by the Exchange. They lock and unlock with two keys. One key is the sun, the other is the moon. One sits here around my neck. The other around hers. Both must be turned together. If we do that, all the ports will close together. Like a drawbridge."

The Laird held up a carved wooden key, one of many necklaces strung at his chest. The base of the key was an intricate, beautiful sun.

He anticipated Ailsa's next question.

"But I won't do it. And I cannot speak to that ... individual," he said finally. "Since, knowing her as I do, that individual in question would never agree..."

"How do you know? Do you think that individual – sorry, Lady Blackthorn – enjoys us humans coming here? Driving jeeps around her land? Exploiting it?"

"Oh, please, that is spring air to her. Dew on the grass. She laps it up. She enjoys the chaos," he said. "Thrives on it. Personally, I find it all exhausting."

The echo of a bell held in the air.

Ailsa froze. They had all forgotten.

"What bell was that?" she gasped. "Which one?"

The Laird listened to the echo, but Tobias already knew.

"Four bells left," he said.

Around them, the twilight that had lit their time was beginning to fade. Even the torches blazing in the clearing were starting to smoke and sputter.

"What happens here after final bell?" asked Ossian.

"You don't want to know," said Ailsa.

"Best you go see the Tally Folk," said the Laird. "The ones who control the Sanctum. Officious little rooster there called Virgil Merrimack."

CHAPTER 46

A GENTLE BREEZE

In the outer circle of buildings around the lightning bolt, a team of scientists were analysing the latest data from their experiment. This frozen bolt, seemingly preserved in form, was outputting its energy at a strong and steady rate.

It was a complete mystery why such a source of power would freeze where it met the ground, and yet still continue to provide millions of volts of pure electricity.

This discovery would change the world, that they knew. So long as they could find a way of harnessing that energy and siphoning it off into their own world, selling to the highest bidder. It was the perfect scenario – they now controlled finite access to infinite resources. The agencies of government were all over them, of course, via a private company called the Compass Group, but there was a deal to be struck. It would make them all rich.

It was thus surprising to most of them when Sandy Munro burst into their operations building, waving his arms and screaming at the top of his voice. The scientists had already heard the shriek from the Brollachan, and seeing how agitated he now was, many of them thought the noise must have been him.

"She knows!" he yelled.

"Who?" asked a bewildered young woman in a white coat.

"*She does!*" he yelled again, pointing maniacally outside at the deepening fog.

"The, erm, Craig child, granddaughter. Judith, remember? She is here and she knows, and she is trying to sabotage us all. I know it! What she knows could bring us all down!"

The scientists and military guards at the facility were used to this man being obnoxious, but they had never seen him be actively dangerous before.

"Dr Munro," said the young woman.

"Professor," snarled Sandy.

"Professor Munro," she replied, rolling her eyes despite herself. "What can a child possibly do to jeopardize our research?"

"I do not want to wait to find out. Stop her, someone!"

His finger quivered as it pointed outside at the rim of the crater where Ailsa's footprints dotted the slopes back up into the forest beyond.

"Sir, the research … we couldn't possibly leave—"

"The guards, then!"

"They are here to protect the equipment and ourselves."

Sandy Munro broiled in his own frustration for a moment.

"Useless idiots! Fine! Then I will track her down myself," he snapped back. "But you must do whatever you can to keep this information away from Cameron Dingwall."

"He's never here anyway, sir. Too busy shaking hands—"

Sandy Munro's cheeks were flushed now. He turned on his heel and ran back out the door into a thick, impenetrable mist.

He was striding back to his jeep, muttering to himself, when he heard the first whisper. The Craig child wouldn't get far, he mused to himself, as a second whisper arrived on the air itself, soon strengthening into a languid, gentle breeze. The air seemed to politely introduce itself, blowing in his ear, wending a lazy way through to his nose.

He swallowed hard as the breeze seemed to spread itself across his lungs and form itself into a voice which vibrated somewhere in his ribcage.

I was looking far and wide.

But there you were all along.

Right in front of me.

"Away!" sputtered Sandy Munro, a stronger fight in him than he had ever imagined. His fists and feet lashed out in all directions, as if trying to rid himself of a thousand ants crawling over his body.

Calm thyself, the voice said.

Your heart only beats, it added, *because I myself allow it.*

You will not take me, rasped Sandy Munro, but the words echoed hollowly inside his skull. There was no light here to fight back with. His inner mind was all shadow. Soon, his tongue, his lips, his voice were not his own any more.

He crumpled into a heap. Then, with effort, stood up again.

His eyes burned like dark cherry coals in a dying fire.

From deep inside him, another voice came.

Home sweet home, said the Brollachan.

CHAPTER 47

TERMS & CONDITIONS APPLY

They found Virgil Merrimack in the Reckoning Room, leaning on the long counter, polishing a lever on a copper machine.

"No one ever asked before," he sniffed.

"The Magic Hour must be stopped," said Ailsa.

"Impossible."

"My grandmother tried. You helped to stop her."

"Oh, that was nothing to do with me, I can assure you."

"So then we can both agree who it really was."

Virgil rolled his eyes and yawned. "If you're talking about Professor Munro, then yes, I imagine we do. It's one thing I've noticed about you people. You don't like working together. Someone always has to grab the glory for themselves."

"Is he here?" asked Ailsa.

"I have no idea. Too late for that now, anyway. It's not up to me. It's Her Ladyship who makes these kinds of decisions."

"So take us to her."

"Out of the question." Virgil's face turned puce and he pivoted on a leather-booted sole. When he saw Credenza, his teeth wrestled themselves into a beaming smile. It looked like his lower lip was attacking his own cheek, using his teeth for weapons. The overall effect was bizarre.

"Even for our best friends, I'm afraid. Although I do admit I am puzzled. You, Credenza, a Dingwall. You would try to destroy all that your father has worked for?"

"He doesn't know what he's doing," said Credenza. "Or the damage he is causing."

Virgil sighed deeply. He had thought he was done for the day, and yet here they were again. Humans.

"I rather think he might," said Virgil. "You Mouldy Ones honestly don't seem to care about consequences as far as I can see," he said.

"You don't see the problem with what you're doing?"

"First of all, may I say, I had no hand in the Magic Hour's design. Secondly, well, it's not as if we don't make the truth abundantly clear to you. I mean, it is all there in the small print."

Ailsa looked blankly at Credenza, who stared at Ossian, who looked back again at Ailsa. Tobias, for his part, shook his head.

"What small print?" asked Ossian.

"You all seem very happy to agree to things without ever looking at what it is you're agreeing to."

"Oh no," said Ossian, who knew what came next.

Ailsa did too. "The orientation video," she said.

"The bit at the end," agreed Ossian numbly.

"The part no one ever reads," said Virgil, "because they're too impatient."

Ossian bit his lip. "Or can't be bothered. It's like downloading an app and clicking agree on the terms and conditions."

"Yeah, no one ever reads that stuff," said Credenza.

"And look where you are now," said Virgil. "I'd say reading is rather important, wouldn't you? It's the first stage of understanding something."

"Don't you realize what will happen if you do nothing?"

Virgil moved closer to Ailsa, and said in a confidential tone, "Look, I'm not over the moon about having to deal with the likes of you either, all right? Like I said, it wasn't my idea. My days used to be spent reading and trying to grow new kinds of cowslips and forget-me-nots. Now I manage a bureaucracy. I do paperwork and have to interact with walking piles of fungus like you. The way I see it, once Mr Dingwall and Professor Munro are finished with their little science project at the frontier, they'll be on their way. We will let them have their fun. But only up to a point."

"At what price?" said Ailsa.

"I don't understand."

"Did you not read the small print too? That science project, as you call it, is a money-making enterprise. And when money gets involved, you get a gold rush. That lightning bolt will bring many, many more here. They want to take free energy and sell it, back in our world. They're exploiting you, even now, and they won't care who they hurt. You'll be overrun. And the damage they do to innocent people back home will be … endless."

Virgil folded his arms and shook his head.

A bell tolled.

"Three bells left. Now, I'm prepared to take Miss Dingwall to see Her Ladyship, if that will shut the rest of you up."

"And what do we do?" said Ailsa. "Stay here and get attacked by the Brollachan?"

Virgil stared coldly at her, taken aback. "What did you say?"

"I met him, you know," continued Ailsa. "Out in the

Wilds earlier. He's not exactly friendly, but then you already know that."

"I beg your pardon, the *Brollachan*?"

"He attacked me," said Credenza. "Until Ailsa drove him out." She leaned in to Ailsa, clearly changed by the experience.

"Are you telling me…" Virgil was trembling now.

"That there's a monster on the loose?" said Ossian. "Um, yep."

"The creature is out," said Tobias. "It is hunting. And soon it will find its final form."

"It lived down there, behind the red door," added Ailsa.

Virgil cleared his throat. "So you know about the Brollachan, fine. But what you're saying makes no sense. Perhaps you're thinking about something else? A badger perhaps? We still get them around here, the old sort. We call them brocs. But the creature that you mentioned, well, it is bonded, restrained and safely kennelled below us, my dear. I wouldn't worry about it."

"Was kennelled," said Ailsa. "Because clearly it got out."

"Or someone released it," said Credenza.

Virgil Merrimack's face froze in abject terror. Ailsa had never seen a mask peel so completely from a face. He looked like a five-year-old child hearing his first ghost story.

"Professor Munro himself ensures that door stays forever shut."

"Maybe an idea," said Tobias, "to check?"

"Morag!" shouted Virgil.

The clerk called Morag arrived, and was soon dispatched downstairs. As they waited, every so often, the machines would whirr, and the clerks would open a vast red ledger.

Ailsa tried to swallow, but found her throat was dry. "The people you take time from. In payment. Do they even know it's gone?"

Virgil Merrimack turned back to Ailsa. "I doubt they have any idea at all. After all, who misses a day or two here and there? An hour even? Not you lot. You don't seem to place much of a value on time, so you never seem to miss it when it is frittered away."

"Why don't you take the time from the people who actually come here?"

"Don't you see? No one in your rotten world ever pays their own bills. We didn't see fit to change that. One generation passes on the debt to the next. And on, and on. It's what makes the trick so very ... tricky."

Ailsa remembered Dad's words at breakfast on a day that now seemed a thousand lifetimes ago.

One minute can mean the world to someone.

Morag reappeared at the far stairwell, a horrified look on her face. She shook her head, and Virgil Merrimack's eyes turned cold.

"Very well, follow me," he said, striding towards a large set of doors in the far wall. "We will see if Her Ladyship is prepared to give an audience."

CHAPTER 48

A PUZZLE

Virgil led the group along a narrow exterior walkway, one of the city ramparts she had seen from the Tron. The stone was mossy and Ailsa's feet slipped now and then.

Down a dark staircase, they found themselves inside a large, vaulted chamber. It was a curiously empty room with a single door on the far side. Virgil signalled for them to wait and proceeded across the space to the door.

The door was opened from inside by a guard, and the diminutive but sprightly form of Lady Blackthorn stepped out into the cold stone of the room.

"Who are you?"

"Virgil Merrimack, ma'am, I run the Reckoning—"

Lady Blackthorn held up her hand.

Ailsa felt her throat tighten.

"Who wishes an audience with me?" asked Lady Blackthorn.

Her words echoed across the high, cold walls. From

somewhere, Ailsa could hear another bell toll. Time was passing, and they had to do something, fast. She ground her heel into the floor and bit her lip with frustration.

"Careful," whispered Tobias into Ailsa's ear. "They renounced the old magic here a long time ago. But only in public. In private, she has powers you would rather not encounter."

"I wonder," said Lady Blackthorn, "if you are worthy of my time? I only meet the smartest and the cleverest people. If you can get to my door, I'll see you. Be sure all of you make it in one piece."

With that, she waved her arms, opened the door and dragged Virgil Merrimack inside it with her. It slammed shut.

The floor began to crack and groan. Before Ailsa knew what was happening, the entire floor ahead of them, halfway to the door, began to rip apart. A great gash appeared through the very heart of the room, to reveal a channel traversing the breadth of the chamber. Into this channel came water, filling it to the brim.

It was like a river had suddenly sprung to life, right there in the centre of the room.

Ailsa was about to turn to her friends when she heard a low growl, followed almost immediately, from the other side, by a loud, rasping *mEEEHHHHHHH*.

Whipping around to see what was causing the commotion, Ailsa was shocked to see – no one at all. No Credenza, no Ozzie, and no Tobias. In their places were…

Other things.

Ossian was no longer a sloping pre-teen and had apparently transformed into a surprised-looking timber wolf. (That was the source of the growling.)

Tobias, for his part, was now a bleating goat.

As for Credenza. Well, sorry to say, she was a cabbage. A small, round, light green cabbage.

Ailsa rubbed her eyes. This could not be happening. *And yet.*

The Tobias-goat spoke first. It had his voice, but with added goaty gravitas.

"The Shee love puzzles," the goat-Tobias said. "She's making you earn the meeting by taking us all across the river."

"What? How?"

"Did you miss the boat?" purred a voice behind her. It was wolf-Ozzie, licking his lips as he stared over at Tobias the goat. Instinct was starting to take over. Ailsa glanced across to the near side of the river where a small wooden boat was tethered to the stone bank, bobbing happily along with the gentle current. On the other bank was a tiny jetty.

"Stop staring at me like that!" bleated Tobias.

He was staring at wolf-Ozzie, who was salivating.

"I can't help it," said Ozzie. "Maybe just one bite?"

"We don't have time for this!" said Ailsa.

"It's our only chance to stop them," said Tobias. "You have to figure out a way to get us all across that river to the other side."

"What is happening to me?" shrieked a high-pitched voice that sounded a lot like Credenza. Ailsa bent down and picked up the cabbage.

"Denzie?" said Ailsa.

Now it was Tobias's turn to lick his lips. If there's one thing a goat cannot resist, it's fresh green cabbage.

"Help me!" said the small green Credenza.

"I'm trying!" said Ailsa. "Now everyone stay where they are while I think."

"How about we all get into the boat," said Ossian. "Problem solved."

"There's only space for two at a time. And I have to be one of the two because I'm the only one who can steer the boat."

"So send Denzie over first," said Tobias.

"Good idea," said Ossian, baring his teeth. "I'll look after goat boy while you're gone."

"Err, on second thoughts," said Tobias, "take him away first."

"Better idea," said Ailsa.

This was more complicated than she had thought.

Ailsa started towards the boat, beckoning Ossian with her. As they walked, Ailsa heard a scream. She ran back to grab Tobias, who was about to take a large bite out of one of Credenza's leaves.

"Don't leave me alone with him!" she shrieked.

Ailsa rubbed her eyes. This was impossible. Wasn't it?

She felt for Grandma's postcard. Maybe the Scientific Method would help.

The boat only takes two, Ailsa thought. *Since I have to be in the boat to steer it across, that means I can only bring one of these three to the other side with me.*

Ailsa decided to State her Problem clearly once more.

"Which two can I leave alone together?"

Which boiled down to a more precise question, namely: *Which two don't find each other appetizing?*

Wolf wants the goat. Goat wants the cabbage, but...

Wolves don't eat cabbage! And cabbages don't attack wolves!

Ailsa tested her hypothesis by picking up Credenza and moving closer to Ossian-the-wolf. Denzie's unease built into a scream as she approached, but Ossian seemed utterly disinterested in any green vegetable at all.

"That's it!" said Ailsa out loud. "Tobias, get in the boat!"

Ailsa put Credenza down carefully on the floor and ran to the boat with Tobias, who was better able to balance in the tiny craft than she was. Ailsa then carefully paddled across to the other side, where Tobias leapt out. Turning back, Ailsa could see Ossian pacing next to Credenza – but neither were paying attention to each other. Ailsa grinned; she had solved the puzzle!

But as she placed Ossian on the boat for the second trip, her heart sunk. She could take him across, of course, but leaving him with Tobias would mean the wolf would eat the goat.

This wouldn't work at all.

Ailsa took Credenza the cabbage with her instead. But then she thought it through a little more. If she left the cabbage on the other side with the goat, then Tobias would eat Credenza. Which would not be ideal. How on earth was she going to solve this?

Ailsa was about to give up when she remembered her Grandma's final words on the Method. "This is really more of a circle than a list, as you will no doubt discover."

If it's a circle, thought Ailsa, *then each trip is its own experiment. Experiment, test, analyse and repeat … each time.*

Ailsa grinned and grabbed Credenza, running back to

the boat. She knew what to do. (You've probably worked it out yourself now too.)

When she arrived at the far side of the river, Ailsa placed Credenza gently down on the ground. But before Tobias was able to make a move towards her, she grabbed him back and pushed him on the boat again.

"Wait a minute, I don't want to go baaaaaack there..." he said.

But that's exactly where Ailsa was taking him.

When they arrived, she leapt out and dragged him back on to the bank, taking care to stand between him and wolf-Ossian.

"Just you now. On you get."

Ossian glared at her, growling all the while, but he sloped off and into the boat, taking care not to get any part of his fur wet. Tobias looked at Ailsa in admiration.

"I get it now," he said.

"Nearly there," said Ailsa.

Returning Ossian to the far bank, she already knew (thanks to her previous experiment) that wolves and cabbages didn't try to eat each other. So, by the time she had returned for Tobias and deposited him on the far shore, all three of her friends were in one piece.

The moment Tobias's hooves touched the far side of the room, all three of them transformed back into their human forms. The door swung open, and Lady Blackthorn could be seen applauding politely within. As she ran inside, Ailsa glanced back for a final look at the puzzling river, only to find it was, once again, a long blue carpet.

"Not too shabby," cooed Lady Blackthorn as they entered.

"You know what?" said Ozzie, brushing the fur off his arm. "I think I'm done with puzzles for a while."

CHAPTER 49

THE SMALL WHITE COTTAGE

They stood in a vast chamber, like the drawing room of a stately home. Lady Blackthorn sat in a chair before a roaring fire, propped up by a tower of purple velvet cushions. There were guards here too, standing ominously in the shadows, the light of the flames dancing on their axe blades.

"The thing you must understand," said Lady Blackthorn, "is that the Laird is an irredeemably awful man."

Ailsa was pacing, wracked with anxiety at the passing seconds. Time was literally slipping through their fingers now. This was their last chance to change things. "This is so much more important than two people," she said. "Why can't you see that?"

"My idea was a wonderful trick. The way things have

gone recently… Well, it's all his fault, of course. That smelly oaf."

"The Laird agreed to help us if you do too."

"Ha! An agreement, with that man? I doubt that very much!"

"But you agree the Magic Hour must be stopped?"

Lady Blackthorn shrugged, like a child getting bored of a game. Ailsa had seen this attitude before. The Shee, for all their powers, seemed to behave a lot like teenagers.

Lady Blackthorn looked up for a second and saw Tobias staring at her. "Don't I know you?" she asked.

Tobias said, "You might remember me from above the hill."

"I remember it now. You were a Mouldy One once."

"You stole me from my family."

"Probably for the best, wouldn't you say? I mean, just look at them."

Tobias broiled in silence.

Ailsa moved closer to him and took his hand. Then, in as calm a voice as she could muster, she said, "Tobias, we can't do this now."

Tobias gritted his teeth but nodded.

Ailsa tried to picture her grandma's face to calm herself down. She had overcome so many more obstacles than this! How would she approach the problem? As she pictured her grandma, the smell of the perfect tomato suddenly came to Ailsa again, wafting over to her, stronger than ever before.

Lady Blackthorn noticed her expression change.

"We are asking you to help us," Ailsa said.

"Yes, I noticed that," said Lady Blackthorn. "But you're troubled. What is it?"

Ailsa felt tears welling up in her eyes. "Why do I keep smelling old memories here?" she asked.

Lady Blackthorn smiled. "That is more than memories. We sit outside of the regular flow of time here. The past and the present tend to fold over each other in places like this. A strong memory, from a time before, can easily germinate and blossom into the present – if only for a few moments."

"You mean … become real?"

Lady Blackthorn nodded. "If the memory is strong enough."

As Ailsa turned away from the fire, she saw it. At first, she thought it might have been a trick of the light.

There was a lead-lined windowpane nearby, giving a view of a large paved terrace outside. Suddenly there appeared, in the centre of that terrace, a small white cottage, trellised and bright.

Her grandparents' cottage.

Happily sitting there.

Ailsa stared. The apple tree in the front garden was wafting gently in a breeze. It almost looked like the sun was shining, a golden beam filtering down on it from above.

"Charming. Must be a strong memory of yours."

"It's real?"

"I'd go say hello if I were you; be rude not to, quite honestly."

"My grandparents…?"

"Well, it's your memory. You'll know better than I."

"But…" said Ailsa, her stomach churning. "But we don't have time. We don't have enough time for that."

"Now then," said Lady Blackthorn, her eyes full of cruel judgement, "exactly whose fault is that?"

Ailsa vowed to herself: she would never be late for anything again. Every second truly counted and this was the moment she knew it for sure. As Ailsa turned, to her horror the cottage faded and vanished. Try as she might, she couldn't summon the memory again; she thought she might collapse in sadness.

But there were more important things to do, here and now.

Things like saving the world.

"Looks like you lost the chance. Ah, you mouldy little

things," said Lady Blackthorn. "There's no changing you, is there? Well, most of you, at least." She winked at Tobias, and he dug his nails into his fists. He knew they needed her. He would have his revenge another day.

Lady Blackthorn's words landed hard for Ailsa, like cups breaking on hard kitchen tiles. She remembered how, in the bad old days, her parents had said things like that to each other, during the divorce. If the volcano experiment had a language, it sounded a lot like that.

But Ailsa also knew how her mum and dad had learned to stop arguing. A common enemy, Ailsa had always noticed, could bring together all kinds of different people.

Which is why, when she turned back to rejoin Lady Blackthorn, she already had an idea. She moved to Virgil, but her words were interrupted by a bell.

Only the final bell to come.

Virgil raised an eyebrow at her.

"We need more time," she said.

Virgil shook his head. "I'm afraid this is all the time you have." Ailsa wasn't sure, but she thought she heard Lady Blackthorn chuckle.

CHAPTER 50

COMMON GROUND

It was a strip of land, halfway across a river, on the road to the Wilds. On one side stood Lady Blackthorn, shivering under a tartan shawl. On the other stood the Laird of the Wilds, arms folded, staring at the ground.

Virgil Merrimack, Credenza and Ossian stood with Lady Blackthorn, while Tobias stood on the far side with the Laird.

Ailsa knew she had never been able to help her parents find common ground, as much as she had tried, and as much as they had told her it wasn't her job. This time would be different, she thought. To save the world it had to be.

The Laird looked down at soggy fronds of kelp as they emerged from the river. They snaked across the muddy ground towards him, curling around his ankles, wrapping ever tighter.

"Tell this *flamfoo*[50] to ditch the cheesy magic," said the Laird, not looking at her. "It's embarrassing."

"Lady Blackthorn, you promised!" yelled Ailsa.

Her Ladyship shrugged and sighed, and the conjured fronds retreated into the murk of the river.

"I told you this was no use; she'd drown me sooner than talk."

"He's not wrong," said Her Ladyship.

This was going nowhere fast.

"Now listen," said Ailsa. She looked to each of them in turn. "We are agreed the Magic Hour must end. For your own sake, as well as ours. To do that, we need you both to work together."

"Fat chance," said the Laird. "We're chalk and cheese."

Or vinegar and baking soda, thought Ailsa.

"And yet," said Ailsa, "Your Ladyship, is it not true that you despise that man?" She pointed at the Laird.

She nodded, sniffing. "Desperately."

Ailsa turned now to the Laird. "And you, Your Lairdship, loathe her equally."

The Laird nodded, arms folded, not looking at Lady Blackthorn. "With a passion."

---

50 A word that is frankly not very nice, so we won't go into its meaning here.

"And yet you both deny you share anything in common?" said Ailsa.

At this, both the Laird and Lady Blackthorn glared at Ailsa, then met each other's eyes. Finally, accepting the point, they nodded.

Ailsa smiled. "It appears you already have much common ground," she said, "in that you both find the other very annoying."

"Your point?" sniped Lady Blackthorn.

"What's more, you are both talented at bearing grudges."

"It's a gift," grunted the Laird.

"But there's another, more potent grudge. One you both share."

"Who?"

"The Mouldy Ones, as you call us. Humans."

Credenza and Ossian stared at Ailsa.

"Um," said Ozzie, "maybe don't remind them of that right now, Ailsa?" Credenza nudged him in the ribs. She was starting to understand what Ailsa was doing.

"We have no problem with you," said the Laird.

"Are you sure about that?"

"You're all ridiculous and annoying," added Lady Blackthorn. "That's why I played this trick on you. And you smell. But the very idea that you little people might cause us problems? Nonsense."

"Virgil, tell them what we have discovered."

"It appears…" started Virgil, unable to utter what he knew to be true. "It appears the Brollachan is now at large."

Both the Lady's and the Laird's eyes popped out.

"How?" they both said at once. "It was sequestered. We agreed it would never be allowed out."

"Professor Munro released it," said Ailsa.

"Possibly by accident," added Virgil, "but from the looks of it, it seems he did open the door."

"He did *what*?"

"As I was saying," said Ailsa triumphantly. "Your grudge involves one mouldy human in particular."

CHAPTER 51

FINAL BELL

The Laird and Lady Blackthorn strode together across the square. All eyes were on the Laird and his retinue of bodyguards, four strong-looking women all holding their Lochaber axes[51] at the ready.

"Your guards try anything, and mine will make soup of them," the Laird growled.

"You're quite safe," said Lady Blackthorn, "so long as you behave."

Ailsa and the others followed at speed as they approached the Tron tower. Tobias caught Ailsa's eye and he lifted his head as if to say *we're going up there*.

"I like what you've done with the place," said the Laird as they approached the tower doors.

---

51   Lochaber axes are just like regular axes on poles, only larger, heavier, nastier. Best avoided.

"Kind of you to say," said Lady Blackthorn. "New carpet."

The two of them stopped at the door. The Laird was holding the door handle next to Lady Blackthorn's hand. Their hands were nearly touching. The Laird moved closer to her.

"You sure about this?" he said.

Lady Blackthorn's face looked like it might burst into another cruel barb. Perhaps it was the proximity, perhaps seeing his face, perhaps a whole host of other things we will never understand, but she met his eye with a look of understanding and respect.

"Restraining that creature was the key to peace."

"It was. I don't want war with you."

"Neither do I."

The Laird nodded, satisfied she was telling the truth. Then a thought landed, and a tiny smile bloomed in his eyes.

"You know, Effeny, the place will be a lot quieter."

Lady Blackthorn's face flashed in surprise. You probably know this already, but fairies like the Shee rarely, if ever, use their true, real names. Names are things of enormous power. When they do use them, it is a sign of friendship and trust.

"Indeed it will, Crannog."

The Laird's eyes burned with the same surprise.

They'd called each other, directly, by their true names. Trust was building.

"There are other tricks to play on them, you know that."

Lady Blackthorn smiled. "Aye, I know."

They looked at each other.

"You've a goosegog berry in your beard," she said.

"That's my piece." He smiled back. "Keeping it for later."

Together, they pushed the door and ran up the stairs.

Ailsa turned to beckon Credenza but saw her eyes were far away, on the Middlemarket.

"They're going to close it down now, aren't they?"

Ailsa nodded. Credenza bit her lip. She was staring at the top floor of the Exchange building. There were still lights on up there, glowing like a beacon in the gloomy light.

A bell tolled. The final bell. A deep, sonorous clang.

The sky darkened further, a wash of ink flowing into the air.

"Credenza, come on!"

Credenza tugged at Ossian. "I need to speak to Dad," she said. "He'll be trapped in here!"

She was already running across the square, making a beeline for the entrance to the Exchange.

Ossian shouted after her. "Denzie, come back! We'll find him together!"

But Credenza wasn't paying attention. Ailsa looked at

Tobias, whose eyes were on the Laird and Lady as they ascended to the roof.

"Ozzie, please, go find her. Then get out while you still can."

"What about you?"

"I'm the one who led you in here, I should make sure I'm the last to leave."

"But Denzie's the one—"

"Just go, OK?"

Ozzie saw the fire in her eyes and didn't wait. He sprinted after Credenza, who was rushing in through the main doors of the Exchange.

"He's probably left already," said Tobias.

"Then they'll have more time to make it to the gate," said Ailsa as she ran up the stairs to the roof.

At the top of the tower, out of breath, Ailsa saw the Lady and Laird move to opposite sides of the flagpole. The Laird removed one of his necklaces and held it up to the light – the shape of a sun. Lady Blackthorn, for her part, did the same on the other side. Her key was a crescent moon.

"We'll have peace?" said the Laird.

"We'll see," said Lady Blackthorn.

"You'll spoil Sandy Munro's peace, that's for sure," said Ailsa.

The Laird and Lady looked at her curiously.

"Good mischief," said Lady Blackthorn, smiling at the idea. "You sure you're not fairy-born? There's something under-the-hill about you, no doubt."

"Born at midnight," said the Laird, smiling. "I'd wager it. With a rowan by her window. She's not like the others."

Tobias looked at Ailsa suddenly, the words landing with him.

"Were you?" he said.

"What?"

"Born at midnight."

"Um, yes, I think so," said Ailsa. "Why?"

Tobias said nothing. Ailsa knew him better now. He usually went quiet when there was something else more important to say.

"Let me guess: you'll tell me later?"

Tobias smiled and nodded.

The Laird and Lady placed their keys in the slots. The sun and the moon, turning together. One full rotation ended in a deep, sonorous click.

There was silence, for a moment.

Then came the explosion.

Not of sound but of light. A beam of vibrant, glowing purple erupted up from the flagpole to the ceiling of the sky. The entire plaza lit up in a violet glow (which is not an easy feat to pull off when you're a plaza).

"What is that?" said Ailsa.

"The old magic," said Tobias. "Don't look at it."

The glow pulsed and warmed, growing brighter and brighter. It began to hum slightly, not a sea shanty or an Irish jig but something more portentous and altogether loud, something akin to a thousand monks singing their lowest note, or the sound continents make when they bump up against each other. The hum deepened and broadened into a rib-shaking, apocalyptic rumble. The beam then flashed and split into four, like a quartet of searchlights seeking out their compass points.

Now the hum was a musical chord – not one of the nice ones, either, but something that promised strange and disturbing things in the very near future.

Lady Blackthorn and the Laird then began to sing in harmony – slow, deliberate, commanding – taking that chord and somehow completing it with their two melodies.

To the north port, the south, the west and the east
Pull up the drawbridge, imprison the beast.

"Take cover," said the Laird.

Ailsa and Tobias were already diving to the floor.

They scrambled over to a corner of the tower balcony for shelter as the southern and the eastern beams of violet light lowered, growing ever brighter in their power, ever louder in their bone-rattling hum, stretching out across the entire Middlemarket to the very ports themselves. Ailsa had clamped her eyes shut. But had she opened them, she would have seen the same thing happen on the other side, with the northern and western beams dipping equally low, their power hitting similar flagpoles on the ports at the other far edges of the city.

"Causeway Port, sealed. Marlin Gate, sealed," said Virgil, crawling over to them as they cowered.

They heard an almighty roar, a deafening cataclysm that drowned out the guttural hums. It sounded like a vast stone wall falling (which is, in many ways, exactly what it was). The beam to the south flared just as bright, and another crunching, grinding noise filled Ailsa's ears.

And then, just like that, all was silent.

"Only the Niddry Port remains, to the west," said Virgil.

"That one you can close yourself, when you leave," said the Laird.

It hit Ailsa that she hasn't even thought about that.

"Only if it's nearly shut," said Tobias. "And right now, it's not even close."

Even the hum had faded away. Ailsa's ears were ringing, but the air was full of nothing else but silence.

Sometimes, silence is a good thing. Peace, tranquillity and calm. Other times, silence suggests that something terrible has happened and that nothing can be done about it.

This was one of those silences.

"Why ever not?" said the Laird. "What happened to the beam?"

"The light … is blocked," said Lady Blackthorn.

There was something in her voice that Ailsa had not heard before.

Fear.

The beam of light aimed to the west was indeed blocked.

Standing there was Sandy Munro. The light striking him squarely in the chest. His mouth foaming, eyes red as coals.

CHAPTER 52

THE BATTLE OF THE TRON

You already know the truth, of course. Sandy Munro was no longer Sandy Munro.

The Brollachan had him fully now.

In his hand, a Lochaber axe, his knuckles white with the weight of it. Dark patches streaked across the blade. Down below in the tower, no doubt, were injured guards, or worse.

"The beast!" screamed Lady Blackthorn.

"Save yourselves!" shouted the Laird. "Guards!"

But Sandy Munro's feet were planted firmly on top of the access hatch. His body, plus the weight of the axe, proved too much for the brave guards pushing and shoving from below. Imagine trying to force open a heavy door using only a piece of cheese, and you'll get the idea of how challenging this was.

But don't imagine it too much. We need our attention here at the top of the Tron tower.

Here, where Sandy Munro was moving.

With his foot, he was pushing the bolt on top of the access hatch. He moved it carefully but forcefully across to the other side, the metal shrieking as he locked the hatch shut.

There was a moment of calm, as if nothing else would happen. But of course, it did. Faster than you're even thinking it right now.

He leapt at Tobias first, a bolt of pure fury and power, grabbing his shoulder with extraordinary strength and flinging him over the side of the tower like he was a pebble.

Ailsa screamed but then remembered Tobias's secret. She listened for impact but heard only an irritated feline screech. Her friend was safe. She hoped.[52]

Virgil shook in his boots, removing a small mini axe from a hidden pouch on his belt. It looked more like a Swiss army knife than any kind of meaningful weapon. (A Swiss army knife, in case you don't know what one is, looks like all the things you might need in the cutlery drawer, all at once, but sharper. But here it seemed

---

52   He was. But go back to the action now, it's getting exciting.

utterly useless. It might as well have been a spork.)[53]
"May I have that please?" said Ailsa. Virgil gave it to her.

"What shall be done?" said Lady Blackthorn.

The Laird stepped in front of her.

"Let him take me should he wish," he growled.

"If the beam is broken, the gate won't shut!" shouted Virgil.

"We have a bigger problem right now," said the Laird.

But Ailsa had an idea. She sprung up, climbing the great stone base of the flagpole, holding Virgil's blade between her teeth. She jumped down the other side, grabbing a length of halyard rope as she fell. She tried to slice it with Virgil's knife, but the blade was too dull.

That was when Sandy Munro swung his axe at Virgil.

Ailsa saw it in time and in one movement pushed him away from the blade, dragging the flagpole rope before her. The axe missed Virgil, but struck the halyard rope with full force, splitting it in two. A shower of sparks rained down over the rooftop, and for a moment the Laird's beard caught fire (Lady Blackthorn swiftly patted it out).

Ailsa passed her length of rope to Virgil and shouted

---

53   A spork is a spoon that's also a fork. Anyway, what are you doing all the way down here? There's a fight going on.

to the Laird and Lady, throwing them the other end of the rope. The plan was clear. All four nodded, and as one they looped the length of rope up and over the back of Sandy Munro, dropping it to his ankles.

Then heaved with all their might.

The rope pulled taut and took his feet away.

As he lay on the ground, the Laird leapt on top of him.

Ailsa pulled the bolt back on the hatch and guard after guard spilled back out on to the roof of the tower.

The Laird and Lady ran down the spiral stairs, followed by Virgil and Ailsa.

Ailsa sprinted into the middle of the square. Glancing up at the Exchange building, she could see that all the lights were out. It was night-time in the Middlemarket now, and as far as she could hear, there was no bell. The air was getting colder by the second.

Virgil looked at her, shaken but grateful.

The Laird and Lady came to her next.

"Thank you," said the Laird. "But I'm afraid the final gate is not yet closed."

Reading Ailsa's concern, Lady Blackthorn continued. "The beam was cut too soon. Instead of pulling it to, after you, you will have to close the whole thing by hand yourself."

Ailsa was about to ask how on earth she was supposed to do that, when the Laird and Lady handed over their sun and moon keys. She took them, one in each hand, and gulped.

"You can't do it yourselves?" she asked.

"With only one port open, the area around it will feel like a whirlpool. To stand on the edge risks us falling into it. We cannot risk being dragged over the hill into your world."

Ailsa listened for signs of the bell but could hear nothing. She could feel sharp stabs of discomfort in her eyes. Tears would not be far away. She gritted her teeth, determined to stay focused.

"What if I can't close it?"

Virgil stared at her and then threw a glance at Lady Blackthorn.

"Let's take one thing at a time, shall we?" said Lady Blackthorn.

"Come with me," said Virgil. "Try not to let anyone see you. In fact, wait. Inside the Tron is a passageway—"

"I know," said Ailsa, already springing ahead of him.

As Ailsa dashed back into the darkness of the tower, the Laird and Lady waited in silence. Far above, they could hear an almighty battle between Sandy Munro and their guards. It wasn't clear who was winning.

Laird and Lady looked at each other for a moment. A tenderness glowed in their eyes.

"I'm hungry," said the Laird.

"You were always hungry, Crannog," said Lady Blackthorn.

"We used to make chutney, Effeny, do you remember?" said the Laird. "Before they came."

"I do miss that," she said.

"Chutney-making is more fun than prank-pulling."

"Depends on the prank."

"And the chutney, no doubt."

"Well," said Lady Blackthorn, plucking a hidden gooseberry from the Laird's beard, "it'll have goosegog in it, that's for sure."

They chuckled, surprised at how pleasant the sound was.

One of their guards broke the moment with a bellow from the top of the tower.

"He has broken through! Run for your lives!"

Sandy Munro burst through the main doors. But the Laird and Lady were already sprinting away into the darkened alleyways of the Middlemarket.

The Brollachan, who at this point was deeply

enjoying this new home's features, turned Sandy's nose up into the air.

The daffodil hat, it thought.

Now there's an idea.

CHAPTER 53

THE HOURGLASS

Ailsa and Virgil emerged from the tunnel next to the blood-red door. Ailsa dashed inside for a moment as Virgil stared, aghast.

"What on earth are you doing?" he asked.

Ailsa appeared a moment later, her yellow hat in hand. "It's my favourite hat," she said.

Moments later they stood in the Reckoning Room, the pencil-thin clerks barely visible in the dying light. They seemed different now, as did everything in the Middlemarket after the final bell. Their smiles seemed sinister. Their skin, parchment. Their eyes, cruel.

But beneath the cruelty was a deeper truth: all of them were, in their own way, a little scared of Virgil Merrimack.

He was, after all, their boss.

Virgil pulled himself up to his full height, which was not particularly impressive. So he puffed out his chest and stomach for good measure, and strode confidently up to one of the clerks.

"Morag, we need an urgent overdraft."

Morag the clerk stared up at him, terrified. She wasn't sure she had heard him correctly.

"Is it pre-arranged?" said a neighbouring clerk.

"It is not."

"We'll need to get to it later," they said. "Unauthorized overdrafts are not…" He searched for the word. "Authorized."

"Well, Morag," said Virgil, "authorize one now, will you?"

She stared at him for a moment, appalled to have been singled out for this test of loyalty. She stood up, sighed audibly, and disappeared into a small cupboard nearby. When she emerged, she held in her hands the most beautiful object Ailsa had ever seen.

An audible tut could be heard from her neighbouring clerks. But Ailsa was too focused on the thing in her hands to care.

"These are the sands of time," said Virgil.

Ailsa stared at the hourglass, a glorious, flowing mechanism of warm woods and burnished metal. The two bulbs were held together by the tiniest swirling filaments of wire, as if they were suspended in air all by themselves. The grains inside pulsed smoothly down from the upper bulb into the lower chamber. They seemed to glow with life itself. They dripped in a hypnotic, steady rhythm that felt, to Ailsa, like a heartbeat.

"Ailsa, the grains must keep moving, do you understand?"

Ailsa nodded.

"Keep the grains moving," she repeated.

"Do that, and you'll be spared. Oh. And whatever you do," he whispered, "don't drop it."

"Don't drop it," she said again.

The grains flowed down and the sands in the upper chamber diminished. She would soon have to turn it upside down again. She wondered how long she had left.

A thought prodded her, and she prodded back.

"But how do I pay for it?"

"You saved me from the Brollachan," said Virgil. "If it comes to it, I'll find a way to settle your account myself. Now hurry, you must reach the west gate and finish the job."

"Me? Aren't you coming?"

Virgil started backing away. "Like the Laird said, I can't risk being pulled into your world," he said. "You will have to lock the gate manually, and the pull of time could drag me under. Use the keys the Laird and Lady gave you. The sun and the moon will lead the way. I'm sure you'll be fine."

"Fine?" shouted Ailsa as he turned and ran away. "But there's only one of me and two keys! Who's going to help me with those?"

As if in answer to her question, a soft furry tail curled around her feet.

CHAPTER 54

HELL'S BELLS

Ailsa and Sydekyck sprinted across the rooftops, and believe me if you could have seen what they could see, you'd be sprinting too. It was after the final bell in the Middlemarket, and the darkness was everywhere.

The colour was leaching from the buildings and the people. Gossamer, moonbeam and silver was all that they could see. Sydekyck was leading the way, with Ailsa lagging behind as she tried to balance speed with her grip on the hourglass, which was slippery and unwieldy; and navigating the shadowy slopes of roofing slate, which was nearly impossible.

They reached the final staircase, ran up to the last gate and gasped. The arch was still there, but a stone drawbridge was visible beyond it, stuck fast with barely enough space for a human to squeeze through. The vortex was dragging Ailsa back, like the first time she had stayed past final bell. The temptation to let go and fall into the void was almost too much.

Sydekyck leapt up daintily on to the chains that held the door open for now and jumped down. When Ailsa looked back, he was Tobias again.

"There are two holes in the pillars, same as at the Tron."

"So we use the keys?"

"That's the idea. But—the second you turn, you run, OK? I'll make sure the portal closes fully once you're over to the other side."

"What about you? Aren't you coming?"

Tobias shot her a look of the deepest sadness and yearning.

"You will survive the journey. I would not." Ailsa placed the hourglass carefully on the cobbled street, taking care as she did so to turn it over. The grains regrouped and commenced falling once more. She then clambered into the space between the stone drawbridge and the infinite black beyond.

"Careful you don't slip," she said, placing her "sun" key in the slot to the left.

"No need to remind me," said Tobias, placing his "moon" key in the right-hand slot. His previous words suddenly landing with Ailsa.

"But wait, I thought you were human. You'd survive if you were human, right?"

Tobias said: "My true name is Mackay. Tobias Mackay of Dalkeith. They renamed me Ragwort when they stole me away. But Ailsa, I may be human, but in your years I am old. I was born sixty years before you. If I was to pass over to your world, there's no telling what would happen to me."

Ailsa absorbed this news as best she could. She also did a quick calculation.

"So your parents might still be alive?"

Tobias nodded, a deep hurt glowing in his eyes. "It's possible, I suppose. No way of knowing now."

Ailsa was in such shock that she lost her balance and slipped down the steep slope of the drawbridge.

Straight into the hourglass.

It shuddered and shook.

Then it broke into smithereens.

"Turn the key!" said Tobias, but then he turned back to see Ailsa, standing over the sand and broken glass at her feet.

A hooded woman approached, flanked by two guards who now stood between Ailsa and the gate.

The woman held out her hand. "Reckoning."

"I'm sorry?"

The hood came down and there was Morag, the clerk. She seemed much less pleasant here in the shadows. Which wasn't saying much.

"Your voucher? But since it's gone final bell, it had better be a receipt. Unless you're trying to skip out without paying at all…"

"But my account was settled! Mr Merrimack said he'd pay it for me."

"How convenient. I assume you have signed paper-work?"

Ailsa looked at the ground, broken.

"Didn't think so." She glanced up at Tobias on the drawbridge. "I'd be careful you don't go to dust looking in there, chaff," Morag said to Tobias, who nodded meekly and clambered down.

Both of their keys were still in the slots, unturned.

"So, I'm afraid you are in default," said Morag.

The way Morag was smiling at her made Ailsa think she wasn't really that afraid at all.

"What about a guarantor? I thought that's how it works here?"

"They most certainly will pay, should you step back into your world. But the debt would be considerable."

Ailsa stared Morag straight in the eye. "I refuse to use a guarantor. I will pay my debt myself."

Morag stared at her blankly for a moment. "I've never heard anyone say that here before."

"Take the time from me," said Ailsa.

"Are you sure about that?" asked Morag.

A smell drifted over to Ailsa in that moment.

The scent of the most perfect tomato in the world. Ailsa looked over and there, before the open gate, like a tollbooth in the sun, was her grandparents' cottage. Seconds earlier, there had been the cold hard stone of the Middlemarket. Now, there was a patch of lush grass and a beam of golden sunlight on the garden gate.

Just sitting there, in the sunshine, in the middle of the road.

Ailsa stared. Morag approached a little more kindly. "Since you're settling your own account, I can let you say hello for a minute. If you like. Not everyone gets another chance to say goodbye to someone properly, do they?"

Ailsa stared back over to the cottage and met the bright smiling eyes of her grandma, pruning shears in hand, as she emerged from the front door.

CHAPTER 55

THE MOMENT

The minutes slowed to seconds and the seconds slowed even further than that. Whatever atomic tick or quantum tock that time really was, the ancient river that carries us all, all of it that was around her and under her feet, between her toes and surging past her ankles. All of that seemed to stop.

Ailsa was in the moment, a moment she had craved for years.

More time with her grandparents.

The Laird was right, thought Ailsa, as all other thoughts drifted away. *We don't move through time, time moves through us.*

She moved over to her grandma.

She was wearing the cornflower-blue shirt she often wore when gardening. Ailsa rubbed her eyes. But Grandma was still there when she opened them again. She walked first, and then ran. She swung the gate open, and the smell of freshly cut grass filled her nostrils. Grandma gathered up Ailsa in a giant embrace. She smelled of sun cream and old perfume and fresh laundry. Ailsa held her back to gaze at her, a big silly smile on her face. When she looked up again, eyes wet, she saw Grandpa in the doorway, also grinning.

"What a surprise! What are you doing here?" said Grandma.

"I don't really know, but ... I missed you..."

"Well, same here, dear. Why, you'd better come in. Grandpa's made some tea, which is cause for celebration in itself."

As they walked in, Ailsa looked back at Tobias, who nodded at her to go, go. Ailsa turned to Grandma.

"Are you real?"

Grandma pinched her forearm. "Feels like it to me."

Ailsa blinked.

"I don't understand how this can be happening."

"It's certainly odd, I agree. An unexplained phenomenon. What do we do, Ailsa, with things we cannot yet explain?"

"We apply the Method?"

Grandma grinned. "Precisely."

"The Method doesn't work here, Grandma."

"You're sure about that, are you?" She smiled.

"Pretty sure."

"The Method works *everywhere* you apply it, my dear. It's whether or not you understand the answers, *that* is the work."

Ailsa walked in, where she was embraced by the smell of the past, the comfort of all things that were. All of it seemed so much smaller, but then of course, all our pasts do that when we visit them. Like the senior school kid walking past the primary school playground; everything seemed bigger back then. She hugged Grandpa, settled herself down on the old brown armchair, and asked them both all the things she had always wondered about, the questions that she had never thought to ask before the moment she knew she could never ask again.

But first, she asked how much Grandma knew about the Magic Hour. About how it was possible that Ailsa had found it. After all, her first time here hadn't been at the usual gates. It had been at home, in the garden shed. How was that even possible?

"You were a midnight child, my dear," said Grandma with a smile. "And midnight children are doubly blessed. Because of the accident of your birth, some paths that are closed to others are open to you. Of course you found your way here."

As she talked, the truth came as clear to Ailsa as

anything she had ever known. That what matters in life is love, and that the memory of those moments mean that love will never die.

When at last it was the moment to say goodbye, Ailsa told them both that she loved them. She spoke her words loudly and clearly so that her words would be truly heard.

They were.

It was then that she heard a scratching sound at the door.

Ailsa glanced up to see Sydekyck pawing at the window. There's a particular expression on a cat's face when things are not to his or her liking. A narrowing of the pupils, and a snarl of concern. If you can imagine a cat doing this, as someone trod heavily upon their tail – this is what Sydekyck's face looked like right.

Sounds of a commotion outside made Ailsa jump up from her armchair and run to the door. She turned back to see Grandma and Grandpa, smiling by the fireplace, a pose she would for ever remember them in.

"Thank you for tea," said Ailsa.

"Anytime," said Grandma.

CHAPTER 56

CLOSING TIME

Ailsa yanked open the door and sprinted outside. Behind her, with every step, the cottage faded into vapour, and a heavy darkness wrapped itself around her like a blanket. Tears came quickly, like a summer mist, and drenched her face as she ran.

Sydekyck was now Tobias and Ailsa felt him take her hand. She welcomed the contact, and it helped her steel herself for what lay ahead.

"The port is closing!" Ailsa said.

"By itself?"

"Worse. Look!"

There in the drawbridge was Sandy Munro, a mere puppet now, every string controlled by the Brollachan. A spindle of white mist had stretched from his fingers all the way to the keys. A single person would never be able to turn both keys at the same time as was required.

A Brollachan, however, could.

The keys began to turn, and a great rumbling shook the streets. Roof slates began to fall, and Sandy Munro stared at Ailsa as he dived back into the darkness.

The drawbridge closed further, its gap now far too small for a human. Ailsa couldn't breathe. She was trapped here – for ever.

Tobias turned to her. "You were born at midnight? That's true?"

Ailsa nodded.

"Then you have the gift. Which means you're ready."

"For what?" Ailsa remembered Grandma's words. *Some paths that are closed to others are open to you.* She was about to ask him again when he grabbed both her hands and closed his eyes. In that moment Ailsa felt a surge of energy spread from her hands to every molecule of her body.

"What's happening?"

"We're the same, Ailsa, you and I. Midnight children. If you truly have the gift, I can bequeath my power to you."

"The power to what?"

Ailsa felt her hair retreat into her head. This is not something most people have ever felt, and it must be said that the feeling is not at all pleasant. Ailsa didn't have time to process much of this as her entire body now began to shorten, her muscles grew taut, her eyes seeing not only the shadows but the light and shape of everything. She could see the veins on leaves, the ears on ants, the cloud of menace that spewed forth from the nostrils of Sandy Munro. In all the confusion and shock, her mind suddenly recalled in perfect detail Dr Matthews's lesson on states of matter. He had made the entire class take a beaker of water, freeze it, then boil it, and condense it again back to water. Solids, liquids and gas. That was the only way she could describe what was happening to her: she was ice and water and steam all at the same time.

She fell down on all fours, a tail suddenly flitting back and forth behind her. Wait, a *tail*? *She had a tail now?*

Looking up at Tobias, so tall and pale and slow now with her new eyes, she suddenly knew what had happened. She had changed state and so had he.

She was a shape-shifter now. A real one.

"There you are," he said. His voice sounded deeper and almost glacial. She was living at a different frequency, a new octave.

"I can change," said Ailsa.

"You just did," said Tobias. "Now go, while you can."

Ailsa looked up to see the gap in the gate. It was tiny, far too narrow for a human. But the perfect size for a cat.

"How can I repay this power back to you?"

"The gift, once given, is gone for ever."

Ailsa tried to speak but found she had no words.

Tobias continued: "There's a cost to everything in this world, Ailsa. I thought you would have understood that by now."

A grinding sound made Ailsa's fur stand on end. Working now on instinct, she sprinted up the ever-closing chain to the highest, widest point of the closing drawbridge.

Ailsa was off in a flash. Behind her, out of her sight, the two guards saw her move and shouted strange words into the shadows. The shadows, as if obeying, moved after her and she thought she heard Tobias scream in warning.

With a single leap, Ailsa landed on the very top of the stone, her claws sinking impossibly into the grooves of rock, somehow finding purchase and toeholds. With a final scrambling leap, she was out and over the side, into a tunnel of profound darkness.

Far ahead, she could see a single point of light.

It would take all her effort to reach it now.

But reaching it was her only chance.

A flash of searing pain hit her as she landed. The tip of her tail was caught somehow. Curling back in fury, she saw them.

Two creatures, dashing into the gap after her.

Two shadows that now pursued her.

Whether it was her feline instinct or her human-based knowledge, we shall never know. But Ailsa knew immediately what those shadows were.

CHAPTER 57

HOW TO EVADE A NIGHT GLOAMING

The Gloamings did indeed have yellow eyes, thick haunches and a metallic tinge to their fur. What Ailsa had not predicted was their jaws. They were sharp, slavering things, pointy like an anteater, wide enough to vacuum up a room. One of them had caught her tail in its teeth and was holding on grimly. The other was racing ahead over her, claws gripping the walls of the tunnel, spiralling up towards the tiny spot of light that Ailsa could see at the far end.

These were Night Gloamings, all right.

As clearly as Ailsa had first imagined them.

They grunted and scroffled behind her, making noises identical to the ones Ailsa had heard in the back garden that night. (Sometimes it's not fun to be proven right.) As one sunk its teeth down ever deeper into her tail, its companion was far ahead of her, ripping and tearing up the only way out for Ailsa. The light, once a shining star, began to fade. The Gloaming was eating the last shred of light in Ailsa's world.

But now Ailsa's claws were getting purchase on the walls of the tunnel. The cold stone was getting warmer, softer. The smell hit her immediately. This was wood. She was climbing up through a dark wooden tunnel.

How could that be?

No matter. First, she had a tail to get back. She flicked it, left and right, the tunnel getting ever steeper now, almost vertical, the Night Gloaming behind her clinging on to her with all its might. An idea struck Ailsa as she ran, and she leapt, suddenly, from side to side inside the tunnel, from wall to wall.

Now the Gloaming knew what it felt like to be the ringer inside a bell. It smashed against the wood, left, right, left again, until its jaw connected with the side and it let go.

Ailsa was free. But the second Gloaming had been hungry.

Ahead of her, there was hardly any light left at all.

But now, at least it had grown larger. She was close. She scrambled up, and the Gloaming turned to her with its boiling yellow eyes and roared. It leapt at her, but as a cat, Ailsa was quicker, nimbler, and frankly Gloamings are far better suited for eating than gymnastics. It tumbled awkwardly, lost its footing, and fell far down the shaft of darkness below.

The tunnel of wood ended just ahead, and Ailsa stretched her body up towards it. She felt a blast of wind and heard a sound like the winding of a clock as she flew through the air.

Pausing at the lip, Ailsa glanced back to make sure she wasn't being followed. As she did, she became aware of something else on the inner surface of the wooden wall behind her. A set of patterns clawed into the flesh of the wood itself. The light was dim, but her cat's eyes could see it clearly. Words she already knew:

EVERY SECOND COUNTS

The Es and the Ss gave it away. This was Grandma's handwriting. But Ailsa remembered very well where she had seen that writing before...

She leapt through the dot of light and emerged into nothing.

Her final thought before the void embraced her was gratitude. She owed her life to Tobias, and she would never have the chance to thank him or say goodbye.

CHAPTER 58

HAPPY HOGMANAY

Ailsa remained still for a long time.

She felt fresh air in her nostrils and the smell of cooking, damp leaves, laundry on the line. A radio was burbling away somewhere. She kept her eyes tightly shut as if she did not want the feeling to end. This smelled like home.

Moment by moment, she felt herself standing tall again, her painful tail retracting. She wasn't sure if she would ever know how to make that transformation again, but she would never forget how it felt.

As she grew used to her two legs again, her eyes refused to cooperate, and she felt as if she was nearly blind. Her hands sought out the ground beneath her and felt the cool caress of wet grass.

Ailsa opened her eyes.

She was sitting at the bottom of the rowan tree at 47 Bothwell Gardens. Her attic bedroom, far above her, intact. The entire house was here. There was no sign of damage.

No explosion had ever happened here.

How on earth…?

Ailsa blinked. Above her, on the trunk of the intact and healthy rowan tree, Ailsa could see a tiny knot of wood. That had been her escape. Somehow.

Everything was the same, but yet everything had changed for ever. Ailsa had new eyes to see her world now. She pulled her yellow hat down over her ears and stood up.

There were crowds of people in the streets, many of them singing. Some were wearing party hats, some drinking from cans. All were in a buoyant mood. The sun was setting, and a thought struck her plain between the eyes.

She was back at Hogmanay. New Year's Eve.

But back then, she'd lived it. She'd been here. It was a few weeks ago, and it had snowed. What had changed? Was this a different year?

"Happy New Yeeeear!" said a voice from down the road.

There was music filtering in from somewhere down the street, an old disco band her parents had both loved. The very same one that had been playing two weeks ago. This had to be the same Hogmanay she'd just lived. Except, simply … how?

Had the Magic Hour warped time?

"There you are," said a voice from behind her.

It was Dad.

Ailsa spun around, just as she heard the snap and crack of a firework in the far distance, and the holler of another group of people as they passed on the street.

"Happy Hogmanay," they said.

Dad nodded to them, then grinned down at her on the grass. "What are you doing out here? I thought you were heading into town with your friends."

Ailsa was about to answer when her eyes locked on to his head. "Dad, your hair!" she exclaimed. His hair was shorter, jet black, with not a silver hair in sight.

"Um, what about it?"

"It changed back?"

"Back from what?"

Ailsa's stomach churned.

"So … you don't remember your hair turning grey?"

"Ailsa, have you had enough water today? I think you may be seeing things."

Dad hugged her on the way in and she leaned in and hugged him tight. She would do the same to her mother later that evening.

I'm back, Ailsa thought. *Right where I started*.

Another firework exploded in the sky towards town.

She was sure of it now. The Magic Hour had indeed turned the clocks back. *The Big Bang*, thought Ailsa. *A new beginning*.

Dad's phone rang and he showed Ailsa – it was Mum. They FaceTimed together. She was still at the hospital but standing outside in a courtyard.

"Sorry I can't see you," said Mum. "It's a busy night for us in the hospital. Is that OK? We'll have to do New Year's Eve tomorrow. I can only spare a minute."

"Every second counts, Mum," said Ailsa.

She saw her father react, but kept her focus on Mum.

When Ailsa hung up, Dad's cheeks were wet with tears.

"Did I ever tell you why I say that?"

Ailsa shook her head numbly.

"Quite a few years ago now, when you were really small, and my own father was very sick in hospital, I had to go to a work meeting up in Fife. It's a train ride away. I knew my dad wasn't doing well, so I wanted to make sure I was close by. But the meeting was really important and if I didn't go, I might not have a job any more. So I went. In the middle of the meeting, I got a call. Grandpa had taken a turn for the worse, and I had to get to hospital fast. I left the meeting, but my boss started arguing with me. I must have spent twenty minutes explaining it to him, but he never listens. So, by the time I got out of the office and down to the railway station, I'd missed the train. Next train was half an hour later. There weren't any taxis at the station. Ten minutes. Then there was a traffic jam. Fifteen more minutes. By the time I actually got to the hospital, the lift had broken, and it took me precisely one minute to climb the stairs and get to his bedside. When I arrived, my brother was in tears. He told me Dad had just died. One minute earlier. I wanted to be there, to hold his hand. Grandma and both my brothers were there, thankfully. But I wasn't. So that was the day I realized how important every second is. How important being on time is, and how we always need to do what's best for the people we love. Grandma used to say it to me when I was a kid, and it was only then that I truly understood. Every second counts, my dearest Ailsa."

Ailsa had sat in silence with her father for a full minute before it hit her. Her head was full of ifs.

If she really had gone back in time.

If somehow that had happened.

If what she had experienced in the Magic Hour had now sent her back here, somehow, to that fateful New

Year's Eve…

    Then her house would still explode tonight.

    In under an hour.

CHAPTER 59

FIREWORKS

Professor Sandy Munro's mind was a piece of Swiss cheese. And not in a velvety, delicious way.

There were parts of him that still knew he was there, he was alive and that his entire being had been overtaken by the creature known as the Brollachan.

But as most everyone knows, Swiss cheese is mostly made of holes. And it was the Brollachan who lived there now, like a knot of twine, tying itself in and out of those holes so much it wasn't clear any more what was Sandy and what was Brollachan.

The creature knew Sandy Munro needed to survive, and to survive he needed to destroy any evidence of the Magic Hour.

He would erase his hard drives at the office, certainly.

He would burn the records in his safe, all connections to his partnership with Dr Judith Craig, from whom he had stolen most of his research.

These actions were entirely under his control.

But there was one piece of the evidence he knew he had to address right there and then. He knew the Craig grandchild knew something, and that more than likely any evidence to support it was in her bedroom, at home.

It didn't take long in the Observatory personnel files for Sandy Munro to find the address. Thus it was that Sandy Munro began his long walk to 47 Bothwell Gardens.

Where are we going? asked the Brollachan.

Destruction, retorted Sandy Munro, realizing he was talking to himself. It was Hogmanay, a New Year welcomed with enthusiasm by all, and fireworks were being set off all over town. It would be hours before the firefighters got there. Plenty of time for the evidence to burn to ash.

The Brollachan warned Sandy that it had seen a picture of the house, and that it seemed that there was a rowan tree in the front garden. The Brollachan warned Sandy's limbs to make sure to remember to give it a wide berth. Everyone knows that the creatures of the Secret Commonwealth avoid these trees if they can, even entities of power like the Brollachan.

Sandy Munro kept up his pace as he exited the office, musing as he did about the satisfaction he would feel when all record of Judith Craig was gone, all written testimony that she herself had discovered the Middlemarket was destroyed. The fact that it was the truth was of no concern to him. He would do this act, of course, without a single thought to the dangers and damage that action might cause. Without a single consideration that perhaps, just perhaps, Judith Craig's granddaughter might have been careful with the evidence of wrongdoing. And copied the entire notebook long before her final departure to the Magic Hour.

The Brollachan assumed this too, of course. But nevertheless, it was enjoying the frenzy of hatred that boiled in the marrow of the man, and let it happen with pleasure.

But he had hardly left the front door of the Observatory before he heard a familiar voice shouting nearby.

"That's him!"

It had not taken Ailsa Craig long to figure it out, and even less time for her to persuade her father what they needed to do. Their house had not exploded by accident. It had been Sandy Munro, destroying the only evidence linking him to Grandma Judith and their Most Extraordinary Discovery.

It had been the glasses that had clinched it.

A pair of gold half-moon glasses. Around his neck. Which, in the past – and, as Ailsa was working out, again now in her imminent future – lay in their garden.

She had seen these glasses with her own eyes, dangling around his neck on a chain in the Middlemarket.

The man had to be stopped.

Ailsa was already out of the car and running.

Dad caught up with her as she found Sandy Munro. He turned slowly to her, his eyes boiling red.

"You!" she screamed. "House-destroyer-to-be! Thief!"

The Brollachan recognized the voice immediately.

Hello, daffodil, it said.

"You won't succeed!"

A scrap of defiant Sandy Munro remained in the centre of the Brollachan, and it was he who spoke now.

"You have no evidence," he sneered. "By which I mean you won't have anything at all when I'm finished. And the wheel will turn again. Crushing you in the process, naturally."

"My grandmother took copious notes. The Magic Hour was hers. Her work, her science, her discovery. A written record. She tried to bring you in, and you pushed her away and grabbed all the credit for yourself. Before turning it into a horror show."

"And yet all of those notes will soon be gone. As will you."

Ailsa swallowed a sob of fear as her dad arrived.

"What the hell is going on here?" he demanded.

The Brollachan's red eyes blazed brighter as it regarded the new prospect.

"Dad, don't get too close."

"What is up with that man's eyes?" asked Dad, peering.

This one won't do either, far too full, murmured the Brollachan as it surveyed Ailsa's dad.

"In any case," said Sandy Munro, forcing out the words with effort, his voice a dry croak, "I mean this is science we're talking about. A mere woman couldn't have possibly made that sort of discovery on her own. Even if she was your grandma."

Ailsa's eyes burned with the rage of a thousand generations of passed-over, invisible women. They flared with the indignant fury of Rosalind Franklin and Alice Ball, of Lise Meitner and countless others.

They also burned bright with a plan.

Ailsa vaulted over a hedge and into the dark gorse and bramble of Blackford Hill beyond. The Brollachan chased after her. As he vaulted after Ailsa, Sandy tripped, half-impaling his shin on a railing. He yanked his leg free after him, the wound meaningless to a man already possessed.

Ailsa's dad watched helplessly as an unhinged figure with red eyes pursued his only child into the night.

Ailsa kept her breath steady as she ran.

She checked her watch. Five minutes to midnight.

Now she knew she had to be on time.

But it was a New Year, as we know.

Ailsa was fast, but the Brollachan was faster. It didn't take long for the creature to catch up with her. She was cornered now, stone and sky around her in the darkness.

As she stood on the windy ridge at the edge of Blackford Hill, Ailsa wondered if this would be her last moment. As we've already said here: we never know, in real life, when our own story is over.

The Brollachan forced a grin through Sandy Munro's sneering lips. His ragged brown teeth were bloodied with effort, a bitten tongue ignored.

That's when the world exploded.

At least, it seemed like it from that ridge.

A vast firework, pink and green, tore apart the sky above.

The Observatory buildings were a flashing silhouette now as more blasts came. The sky was alive with noise and fire.

The Brollachan screamed and ran.

As it did, the last remnants of Sandy Munro, such as they were, began to wither inside the Brollachan's latest house. The Brollachan staggered towards the ridge when boom! another firework exploded like a supernova on the other side of the building, a vast sunflower of bright pinks and greens, whistling, rumbling. Another joined it in the sky with a rib-shattering boom, this one the colour of diamonds, flashing bright and loud.

There were vast starbursts of fireworks everywhere now, crackling explosions of colour and sound. And then, at the climax of the show, a vast waterfall of white sparkling down into the golf courses of South Edinburgh. Ailsa could hear a crowd below erupting in a roar as the bells chimed. And everywhere the Brollachan turned, there was light and fury and pain.

Not fair, it screamed.

Make it stop.

Leave me alone.

It pushed Sandy Munro's body along the side of the sharp ridge of the hill where it had no desire at all to be near such a fatal drop. But all control was lost to the Brollachan now.

At that moment, the largest firework Ailsa had ever seen exploded right in front of them. It was every colour of the rainbow at once and sounded like the barrage of an army battalion.

That was enough for the creature.

It was time to move house.

Sandy Munro, what was left of him, crumpled into

himself like a tumbling house of cards. A thousand years of debt came rushing back. Even as Ailsa ran to him to stop him falling, the shell that was Professor Sandy Munro stared back in regret at her, as he fell, at last, to dust.

What remained on the ground blew off the cliff in a flurry, peppering the darkness and the gorse bushes far below. Peering through the murk, Ailsa could almost make out a faint mist, swirling in the breeze, snaking off down the hillside towards the darker part of town. It seemed irritated and hungry.

There were thousands of prospects kissing and hugging below. Some were singing "Auld Lang Syne". Many of them seemed particularly spacious, and it occurred to the Brollachan for the first time that it might try to live in two places at once.

Another sound came to Ailsa as if on a breeze.

Tioraidh an-dràsta,[54] it said, and all was silence.

---

54   A phrase in Scots Gaelic that Ailsa didn't know but means "bye for now".

CHAPTER 60

UNFINISHED BUSINESS

The memorial for Grandma was held that week. It was something they had been planning to do for years but had never been able to organize. (There are a lot of things in life like that.) At Ailsa's suggestion, the evening had a dual purpose: to celebrate both the life and work of her grandma, and of all the many other women scientists who had been passed over and forgotten for so long. Ailsa had once started making a list of them, and to her shock, and history's embarrassment, the list was very long indeed.

The invitation gave the time as "8 for 8:30".

Ailsa arrived five minutes early. She wore her favourite outfit but kept her yellow hat on. Denzie and Ossian were the first guests to arrive, and from the looks on their faces, they were proud to be there.

Soon the main reception area at the Observatory was packed with people. Ailsa spotted Dame Zara, alongside Cameron Dingwall and Credenza's mother, who was healing well after her fall. Ailsa's parents were here too, relaxed and happy. Ailsa was relieved to see them both smiling. Mum had even brought her cats, the two Steves, who seemed nonplussed about the whole thing.[55]

Ailsa kept to the back of the room, near the door. So it was Priya who took centre stage and began to speak.

"Thank you for your time this evening," Priya began. "The biggest gift of all is time. Because in the end, time is all we ever truly have. It's the very currency of life. But time can lose all meaning when we lose someone we love. We are here to remember Dr Judith Craig and all the other women of science whose work might go unsung as time marches on. These strange years we have all lived through have warped all sense of time. It has been hard on us all but" – she looked directly at Ailsa now – "I think it has been particularly hard on children. Because for them, their experience of time is more like a physical place, a landscape. Which Einstein, of course,

---

55   If fact, it was rare for Ailsa to see her cats plussed in any way at all.

would agree with. Time is space, and space is time. The stars shining beautifully above us tonight are merely maps of the past. The sun's rays are eight minutes old; the light we see tonight from Betelgeuse left the Orion constellation seven hundred years ago, the same year the Declaration of Arbroath was written."

Ailsa heard a grunt of agreement at that.

"Fine declaration, indeed," said an earthy voice behind her.

She whirled around and saw a foot leaving the open doorway. A bare foot, its shin blistered red with cold.

A distinctly familiar foot.

As she ran out into the car park, Ailsa felt a strange shape in her pocket. Reaching in, she pulled out a note. But before she could read it, she stopped dead. There on a ridge, half-shielded by moonlight, was what looked like the Laird of the Wilds. Two wary guards by his side. She ran over to them. It was only now that Ailsa could see both the Laird and his guards were dripping wet.

"How come you're all soaked?" said Ailsa.

"How else were we going to get here?" said the Laird, as if that made any sense.

"I don't understand," said Ailsa. "I thought you couldn't survive outside of the Middlemarket. What's going on?"

"You've made quite the mess of things," he said.

"But," said Ailsa, "you gave me the keys. We had to stop it."

"And we did, true enough. But. Problem's not what you stopped." The Laird was pointing behind her now. "It's what you started."

Ailsa turned to look.

There, on the far edge of the car park, was a girl. She was staring at Ailsa, but Ailsa already knew who she was. After all, she saw her almost every day in the mirror. The girl had a yellow, knitted hat, chaotic curly hair, curious green eyes, and a pair of glasses that kept sliding down her nose.

It was Ailsa.

But, thought Ailsa, *I'm Ailsa.*

And so if I'm Ailsa, who's that? Strange though it may seem, at that very moment, the other girl, the second Ailsa, was looking over at our Ailsa and thinking exactly the same thing.

Ailsa looked back at the Laird, who nodded grimly.

Her hand tensed and she remembered the note. She removed it and gazed down. It was in Tobias's handwriting. It read simply:

HELP

Ailsa felt a chill hum through her bones. Looking over the rooftops and down to the streets, she could see wisps of mist roaming the town. Mist that shouldn't be there. Mist with two red eyes glowing in the centre. The air felt sharp, frostier with every moment.

And from somewhere, in the dark shadows of the city, Ailsa could hear the tolling of an ancient, very familiar bell.[56]

---

56 Well, that is the end of this book, I think. I know I'm only a footnote, but honestly? I was gripped. I didn't think Ailsa would make it and I certainly didn't think that this was the kind of story where a red-eyed mist might be on the loose at the end. Fireworks too. Some nice stuff about time, I thought, which delivered on the promise of the title. I'm generally quite punctual myself. But since I'm a human foot, it's hard not to keep in step (STEP! Foot joke!) with the author. What's that? Oh. You did know that most footnotes are written by feet, didn't you? I wasn't sure if anyone knew. I mean, it's obvious once you know, or if you stop to think about it for a moment.

Do it now. Think about it. Foot. Note. See? Makes perfect sense. A few authors with special circumstances are given permission to write them in other ways, but that's our basic point of view. It's quite hard being a footnote, to be honest. Most people zoom right past us. We're not exactly top billing. Bottom of the pile. Readers like you are generally far more interested in the main story, with all the bigger, fancier fonts and chapter art and whatnot. Some people look down on us, and think we're "interrupting the flow of things", but honestly they're wrong. Generally footnotes have had bad press over the years. We tend to be given boring jobs normally, going on about stuff like "mouldy potatoes in the French revolution, see appendix seven paragraph one chapter 2 ibid IIII". And things like that. But I think we provide a unique perspective. All the same, it's a hard life below stairs. I belong to the footnote union. So we have some rights. But honestly, I tend to avoid the meetings, since it's just a bunch of feet hanging around and it's not a particularly fresh atmosphere. Sometimes when it's hot, I can see more of things, since the author tends to wear flip-flops. Doesn't last long, sadly. When the weather turns cold again, I'm sure I'm going to be down in the socks once again. The good news is, being an author, most of his socks have holes in them. So I always get a peek of something. By the way, from a FRP (foot-related perspective), I must tell you that the next book in this series is even better. There's more running, jumping, dancing and kicking. FRP-wise, that is a real winner, let me tell you. He may even have written a couple of chapters which you can find at the back. Anyway, now you know the truth about me, and I hope it's been fun to read my contributions. I've certainly enjoyed giving them to you. So next time you see a footnote, please stop to say hello. We're always here to help.

ACKNOWLEDGEMENTS

Thanks doesn't even cover it, but I'll give it a try. Help and support takes time, and *time* – I hope you figured out my viewpoint on this subject now – is the most important, valuable thing in the world.

I'm hugely grateful to my friends and family who have patiently stuck by my side on this long road to publication. Thank you one and all for your time.

Epic torch song rock ballad candle held far aloft to my amazing editor at Scholastic, Yasmin Morrissey: thank you so much for your unbridled enthusiasm, confidence-boosting, laser-like editing eye and raw instinct! Ailsa wouldn't be here without you, and I am eternally grateful and very lucky to have found you. You know and love Ailsa and her world like I do, a rare blessing. Thank you, too, to the wonderful Tierney Holm for your terrific suggestions and counsel.

Everyone else at Team Scholastic: thank you so much for everything, I'm so grateful to you all for believing in this story. Harriet Dunlea, Sarah Dutton, Sarah Baldwin, Jessica White, Ellen Thomson, Lucy Page – thank you so much for the wonderful warm welcome, and I couldn't be happier or more excited about these words, and the words to come. Thank you for all your tireless efforts.

I am indebted to – and so grateful for – the luminously talented Alessia Trunfio, whose beautiful illustrations have shone a mesmerizing new light on Ailsa and her story that I didn't know existed. I can't wait to work together again.

My friendly neighbourhood Curtis Brown family – Isobel Gahan, Stephanie Thwaites, Jonny Geller and Lily Williams – thank you all for your belief, reassurance, patience, philosophy, excellence in all things agenting and beyond. You are all legends. I couldn't have had better partners getting this world out of my head and on to the page. Thank you to Scott Seidel and Kevin Marks, at WME and Gang Tyre respectively, who didn't blink an eye when I said I'd be doing this. Mr Lindsay Williams, you joined the team mid-flight, and I'm so grateful you did.

Huge props to my pal Molly Ker Hawn, a cheerleader

for this book despite knowing nothing about what's inside other than that I was writing it. That's trust and friendship right there – I kept going, Molly. Thank you. I owe you a beer.

To my supremely talented pal Mark Evans Esq, thank you for your generous support and help, plus your swift and incisive reads of early versions of this. Your notes were brilliant, naturally … your support and friendship has meant the world to me.

To fellow Auld Reekier, Sir Ian Rankin: you'll never know how much your encouragement has meant to me over the years. Even if you asked me, I won't tell you. So there. Only to say: thank you so much.

Thank you to my wonderful and supportive mum, Susan Wolstencroft, for all your love, humour and help over this and many other years. I'd also like to thank my dear departed dad, Dr. Ramon Wolstencroft, who loved the stars but adored his family more. Leiomi, thank you for being there, always. And Mark, thank you for being my brother. I love you all.

To my wonderful wife, Flore, who I still can't believe said yes, who shared a beer and a laugh with me and somehow understood me long before we met, who gets how the whole puzzle fits together, your unceasing love and support has blown me away all these years. *Merci mille fois*, every day. I'm so grateful to be spinning around on this planet with you. The coffee's ready.

Lastly, my one and only Vida, my super stellar daughter, you're at the front of this book for a reason. Your heart, imagination, love, humour and passion for stories has inspired me through every page of this book. I wake up every day feeling so lucky to be your pappa, and I love you to the moon and back … and while that is, strictly speaking, only 477,710 miles, imagine making that journey, and then heading back again, ad infinitum, and somehow that journey being comprised of love. That might just start beginning to cover it.

COMING SOON

Book 2 of *The Magic Hour* series…

THE INFINITE MINUTE

TURN OVER NOW
for an exclusive

**SNEAK PEEK of
CHAPTERS
1 & 2**

CHAPTER 1

THE FUNNIEST THING
THAT EVER HAPPENED

It all boiled down to this:

  1) the sheep had a purple cowboy hat on, and

  2) it was the funniest thing that had ever happened.

To be clear: the sheep wasn't particularly aware it was wearing a hat. It was nestled between her ears, set back at a merry angle. This sheep did not seem to care that the hat belonged to Lulu Craig, Ailsa's big sister, who was back after two years, and had been gifted the hat during her travels.

In any case, it was the sheep's hat now.

And frankly? She looked great in it.

They had come up the north side of the Pentlands, which up here was a mess of gorse bushes, dark wet grass, and rabbit droppings. The kind of strenuous uphill walk that Lulu called a *yomp*. On a patch of rock and gorse bushes, they had huddled together under Lulu's parka and talked, watching the sun move across the sky (being summer in Scotland, it meant that it was rarely dark before eleven at night).

Then the wind blew.

The good news was that from the moment the sudden gust plucked Lulu's hat from her head, Ailsa's sister had grabbed her phone and started filming. She caught the hat just after take-off, spiralling up and over a fence and into a nearby field, then gliding in to stick the perfect landing on the head of the solitary sheep (who had been chewing grass and minding her own business). This would have already been a perfect hilarious moment, until the sheep, now sporting the hat, and as if on cue, suddenly turned to camera and *BAAAAAAAAAAA'd* in such a bizarre and unexpected way that made this a moment for the ages.

Both girls collapsed in helpless laughter.

You know the kind. Those hysterics that feel like they'll never stop, the ones that make your cheeks hurt and the tears run down your face. Where you wish life had a remote, so you could replay this moment for ever.

"Alrighty, I am for sure GIFing that," said Lulu, and with a few judicious swipes of her finger, that's exactly what she did. Ailsa watched in awe as the funniest thing that had ever happened now became the Funniest GIF in Existence. Now this moment would repeat for ever, if they wanted it to.

Leaving the hat with the sheep[1], they started down the slope towards Dad's house. Ailsa kept up a brisk pace. Despite her previous reputation, Ailsa did not want to be late.

After all, today was her twelfth birthday.

And there was cake at the bottom of this hill.

Six months had passed since the strange events of Hogmanay, the time she discovered the Magic Hour and watched the Brollachan wreak its vengeance before disappearing into the city of Edinburgh like a prowling wolf.

It had also been a few months since Grandma's memorial up at the Observatory, the night that Ailsa had seen not only what looked like her double, but also the Laird, who had told her ominously of problems. Since that night, Ailsa was sure, she had heard nothing more. From anyone.

It was as if the entire business of the Magic Hour had never happened. It had, of course.

---

1   It's extremely impolite to ask a sheep for your hat back, even if they have it by accident.

Hadn't it?

Ailsa smiled as they walked. Lulu was back. Her sister understood her in a way that no one else did. She anticipated her moods, understood her silences and always seemed to appear with a perfectly grilled slice of toast, at precisely the moment that Ailsa was starting to think that's exactly what she'd like to eat.

Ailsa had missed Lulu so much.

Having her back was the biggest birthday present ever.

Dad's place had finally been rebuilt since the Hogmanay explosion which had started Ailsa's adventures. There were leaks now where there never used to be. Floorboards would squeak, and draughts would whistle in through the gaps in the window frames. Ailsa sometimes heard Dad grumbling about insurance companies, rush jobs and cost-cutting. But Ailsa still had her bedroom upstairs, so she was grateful for that.

Back in the kitchen, Ailsa smiled over at Mum and Dad, standing together alongside their new partners in front of Ailsa's chocolate, vanilla and strawberry layer cake.

"Happy birthday!"

Lulu led the cheers and applause, which filled the room as Ailsa blew out the candles. As the smoke wafted to the ceiling, Ailsa smiled to herself that for the first time in her memory, she was on time for her own birthday.

But she was wrong, of course.

Why, you ask?

Well, you see, no one quite understood it yet.

But something terrible had happened to time.

It wasn't that there was too much of it, or not enough of it to go around, or even that some of it was being stolen from others (as Ailsa had discovered to her horror some six months earlier).

It wasn't working as it should.

It was just – broken.

It had to do with something Ailsa had done, in a strange island of time near the Bridges known as the Magic Hour. Something that was about to plunge Ailsa, and the entire world, into a gruesome, churning mass of chaos.

(Well, you did ask.)

The first that Ailsa knew about it was a wet footprint.

CHAPTER 2

THE VISITOR

In the total darkness of deep night, Ailsa half-thought she was still dreaming. She had felt so cosy and happy under the covers, full of cake and her face still aching from all the laughter.

Best birthday ever, she had mumbled as she fell asleep.

It hadn't all been smiles, though.

There had been two empty chairs at her celebration. One had been for Ailsa's school friend Credenza, who had cut her hair very short over the summer. The other was for Credenza's older brother, Ossian, who hadn't cut his hair in months.

They had promised to be there. Both of them.

Mum had said there were problems with the buses these days. All the same, Ailsa felt the tiniest bit hurt.

They hadn't even sent a text.

Now, however, it was dark and chilly in her room, and Ailsa was awake for some reason.

There was an icy breeze coming from somewhere in the corner of the room. Maybe this was what Dad meant when he'd complained about builders "cutting corners".

Perhaps this breeze was what had woken her.

Ailsa was about to roll over and try to catch her dream again[2] when she glanced over at her little desk by the window. In the centre of the surface, glistening in the moonlight, was a footprint.

It looked fresh, with a blob of heel and five chunky toes. There were drips of water all over the windowsill, too, and in their reflection she could see the full moon, flickering. The window was open, the source of the frozen air seeping into her room.

Hang on, Ailsa thought. *Rewind for a second.*

I shut that window last night.

And what's more: *moons don't flicker. Not that one, anyway.*

That's when she saw the shadow.

It was square-looking, solid, and a little monstrous, as if someone had decided to carve a troll out of stone. It

---

2   It can be done, but only through stealth and surprise.

was perched on her window ledge, with two strong legs, and a muscled arm holding a torch that glowed orange against the night sky. It almost perfectly matched the colour of his vast, woolly beard.

The shadow moved and cleared its throat.

The last time Ailsa had seen this strange man, whose full name was the Laird of the Wilds, had been six months earlier, at her Grandma Judith's memorial. He'd been soaking wet then, too.

Now here he was, drenched and dripping all over her pencil case.

"Trouble," growled the Laird.